Time Will Tell

By
Mary S. Palmer

Copyright © 2016 by Mary S. Palmer
ISBN: 978-1-68361-145-5
Cover art by Fiona Jayde

Published by
Decadent Publishing Company, LLC

Look for us online at:
www.decadentpublishing.com

~A Note from the Author~

Dear Readers,

What is it that entices you to buy a book? Is it the plot, the characters, or are you looking for something different? *Time Will Tell* provides all three—appealing characters, an intriguing plot, and a strange, new universe to explore. But it isn't too strange. These extra-terrestrials aren't stereotypical little green men. They are similar enough to humans to be able to integrate into society on Earth. The Svarians have come to help Earthlings by sharing their cures for fatal diseases. To do so, however, they must keep their enemies, the Torpians, at bay. Reporters Mona Stewart and Rob Parker act as their worldly liaisons to help them achieve this goal.

It's important to me to also show how a life without chores might seem idealistic, but it becomes boring. Man needs challenges and life without them is meaningless. Although this novel is set in the South known for its leisurely lifestyle, it is an action-packed story that moves into outer space and back at a fast pace.

If you like diversity in your reading, seek characters you can relate to, and enjoy experiencing a thrilling, suspenseful adventure, I believe *Time Will Tell* will satisfy your expectations. I hope you will give it a chance.

Happy reading,

Mary S. Palmer

Dedication

To my mother, Janie C. Schluter, who made sure I had a good education.

Acknowledgments

Many thanks to the people who critiqued this book, especially my editor, Laura Garland, and line editor, Autumn Knight. Also, thanks to J. Nolan White, Daniel Schuler, Robert O'Daniel, B.A. Davis and Linda Brewton Strong. All their help and encouragement is appreciated.

Chapter One

In the heavy rainstorm, Mona's car skidded, swerved sideways, and spun around three times. As it flew off the road and plunged into the gully below, her body became light, lifting out of the driver's seat. Fear ripped at her lungs. *Oh my God! I'm not wearing my seat belt.* Twin headlight beams revealed only darkness in front of her, and air rushed around the car as the engine revved.

The car arced, gravity pulling it down. A wall of gravel filled the windshield, and she clutched the steering wheel. "No, no! Dear God, no!"

The front end of her VW slammed into the ground, the impact catapulting her from her seat. Her head smashed into something...through it...and then she flew into the darkness. Pain engulfed her to the point of madness until, at last, everything stopped.

When she woke, she ached all over. She opened her mouth to yell, "Help, somebody help me!" But no words came out. A heavy weight lay on top of her. She opened her eyes, staring in horror at her little red Volkswagen bug, which pinned her to the ground. Intense pain jabbed at an area near her belly button. Reaching down, she discovered a sharp piece of twisted metal piercing her abdomen. She groaned as she tugged on it, but she didn't have the strength to pull it out.

Fear gripped her. No houses faced this stretch of the sparsely populated road in west Mobile County, and traffic became light at one a.m. Who would know about her accident? She panicked at the thought no one had heard her earth-shattering screams, the trees snapping, or the crunching metal when her vehicle hit the bottom of the ravine.

Exhaustion overcame her. Mona Stewart lay motionless in a pile of pine straw. Her head swam, and she gasped for breath as life oozed out of her twenty-eight-year-old body.

Remembering her little beagle had been in the car with her, she turned her head to the side. A few feet away, a small, furry body lay in the mud. Her heart squeezed with fear. "P-Pep." The word came out on a breathy moan. The pup's ear perked then he lifted his head. Rising onto shaky legs, he staggered to her. Tail low, he sniffed around then crawled under the car, snuggling as close as he could to Mona.

She set her hand on her pup, digging her fingers into his damp white fur. Her eyelids fluttered, and it seemed each breath required a herculean effort. *So tired. But at least I've got Pep. Not alone.*

Behind her lids, lights flashed then melted into images—her parents' funeral after their death in a plane crash, her marriage and divorce, a couple of dateless years for fear of a failed relationship. The scene of her boyfriend breaking up with her played out in her mind.

"What did you expect?" Lee laughed. "I promised you nothing, and nothing is what you're getting. There were no commitments."

Crushed and outraged, she fled her apartment, hopping in her car and speeding away into the humid summer night without fastening her seat belt. She didn't know or care where she went.

"Hurricane Dennis is swirling around in the Caribbean Sea near Haiti. Its projected path is the Yucatan Peninsula. But hurricanes are unpredictable. Once it reaches the Gulf of Mexico, it could change course and take a turn toward the Gulf Coast and Mobile, Alabama." The radio announcer's voice blared through her car's speakers. "Winds are in excess of 130 miles per hour. Stay tuned and we'll keep you posted."

Hurricane Dennis couldn't match the storm within her, so she clicked off the radio. She couldn't run from either one. A sudden downpour blurred the windshield, the wipers unable to keep up.

The wheels lost traction.

She spun around—

Mona's eyes flew open.

A bright light hovered over her. With it came a complete sense of peace.

Pep growled and then barked, which sounded more like a

frightened yelp than a threat.

Two people walked toward her, and she stared up at them. *My prayers have been answered. Help has come.* The car shifted up and off her. Rain splashed on her face as hands lifted her from the ground. The dog gave another warning bark but then backed off, following as two men placed her on a gurney and took her out of the ravine.

"She's almost gone. We'll have to work fast." The taller of the two had a husky voice.

Wait, where did the paramedics come from? I didn't hear any sirens.

The rain stopped battering her face, and she realized they'd carried her inside a shelter. They laid Mona on a thin mattress and worked to remove the piece of metal from her stomach. Her mind whirled; she felt their tugging but no pain. Working fast and with dexterity, it seemed they stopped the bleeding in seconds. Her strength returning, she watched in detached fascination as they closed the wounds and pressured the swelling to a nonexistent state. *How are they doing that using no medical instruments, no sutures, no bandages? Nothing but their hands.*

"Just a few scratches remain." The taller one's monotone got her attention.

She peered up through squinted eyes, but everything was a blur. When her vision cleared, the faces of two people leaning over her were obscured by a brilliant light in the background. She could make out silhouettes but not their faces.

Oh God! There's the tunnel of light. I'm dead or dying. Her head swam, and the world faded into blackness.

When she awoke, she stood with her back propped against a wall. Half a dozen people with pug noses and round faces studied her. She felt no pain or desire to resist as they punched and poked at every part of her anatomy. It didn't hurt or impair her ability to think straight.

She tried to speak, but when she opened her mouth, no words came out. Terror caused her body to shake. *What are they going to do to me?*

The people resembled humans and spoke the English language, but, at a second glance, the unusual shape of their faces and noses made them appear somewhat different, along with their clothing looking like it belonged in a long-past century.

Cortisone. Those round faces make them look like they've been

3

taking large doses of it. Her friend, Della, had to take massive doses of the drug. After a couple of months, her face had become as round as a ball. She'd had terminal cancer, and they tried cortisone—the sole known treatment at the time—but to no avail. Della had died anyway. Were these people all cancer patients on cortisone?

Even so, it doesn't explain the pug noses. She had seen lots of people with pug noses, but never so many together in one place. She glanced around for an exit and, when she spotted one, she took a deep breath. When she attempted to leave, though, she could not move a muscle; she was glued to the spot. Newspaper headlines from the past flashed through her mind, and she shook all over: "Two Pascagoula Men Abducted by Torpians." *That happened just thirty miles from Mobile, forty years ago, but it's still talked about. Those men were released to tell their experience, but I might not be so lucky.* A chill stole through her. *How in the world am I going to get out of this?*

A man on her right wore a white tunic belted at the waist. His long, golden hair draped over his shoulders. Piercing gray eyes seemed to dig into her soul. He reminded her of the men in the documentaries she'd watched about ancient Greece or Rome.

"We are moving along in space at faster than the speed of light." His solemn voice had a hollow sound. "Do not be afraid. We will not harm you. From your credentials, I know your name is Mona Stewart and you are a reporter for *The Daily Times* newspaper in Mobile. It is fortunate you happened to have your accident in our hidden Earth area. Otherwise, you would have died. You see, we have technology unknown to your medical men. Besides, they would never have found you in time. The scene of your wreck is in a deserted area."

Mona's body tingled. She wiggled her hands and toes to regain sensation in them. *Did they drug me?* Someone pushed a chair under her. She slid down onto it and opened her mouth to speak, but words would not come.

"Your speech will return. We will explain more later." Someone patted her shoulder. "You must rest."

As much as she fought it, she could not control her exhaustion. Her head slumped forward, and her eyelids drifted shut.

Sometime later—could've been ten minutes or ten hours, she had no clue—her eyes opened to the bright light of high noon on a sunny day. She glanced around but couldn't find any visible source of the illumination. *I'm in the same room, the same chair. Maybe somebody is nearby.* "Hello," she called out in a quivering voice. "Is anybody there?"

No answer.

She managed to get to her feet, stumble to a window, and peer out. No sun, no artificial light. What produced the light?

Glancing around, she realized she was alone. She pushed the knobless door but it didn't budge. She shook her head. That door offered no means of escape. *Escape?* She smiled at her own stupidity. *Escape to where?* If, indeed, she was in space or on another planet, she had nowhere to go. *This might all be some sick joke. Could it be possible some cult found me and decided to play tricks? No. What can explain the lack of cuts and bruises caused by the wreck?* She examined her body. No scars, only places where it appeared the skin had been knitted together. This was no joke. Her injuries were real, but the healing process was unreal. Still, she was alive.

Or am I? Can this be a place between death and eternity? Mona shuddered.

The door opened, and three men followed by two buxom women entered. The men's body structure was much the same, and all were muscular and not overweight. Both the men and the women had pug noses and round faces, gray eyes, and blonde shoulder-length hair. She straightened to her five feet three inches and realized her captors were taller than she thought, close to six feet, every one. "Where am I?"

"We will show you. Come with us." One of the men led her through a door opening on a hand signal. The others followed.

As they walked outside, Mona shielded her eyes from the light, glancing around, hoping to discover its source. If they were through experimenting on her, what next? Maybe they were taking her to be executed. But, as far as she could tell, they carried no weapons of any kind. Their lack of artillery gave her some hope they wouldn't harm her, but no clue as to what to expect. "Where are you taking me? Am I on another planet, or what?" *Good Lord, I must be!*

Chapter Two

Mona followed the man and two women down a cobblestone street. In less than five minutes, to her amazement, an entire village spread out before her. The bright light spilled onto streets made of a hard, clay-like substance. Small huts of stacked polished rocks lined them. People, all dressed alike in their belted tunics, walked to and fro, as if they had no place to go and nothing to do. One woman made a real production of doing her laundry. Basket in hand, she stopped at every door and discussed where she was going and how long each step of the procedure would take. A bored, solemn nod was the reply. *They all seem so serious. Not one of them is smiling.*

"My name is Eric," the leader told her. "They call me King. We are living in a future dimension of time. Back in 2010, we had a brief atomic war. Many of the people of Earth were destroyed, but quite a few survived. Some citizens of different nations managed to commandeer rocket ships, and they went to a space station. From there, they searched the universe until they discovered a way to survive on another planet. Fortunately, there were enough scientists to accomplish the feat. This planet, which we call Svar, has water and plant life, but its plant life is not edible. Unfortunately, we brought no seeds, so we had to develop a life-sustaining substance from available materials. We can produce energy. We're in the twenty-second century. What I have just told you is history. Here, you are in the year 2105. No matter, we can transgress time."

What's going on here? There wasn't a bomb on Earth in 2010. Is their time different from ours? That must be it. She scratched her head. *This is mind-boggling.*

"You see," Eric drew her attention, "we live in another era, another time frame."

6

Mona shook her head. *What?* She'd been transported to another planet, another time dimension with an alternate history of Earth, a century in the future. *Is what this odd-looking creature telling me true?* She bit her lip. *Oh, dear God, I don't know. Nor do I know what to ask. I might not believe his answers anyhow.* So, instead of addressing the real issues, she asked, "Why do they call you King, and why do you wear those old-fashioned clothes?" *Better to stay with safe topics.*

Eric nodded. "When we formed our community, we needed a leader. Since I had the most education, they chose me. As a group, they decided they wanted a king, but as a real leader, not a figurehead. In many ways, we are different from Earthlings. You may have noticed we use formal language, too. We find it is befitting to our situation." He glanced down at himself. "As for the clothes, well, they're easy to make and simple to keep clean."

Mona shrugged. "I guess they're comfortable, once you get used to them."

Eric tapped his pug nose. "Our facial features are quite another matter. We must take certain medication to survive in this atmosphere, and it changes our physical appearance somewhat. It gives us unlimited longevity. However, we have two factions on this planet. Some broke away from our government and started their own. They have managed to kidnap some of our men and women, and, by withholding the medicine, allowed them to die."

"Exactly how old are you?" His almost unlined face didn't give her the answer.

"One hundred and forty," he replied. "I was an American nuclear scientist when the war came, and I also had a medical degree. We pooled all our brainpower for how to survive and to find the answers for an almost work-free and stress-free life, along with the possibility of immortality. After we accomplished those goals, our reason for unity diminished. As in Earth situations, men became jealous of each other." His voice sounded weary. "Even here, in so-called ideal circumstances, compatibility is impossible. After a time, Torpi, the instigator of dissent, became power hungry. He broke off from us and took some people with him. He also built some ships, identical to ours. So, we are divided and live on different sides of this planet, each in fear of the other."

"Did Torpi attack your group?"

"No, for a while, the power he had satisfied him. At that time, we had no weapons, nor a reason to need them. Now, we are afraid the ones who call themselves Torpians are fashioning weapons from rocks and stones."

"What happened to cause trouble?"

"Greed, for one thing. Also, Torpi is ill but he wants to live forever, and he knows I can help him."

Mona raised her brows but didn't ask any questions.

Eric didn't explain further. "Another problem is their water source is drying up."

"But from what you've shown me, you have everything you need and enough for everybody. It seems this is a paradise on Earth.... Well, we're not on Earth, are we?" She chuckled at her error. Then she leaned forward. "But why do you want me? What can I possibly do for you?"

For the first time, Eric smiled. "Ah, you do not understand, but I will explain shortly. Even though I am sure you have seen a lot as a reporter, I have the advantage over you—I have been twenty-eight years old, but you have never been a hundred and forty. In your innocence, you want to believe people are altruistic. It's difficult to understand people like Torpi are not willing to share. They want it all."

A perfect description of Lee Black. He fooled me. Maybe I am naive.

"Besides"—Eric took a deep breath—"none of us are happy here. We soon found out permanent leisure is boring. Being nonproductive is worse. What we thought would be an ideal life turned out to be just the opposite. All creatures need challenges, and we have none here. So, we want a place where they are once again available to us."

Just like normal human beings, always wanting what they can't have. Never satisfied.

"You see, when we first found a way to travel back in time, only those involved in research were aware we were working on such a project. Some of the others became suspicious and thought if we returned to Earth, we would leave them here. Our intentions were to go back to Earth, gather information, and try to find a way to exist there without using the drugs, which cause our features to distort. As you can see, it would not be possible to live on Earth until we once again have the appearance of Earthlings. We would not be accepted."

He sighed. "We must find the way to conquer this problem soon, for we do not reproduce. Sometimes, one of our clan does die, and we have not yet discovered the cause, so if we do not soon solve this problem, we will become extinct. Let me explain how the situation affects you as well as us."

He turned to stare into her eyes. "We returned to Earth for the purpose of bringing a subject back. But you were not to be the one. Our motives were unselfish. We planned to choose a person dying with cancer. We found a young man. However, for some unexplainable reason, he continued to live. We can make ourselves look more like humans for a while, but it wears off. And every minute we waited increased our chances of being recognized as extraterrestrials, of being caught on Earth."

Mona wrinkled her nose. "I don't understand."

"We know the cure for cancer. We planned to disguise ourselves as morticians, persuade the victim's family to have a closed casket then remove the body we had already put in a state of suspension." He steepled his index fingers. "Our plan did not work. We were searching for another subject to act as our liaison with Earthlings when you happened to fall into our hands. We revived you. So we felt entitled to your remains. When we get back to Earth, you should have many more years to live there. With your help, we can do a great service to mankind with our cancer cure."

Hmmm. Am I getting this or am I being conned? If they're the great humanitarians they claim to be, a lot of lives could be saved. If not, I'm in big trouble. I need to get real. Can't trust everybody. Hell, these are space people, not even humans. I'm just their pawn.

Eric gazed at her, and she lowered her eyes to the ground.

Damn, is this stodgy old dude reading my mind? Does he know I want to be the reporter who breaks the truth about the aliens to the world? I need to learn all I can about these creatures and—oh, man—the next Pulitzer's mine. What will I wear to the event?

Eric cleared his throat, and she jerked. *I've got to think of something else. Pep, water pollution, hating Lee. If he knows my motive, no telling what he'll do.*

"Come with me." He took her hand.

She swallowed hard, *God, did I blow it? I hope he's not going to turn me over to his enemies, the Torpians.*

He led her through a pasture to a stream with a sandy bank and deep blue water. He motioned for her to sit. She took a deep breath and inhaled the fresh air. The softness of the sand, combined with the smoothness of the stream, brought peace to her soul.

"We still control the water." His manner reassured her. His

9

sincerity inspired confidence. "The Torpians cannot use it without coming through our area. And though we have no weapons, there are more of us than of them. Even on this planet, strength is in numbers."

"Okay. Seems like there's only one way to get out of this, one way for me to get home. If you promise not to hurt me and to protect me from your enemies, I'll help you." *You don't know it, but you'll help me, too.*

"We will not harm you, and the Torpians will not know you are here," Eric promised. "When we go back to the hut, you will need to stay there. Let me clarify the reason we all wish to return to Earth."

"Because of the original lack of food, we invented pills to replace it. Our supply will last another hundred years." He pointed to some equipment partially hidden behind huge bushes, a type of shrub she'd never seen before. "Also, our permanent energy supply needs no maintenance. Because of the use of *static* electricity, our environment is so clean even the most menial housekeeping chores are unnecessary."

A woman walked past carrying a small bag, and he waved to her. "Our most difficult job is washing our simple garments every week. Oh, we could even eliminate the washing, but we choose not to. We must have something productive to do. Since we do not use money, there is no reason to work."

Wrinkling her nose, she looked at him. "Don't you have television or radios?"

Eric shook his head. "No, we don't have anything to amuse us. Our life is simple and dull."

"But you have computers, right?"

He shook his finger at her. "Only for space travel and communication with other planets, like Earth."

Good grief, it's too damn quiet here. I can't imagine a life without computers. She looked in all directions, seeing nothing, no movement. She stared at the blue sky, a reminder of watching a sunrise from her apartment. The same blue sky hovered over Earth. She shuddered. *No cars, no bars, no noise. My life may be hectic, but I'll take it any day over this. I want to go home.*

She turned to Eric. "What about the children? Can they use the computers? They'll need to know how if they're going to function on Earth someday."

"There are no children."

Mona slapped her hand against her cheek. "Then you're going

extinct."

Eric shook his head. "Not necessarily. Remember, we're close to finding immortality. We've lost a few people, and when someone dies on occasion, we disintegrate the body."

She frowned. "I realize I can't relate to your lifestyle here, but how can you stand this kind of life?" She picked up a rock off the ground and studied it. *They have no more life than this. Dullsville personified.*

Eric rubbed his chin. "For a number of years, we were content and did not even try to find a solution to the problem of boredom. Now, our interest is in trying to return to Earth. We feel a deep desire to serve others, for without ambition or goals or challenges, man cannot live. And, as I've already told you, we cannot choose to die. So our 'perfect life' is quite imperfect. It has caused much dissatisfaction, and we cannot go on this way, or we will soon lose our minds."

"Well, what kept you content before you decided to try to get back to Earth?"

"We used our brainpower to develop new medical techniques, techniques such as the method we used to revive you. Preventions for heart attacks and strokes, cures for AIDS, MS, cancer, and other fatal diseases. But once all our people were in good health and we had no reason to practice, boredom set in, and we had to find something else to occupy us. Then, the division in forces came, and we have spent some time studying how to protect ourselves. You see, we still have the will to live. Even here, it is any creature's strongest instinct."

"I can relate to that." She rubbed her queasy stomach. *But I want to live on Earth. What if they're lying to me and plan to keep me here on Svar?* She bit the corner of her lip. *Lots of days I'd loved to have slept in, but the prospect of staying on Svar forever scares the hell out of me. It would make me question whether I'm glad they'd saved my life.* If she had to remain on this planet, Eric's description led her to believe her life would be far from ideal. It would be uninteresting. Her thoughts were short-lived because, just then, a woman came up.

Eric bowed and held out his hand. "Mona, this is my wife, Lydia."

Behind Lydia's skirt, a tail wagged.

"Pep!" Overjoyed to see him, she jumped up from the soft grass and grabbed him, pulling him so close he squealed.

"Oh, Pep, I've never been so glad to see anybody in my entire life. I thought you were gone forever." She squeezed him again.

"Mona, your dog may not live long," Eric warned. "We have no assurance our pills will suit a dog's needs for food. We have never tried it on an animal before."

"Not live?" She peered down at her beloved companion who licked her face. "But he's my best friend." Tears ran down Mona's cheeks as she contemplated the consequences Pep might face. But she also realized she might be in more danger than Pep. She was the one being experimented on.

Nevertheless, when they went inside, she accepted the pills they gave her without comment. Since they had no food, it would do no good to protest. If they could find a way to achieve their goals by using her, they'd all soon head for Earth. Once there, after she'd served her purpose, it was a good chance they'd let her go free.

A man came into her hut, carrying clothes.

"I am Marcus," he announced with a bow. "It will be best if you wear the same garments we do. Then, if any Torpians come around, they won't notice you. Just cover your face." He handed the garments to her.

Mona removed her jacket and slipped the tunic over her black pants and white blouse and tied the long sash in a bow. She also took off her shoes and put on toeless sandals. They felt strange but not uncomfortable. Like everything on Svar, they were different.

She strolled through each of the three rooms in the fiberglass-type dwelling. In the front room of the unit, she sat in one of the two upholstered chairs.

"Very comfortable," she told Marcus. "I could sleep in this chair."

"You don't have to." He led her into a separate room and pointed to a flat pallet covered with a mattress. It had sheets but no blanket.

"I'm cold-natured." She patted the sheet. "Do you have any blankets?"

"No, since the weather remains constant at seventy degrees, we don't need covers."

Mona shrugged and moved to the last room, which contained a commode and a washbowl. She flushed the commode and then turned on the hydrant. Both worked. *Thank God they have running water. But there's no bathtub. I wonder if they all take a swim in the creek to bathe.*

She searched for a mirror to check if all her telltale dark-brown hair was under the hood of her garment but found none. So, she tucked her hair deeper beneath the hood. *It'll sure be strange to dress without a mirror. Just one more thing I'll have to get used to.* But it bothered her even more when it occurred to her she didn't have a toothbrush. She opened a couple of drawers, hoping to find one still in its wrapper. No luck.

As Marcus turned to leave, she stopped him. "I have a question. Can you get me a toothbrush, please? I can't stand to get up in the morning without brushing my teeth right away."

He laughed. "You never need to brush your teeth on Svar." He bared his gleaming white teeth. "We do not eat food. The medicine we use takes care of our hunger and our teeth, too. Your mouth will never feel dirty."

She ran her tongue over her gums and rinsed her mouth with water from the washbowl.

Marcus stepped close. "If you put the water in your mouth, it will have a bad taste, and it may make you ill."

She spit it out and frowned as she pressed the palm of her hand against her forehead. "My head hurts. I-I feel awful."

He handed her a pill. "It takes time to get adjusted." He took her arm and helped her to the bedroom. "Lie down and rest. Once you become accustomed to our planet, you will never be ill again."

Lying down, she closed her eyes and relaxed. *They don't know me. I'm Earthbound and hell-bent on leaving. But this is the story of the century. I smell Pulitzer here.*" Drowsiness washed over her, and she yawned. *I'll do what they say long enough to get my prize-winning story, but I have no intention of becoming used to this planet.*

Chapter Three

Sometime later, she awoke with a start. Loud voices echoed in her ears. Two men she hadn't seen before blocked the doorway to the small bedroom. Behind them, Marcus stood, silhouetted by a bright light. *Who are they? What's going on?* She made a weak effort to ask those questions, but fear prevented her from speaking. Marcus told the men to leave, but they did not. He tugged on their cloaks, and one of them shoved him to the ground. The other man came toward her, pulling out a primitive knife made from stone. Mona swallowed hard.

"Come with me," he ordered, flashing the knife in her face.

Unable to move, Mona shook her head and backed away.

"I said come with me," he growled as he tugged on the neck of her gown.

Then, Eric barged in. Grabbing both men by the collar, he banged their heads together. The knife fell to the floor, and Eric picked it up.

"What are you doing? You are supposed to be one of us. Why did it have to come to this?" He stared at the knife. A sad expression crossed his face as he told the men, "Go." With the knife still in his hand, Eric shoved the intruders out.

Mona stood immobile, watching it all happen. Then she sighed.

Eric told Marcus, "Wazi and Cardrian have been troublemakers before, but this time they've gone too far."

Mona's eyes widened as she listened to Marcus's reply.

"Yes, it's obvious they're turncoats."

"By kidnapping Mona and turning her over to Torpi, they would use her as a pawn to try to force us to give up our secrets of stopping disease and achieving immortality." Eric creased his brow. "They'll

14

try again."

Fearful for her fate, Mona found her voice. "You said the Torpians wouldn't know about me. But they do." She jerked off her tunic and slipped out of her sandals, retrieving her shoes and putting them on. "They know I'm here. No need to wear these." She slung the tunic on a chair. "Now you're saying they'll come back. What are you going to do about it?"

Eric rested his hand on her shoulder. "We didn't know those two were spies. Don't be afraid. I'll take care of them. We don't tolerate such things on Svar."

"Do you have a jail?"

With a half-smile, Eric shook his head. "We don't need one. I can banish them from our ranks, put them out, and let Torpi dole out their punishment. He is much more ruthless than I am." He curled his lip. "Especially on men who have failed in their assigned tasks."

Although Eric's reassurance didn't satisfy her, illness and weakness overcame her, rendering her unable to pursue the issue. It even overwhelmed her fear to the point she dropped back down on the mattress and fell asleep.

***

Eric shook his head. "Marcus," he said with deep concern, "we must do something quickly or she won't survive."

"Should we change the medication?"

Eric nodded. "Give her the anti-serum, and I think she will be all right by the time we prepare the ship. This is the plan: you, Lydia, Mona, the dog, and I will go. We will return to the site where we picked up Mona. She will act as our liaison and, hopefully, we can change and rework our physical appearance. That will allow us to reenter the point in time we left. We may still have to face the atomic war, but maybe with wisdom we can avert it. We will all be much younger, and we will eventually lose the technology we have gained, so we must transmit the knowledge to Earthlings as soon as possible. Also, we must pick the proper time to return to Svar to get the others."

Marcus frowned. "Pardon me, sir, but the Torpians will take over as soon as they realize we are not coming back right away. The rebel Torpi will say we abandoned them and have himself declared their new leader. He will do his utmost to convince our people to join their forces."

"I know. But there is no alternative. We must either act right away or give up forever."

The king had spoken, settling the question. They left the next evening.

***

The ship sailed through space faster than the speed of light. When Mona awakened, she found herself on board. Her malaise had subsided. Once she was told the ship had radar plus equipment with more elaborate refinements, including radio facilities, her mental attitude improved, too. But she was still uneasy. Where they were going had not yet been revealed to her.

The dark night sky was a welcome change from the bright light of Svar. She stared into the vast, empty space, hoping to be headed for Earth. She dare not ask; the answer might not be the one she wanted to hear. Disappointment would be unbearable. But when she stirred, Eric volunteered information. He told Mona, "We are returning to Earth. You will find we chose not to transgress time; we let it move forward."

When he told her the entire plan, she agreed to act as their liaison for as long as necessary. Explaining how she escaped injury in the wreck that had demolished her car wouldn't be difficult—she could claim she'd jumped out before it tumbled over the embankment. Although it would require a stretch of imagination, it would probably be accepted. After all, Pep had not been hurt. Her speculation triggered thoughts of her dog.

"Pep, where is Pep?" Mona inquired in a frantic voice. But she discovered she did not need to worry. At the sound of his name, Pep came running to lick her hand. She sighed. Pep was with her, and she did not care what happened on Svar. All she wanted was to make it back to Earth.

As Mona scratched behind Pep's ears, she surveyed the ship's stark white interior. Unlike American spaceships, it didn't have all of the equipment they used. The control cabin resembled one in a large commercial airliner. Every so often, Eric went in there and checked controls, but she couldn't tell what he was doing. Twice, jumbled words came from a radio transmission, but not clear enough for her to discern who spoke or what the speaker said.

Wandering around, she discovered the rest of the ship appeared to be much like the inside of a mobile home. She sauntered through the area divided in two sections, into the kitchen, and ran her hand across the smooth ceramic cook top. Why in the world did they have a cook top when they didn't cook? No one sat in any of the four chairs bolted to the floor, nor was anything on the table. Stepping through a wide-open curtain, she sauntered into a sleeping area with a couple of mattresses on the floor. Then she peeked into a small bath next to the sleeping section and washed her hands in the lavatory, the sole object in the room except for the commode, no shower or tub and no mirror.

A realization surprised her. She could sit, stand, or walk without floating to the ceiling, so the ship must have gravity. She could also breathe, so they must have oxygen. She was curious, but she didn't have a scientific mind. No need to ask Eric to explain the phenomenon; she wouldn't understand if he did.

As if sensing her uneasiness, Eric came over and sat beside her. "Mona, I know what you must be feeling. I'm sorry we took you to Svar, a place so strange to you, but we need your help. We have visited Earth, but we have not tried to mix with your people there for a long time. We need to know how it is at the present time before we land again."

All that had happened rushed into her brain. Mona gritted her teeth then lashed out. "How can you know what I'm feeling? You're not even human." Using her fingers, she wiped tears from her cheeks. "Wazi and what's-his-name could've killed me."

"Ah, Mona," Eric murmured. "Give us a little credit. Consider this: you were already dead when we found you." He raised his index finger. "We brought you back to life."

Mona gasped and slapped the palm of her hand over her mouth. Dropping it, she said, "You're right. I wouldn't be alive if you hadn't saved me." She moved her head side to side. "I don't mean to be ungrateful. All right, tell me what you need to know, and I'll do the best I can."

For the next couple of hours, she told Eric about technological inventions, cars, political situations, and even about space exploration. He seemed to know about some of those but not all. So many changes had happened in the last century she couldn't address them all, but when she finished, Eric patted her arm. "Thank you, Mona. I am much better prepared to return to Earth than I have been."

"Do you think Torpi will follow us?" The possibility made her shudder.

Eric rubbed his hands together. "I will be honest; I think he will. But I can reassure you we're prepared to deal with him. And all this should not take too long. Don't worry; you'll be back in your own home soon, very soon."

Lydia's quivering lip made Mona question his statement, but she turned away, determined to keep her hope. She refused to let fear raise its ugly head again.

By the time Eric left to take a nap, Mona had second thoughts. *He's much more understanding and compassionate than I gave him credit for earlier. Okay, now I feel a little safer in his care.*

Mona was tired, too, but on her way to take a rest, Lydia pulled on her sleeve, stopping her. "I know you're exhausted, but could we talk just for a moment?"

They sat at the kitchen table. "Woman to woman"—Lydia smoothed a strand of her blonde hair—"I think I should tell you a few things about us." Her eyes darkened. "We have customs somewhat different from Earthlings. We aren't exactly betrothed, but our marriages are arranged in a way. From childhood, we associate with those our parents want us to intermingle with. In other words, we only know and mix with certain people. We have some choice in choosing our mates, but it's limited."

Mona squinted as she thought of eugenics. *Are the Svarians planning a master race?*

As if reading Mona's mind, Lydia explained. "It is not eugenics, at least not exactly. But our plan for the future is to have children and we want to produce children with good genes, both physically and intellectually." She cut her eyes sideways at her sleeping husband. "I chose Eric from three other men. He is a good person. He loves me, and I love him in a way that transcends time and space. It is spiritual. I want to spend my life, or eternity, with him. Can you understand?"

Mona swallowed hard. Was this a revelation about love? In the trauma of the last few days, she hadn't given her ex-boyfriend a thought. *So, I've forgotten him? Did Lydia's statement show me what true love should be? Maybe make me aware Lee Black, III wasn't worthy of my love?* She clasped her hands together. *Hmmm. Maybe this was a test, and Lee failed.*

Chapter Four

By the time Mona got back to her apartment overlooking Mobile Bay, she'd ridden in vehicles of many types—a spaceship, a private car when she'd hitched a ride, a taxi, and a bus.

She sighed. *Well, I'm finally home again.* She'd been elated they set her free as soon as they landed. And they trusted her to return to the spaceship as per their agreement. *But I have no idea how much time has passed or what day it is. What a ridiculous position to be in! How can I find out without arousing suspicion?* She snapped her fingers. *The paper. I can check the date on the last paper delivered.*

Her newspapers had all been shoved through her mail slot. As she picked them up, she realized she'd been gone for a week. The last date read July 2.

"Wow, but look what's happened in those seven days. It's unbelievable. My vacation's over, Pep." The dog wagged his tail as he stood by her side. "And I can truly say it was out of this world." She laughed. "Did anyone besides you miss me at all?" She scratched under his chin. "I guess not, since I told everyone I'd be out of touch."

Being a reporter, she couldn't help but form a story in her mind. The headline would read: *Reporter Taken to Outer Space.* Still, she knew it would never appear in print in *The Daily Times.* "Document, Mona, document. You know the routine," her editor would say. And she had no documentation. Besides, even if she did, Frank Dees could punch holes in the best of stories. Anyhow, he'd think she was loony, and she'd probably end up losing her job. She could hear his voice.

"Mona, for God's sake, I can't believe you, of all people, are trying to hand me a faker like this. Your week off must have been a dilly. What did you do—get high and hallucinate?" And off he'd go, laughing. If she pressed the issue, it would be, "Sorry, babe. Take a couple of days off. Come back when you get over it."

Mona sighed. It was sad to have nobody to talk to. She'd become a little cynical about people because she knew quite often their interest and concern about others' problems disappeared once they were out of sight. If this got published, the gossip would begin and big, wild tales would be spread all over town. She could visualize how her tale of the spaceship would be received. The whispered words echoed in her mind:

"Do you know reporter Mona Stewart from *The Daily Times*? Well, her best friend told me she claims to have been taken up into space and even into another era—the future. She's always been, well, way out, but this proves she's flipped completely. What a tale. I don't know what's happened to our newspapers these days. Hiring people like that. They just don't insist on competent, qualified employees. Just so they sell papers."

But her eyes lit up when she made another decision: *No matter. I'm still going to write it. I'll submit it to a couple of major publishers. Maybe they'll be more broad-minded. I'm still looking for that Pulitzer Prize.*

She stopped speculating, took a shower, and fixed her first meal in a week. Her last four pieces of bacon smelled good as they sizzled in her iron skillet. Analyzing further, she realized the main reason she'd delay telling her story wasn't because of its effect on her, but because of its effect on those three people depending on her. When they had complete power over her, they had seen fit to protect her and bring her back to her own planet. She vowed to return the favor. When it was all over, though, she'd write it and maybe become famous.

An unexpected buzz of the doorbell brought her back to reality. She shook; everything startled her. She took a deep breath to regain control of her emotions before she answered. The bell rang again.

"Yes, who is it?" She stood behind the unopened door.

"Paper man."

For once, Mona was glad her former boyfriend insisted on having a paper delivered, even though she got one free at work. Letting the delivery man in while she wrote a check, she decided it would be a good chance to verify the date. "Let's see, Mr. Swift, this is the eighth and I owe you for two months?"

"Yessum," he said, satisfying Mona today was Friday, July 8.

"I came by on the first," he told her as he removed his cap, "but you weren't home. Been on a trip?"

She nodded. *I've been on a trip all right. Thank goodness he didn't ask where I went.*

Instead, Mr. Swift looked up over the top of his horn-rimmed glasses. "Could you do me a big favor, Miss Stewart? It's my grandson's birthday next week, and I promised to buy him a bike. Do you suppose you could pay me for six months? Then I'll get my commission early. I apologize for bothering you." He stared at the floor. "I guess I shoulda saved up for this, but since the wife died.... Well, I jes' ain't much good at managing money."

"Of course I can," Mona agreed without hesitation. "And don't worry about it. I know how it is. I work for the paper, too."

He brightened up and flashed a broad smile. "Oh, Miss Stewart, you don't know how much this means to me. Eddie's turning nine, and he wants a bike so bad. All his friends already got one. He don't have no daddy, and his mama jes' can't afford it. You're so kind. I know I'm imposin'. If I can ever do somethin' for you, jes' let me know." He patted her hand.

She liked the little man anyway, but after her experience, money didn't seem as important as it did before. All she had on her mind was her outer space experience and her promise to help the king. She imagined the feeling would soon pass and she'd be Earth-oriented again in no time.

When Mr. Swift left, Mona returned to the kitchen to the tempting aroma of cooked bacon. Pep begged for some, and she took a piece from the pan to give him his share. With the other three pieces, she made a pumpernickel sandwich, layering it with mayonnaise, cheese, lettuce, and tomato. She savored the flavor with every bite. *At this moment, not even a tenderloin filet could taste so good. Better yet, things seem to be returning to normal.*

After topping off the meal with a bowl of strawberry ice cream, she called her insurance agent and advised him of her wreck. She'd have to buy another car right away since today was the last day of her vacation. Monday, she'd need transportation to go back to work. She thumbed through the paper and the telephone book and decided what she wanted, happy her agent promised to take care of her claim right away.

After phoning a couple of automobile dealers, she talked to one salesman who promised, "I have the color and one loaded with everything you want. Come on down, and we'll put you in a fine little car today." She would go there first, but she'd shop around if necessary.

She slipped on a dark-green suit with a matching blouse of a lighter shade, wanting to appear professional in order to have a bargaining edge. Then, she called a cab. At the first dealership she tried, she found exactly what she wanted. Better yet, in thirty minutes' haggling, they agreed on a price. So one hour after she reached the showroom, she signed papers to purchase a vehicle.

For the first time in her life, she had a brand-new car, a bright-red Toyota Camry with all the extras. The purchase excited her enough to set aside the spaceship and the accompanying problems. However, she'd learned one thing: life is short. Because of her harrowing experience, she decided to enjoy living and hang the consequences. On the way home, she stopped by a coworker's house to show him her new prized possession.

"Hey, you've got a mighty fine looking automobile. Mmhmm, air, keyless entry, CD—it's got it all, even real leather seats." Rob Parker ran his hands through his graying dark brown hair. "Say, Mona, I'm surprised. Back from vacation with a new car? How come?" He stooped to lower his six-foot body enough to inspect the inside.

She replied without emotion. "I had a wreck. My car went over a ravine. Luckily, I only had minor injuries."

"My God!" Jerking his head around to glare at her, he wrinkled his brow. "I didn't hear about that. When did it happen? Where did it happen? How'd you escape without serious injuries?"

"Oh, on some country road. I slowed down and jumped. They haven't gotten the car out yet. Pep was with me, but he's okay." She paused before saying when. Until this moment, it hadn't occurred to her someone might wonder how she got back home and managed to do without a car for a week.

Talking to Rob, also an experienced reporter, made Mona cautious. She feared if she said more, he'd see right through her fabrications. It dawned on her nobody except her and the Svarians knew when the wreck happened. She could say she walked from the site—which she did—without saying when. Her insurance agent didn't even know because he'd gotten an emergency call while they were talking. In a rush, he'd said, "Yesterday, wasn't it?" and hung up. She'd report it happened yesterday. Although a person jumping from a moving vehicle would normally be at least scratched up some, she made no claim for injuries. So they wouldn't have any reason to insist she go to a doctor. It ought to work.

She was glad Rob took her word for what happened and let the details drop. Maybe he assumed her injuries were on private parts of her body. "Well, you sure were lucky. Looks like you're not even scuffed up." He diverted his gaze to the sleekness of the Camry. "Mighty nice car." His sideways grin caused the dimple in his chin to deepen. It also made Mona aware that, even at age thirty-four, he was very handsome, and unattached.

She reminded herself she'd just come out of a bad relationship, plus having an experience in outer space and making a commitment to help the Svarians. This wasn't the time for romantic thoughts. Nor was it the time to open up any doors. To avoid further questions, she left as soon as she could break away.

Chapter Five

The newsroom buzzed when she arrived at work the next Monday morning. A downtown building on fire had their attention, and Mona caught the assignment. She'd planned to sneak a few minutes to start her story about her experience, but this took precedence. She went to the location and found a dilapidated boarding house burning to the ground. Derelicts sat on the curb and watched the firemen attempt to put out the blaze.

She queried the firemen, "Could you tell me how the fire started, sir? Were any of the building's occupants hurt?"

Both answers were negative. After a couple more questions, she left the scene. She returned to the newspaper office to write her story.

Rob plopped a typewritten sheet on her desk. "See if this is accurate, Mona."

With a sly smile, she scanned the story of her wreck and handed it back. "Looks okay to me."

Rob reached in his shirt pocket. "Oh, hell. My Parker pen's gone. I must have lost it in the gully when I was checking out your wreck. It's my favorite. I'll have to go back and search for it."

Mona cringed. She hoped he wouldn't snoop around too far.

Dees stood at her desk waving a paper. "Damn it all, Mona, you could tell me when you almost kill yourself." He slammed his fist on the desk, almost shaking her keyboard to the floor. "But, no, I have to wait and read the copy."

Dees had a reputation as a hard man, but Mona knew he cared about her welfare.

"Sorry, Mr. Dees. But I saw no need to worry you with my problems."

24

"Worry me? Who the hell's worried? I just like to be in on what happens around here. I suppose if you'd been killed, I'd have to find out when I read your obituary." He left in a huff, but she smiled at the concern he failed to conceal.

Life on Earth doesn't seem so bad after all. I'll take it over Svar's dullness any day. She still wished she had somebody she could confide in—somebody who would believe her. Frank Dees might be that man, but she couldn't bring herself to take the chance.

All day long, she tried to find an assignment near Wolf Road, but nothing newsworthy happened out there. She'd need some excuse to go to the isolated vicinity after work, because if someone saw her there, they'd wonder why. She decided to tell her coworkers she'd always liked the area where the wreck occurred and planned to buy a parcel of land nearby. It might sound ironic, but it gave her a reason to go back more than once. She made a big deal of it. With vague interest, her coworkers listened while she expounded on the advantages of living in a quiet, woodsy place far removed from the hustle and bustle of city life.

Heading toward the gully off Wolf Road after work, she jolted. *The people from the wrecking company are arriving to pick up my demolished Volkswagen. Good Lord, suppose they see the ship!* Floor-boarding the gas pedal, she hurried to the site, not sure at all what she'd do when she got there.

Climbing down the embankment, Mona checked out the area. The VW hadn't been removed. Nothing had been disturbed. Reaching the bottom, she could not find the spaceship. A couple of times, she thought she heard someone behind her, but when she turned around, nobody was in sight.

She soon found out why when Eric appeared. "We have hidden the ship. Come with me." He grasped her arm and led her to a stand of trees and brush. The camouflage job was excellent. He pulled back limbs so she could enter.

As agreed on earlier, Mona brought food. Eric had told her their plan. It was to substitute real food for the one pill a day they'd been taking—over time, building up to a complete food diet, which they believed had the vitamins needed to make them look more human. They hoped, after a time, the anticipated reversal of facial and nose distortion would take place. But they had no assurance it would happen. They also expected to return to the age this era would make them. But the results of this experiment were yet unknown. Things could go either way.

In any event, they'd decided to try. A light diet was the starting fare. They chewed up the bits of chicken in the soup and forced down one slice of bread each. It seemed to be a chore.

"Well, how did you like it?" Mona realized the small eating exercise exceeded what the three inhabitants of another planet were accustomed to.

"Thank you for bringing it." Lydia wiped her mouth with a napkin. "It's all bland to us. Our taste buds do not work, so food has no more flavor than our pills."

Mona was disappointed because she hadn't realized they wouldn't taste the food. "I'm sorry." Thinking exercise might help, she made a suggestion. "You're trying to get back in shape. Why don't you sneak out every day and walk around a bit?"

Eric replied, "Not yet. We cannot risk discovery. Maybe when our appearance changes. I am confident a change will come, and I encourage my people to believe it will, too. They want to look like normal humans and be useful again."

Every few days, Mona brought them nourishment, each time adding a little until they built up to two meals a day and just one pill. By the end of the third week, they were ready to eliminate the pills. But it was risky. They might all become ill, or they could die. Still, the time had come to take the chance.

The next evening, Mona had a late assignment and could not get to the hiding place until after dark. Pulling her car into the secluded area where she parked every day, she clambered down the slope.

Eric met her saying, "Lydia is ill."

When Mona neared the place where Lydia lay resting, her burping prompted Mona to take an antacid from her purse. "Here, Lydia. This'll help."

Lydia took the pill. In just a few minutes, she tapped her throat. "My indigestion is gone." The simple solution worked, and Mona was relieved Lydia had experienced one of the minor irritations plaguing humanity. Maybe it was a good sign.

Monitoring the radio, Marcus frowned. "Strange noises are coming from outer space. I can't tell where exactly, but it might be a problem." He turned some knobs on the console. "I think the Torpians have managed to crank up one of the ships left behind, plus they have their own, identical to ours."

"We do not know, but they could have gotten hold of our records from the previous trip." Eric spoke up. "If they did, they will use them and try to come right here. They know we have information and knowledge they do not have. I am convinced Torpi and his clan will follow us if they can. Torpi wants to be immortal, and he knows I'm the only one who can give him the heart transplant he needs."

Worry lines creased Eric's brow. Torpi would not hesitate to endanger all of them if necessary. But all they could do was wait and see what happened.

The signals continued, and, two days later when Mona was there, their worst fears were realized. Torpi himself spoke on the airwaves. All of them listened.

"Fellow Svarians," he began in a sarcastic tone, "you are traitors and have betrayed those of us who have become Torpians. We will seek you out. You are not as safe as you were on Svar. We will get all of your secrets—one way or another—and then destroy you. Yes, and we want the Earthling, too. The job must be complete." He gave a loud, wicked laugh and signed off.

This new development presented a double danger—first, being confronted by Torpians, and, second, if Earthlings were notified, they'd investigate. Pressure would come from both sides.

Mona bit the corner of her lip. *What might be the best course of action?* She turned to Eric, "Look, here on Earth they'll need me to provide them with food just as you do. Maybe you should reveal yourselves and take the chance of favorable consequences."

But Eric would not hear of it. "Torpi is smart. Maybe he couldn't resist bragging, but I bet he has devised new weapons. He has probably found a way to survive hunger, too. His threats aren't idle. He will keep his word. He won't hesitate to kill us. Besides, I want to come back in time as a human and stay as long as I wish. If I can't, then I don't want to exist at all."

Marcus and Lydia made a weak effort to persuade him otherwise, but nothing swayed him from his stand.

"You need a way to defend yourselves," Mona told them. "I can provide some weapons."

But the only thing their leader would agree to let her bring to the ship was knives. However, on her drive home, she remembered her father's gun collection. In a fight, guns would be much more useful than knives. Regardless of what Eric King had said, she planned to bring back both.

The ten o'clock news had no startling reports of spaceship sightings, so Mona switched off the television set and unlocked the closet where she stored the guns. Handling those guns brought back memories. Her father taught her respect for guns. When she was a teenager, he'd often take her to the rifle range and let her shoot. But when he died, she locked them up and had not touched them since, never suspecting she'd take them out for such a bizarre purpose. Her heart ached as she placed them on a table one by one.

They were all shapes and sizes. It was quite a collection, more than she remembered. Many were handguns, both pistols and revolvers, somewhat like Colts and Smith and Wesson's without a brand name on them, but two rifles and a shotgun were in the collection. All were in good working order. She had cartridges and bullets for each. Mona wrapped the box of small guns in brown paper and used an old violin case of her mother's for the dismantled rifle. She giggled, thinking of all the gangster movies portraying characters carrying guns in a violin case. The shotgun she chose to leave behind. It was late, so she put them back in the closet.

The next evening, when it turned dark, she piled the box of guns into her car trunk. *What will happen if I get stopped by the police?*

She closed the trunk and slid into the driver's seat. Pep panted on the seat beside her. She leaned over close to the little dog's ear and confided in him. "Pep, old boy, if I get arrested tonight, we may both be in jail for a while."

He wagged his tail and stuck it in the coffee she'd set in the cup holder. As she dumped out the remaining liquid, she clicked her tongue. "Oh, damn. I forgot the knives." But she dismissed them. The guns would do. She could bring the knives tomorrow. She wanted to pick up tacos on the way, and she needed to get back to the ship.

Reaching the top of the gully, Mona found another car parked in her spot. It scared her at first, but its occupants were just two teenagers making out. She pulled up behind them and shined her bright lights into the car. Their eyes widened liked scared rabbits. Mona backed out. She finished the last bite of a taco that was her dinner then folded the wrapper into a small square. It fell on the floorboard and stuck to her shoe. She ignored it and waited. The kids wheeled out as fast as they could. Mona smiled. *They think I'm the police. All clear.* She pulled in and braked the car.

Contrary to the struggle she'd expected, sliding the box of guns down the hill was an easy task. She pushed it with her foot, and it slipped along on the dew-moistened grass as if it were greased. When she leaned over to guide the box, the taco wrapper stuck to her shoe fell to the ground. Despite the anti-litter ads she'd just passed on the highway, and though it was uncharacteristic of her, she just let it lay. No need to risk getting found out. She could pick it up on her way back.

Nothing stirred in the ravine, and nobody came out to meet Mona. When she reached the ship, Lydia let her in. The others didn't speak right away. They were all listening to the radio, and it seemed the Torpians' spaceship was about to land. Mona shoved the box inside, again using her foot. Opening it, she held up one gun.

"We do not need those." He lifted his chin. "We are peaceful people. I have been thinking about this, and I have changed my mind. I think the Torpians are just trying to bluff us. I do not believe they will harm us." His hesitant tone lacked conviction.

Mona hung her head. In reality, they all knew Torpi would attack, but she couldn't dispute the word of their leader.

The radio became full of static, and words were no longer distinguishable. The last transmission announced the spaceship prepared to land, but where or when they could not tell. Torpi and his group were close, but how close?

The radio stopped working. Silence, deafening silence. Mona turned on a police monitor she'd brought with her. She also spread out a city map and listened to see if any strange calls came from this area. Nothing. Calls about spaceships came in from all over town, but none were in the Wolf Road vicinity. After a second of squawking, the operator broke in.

"We have a 13 on Wolf Road, two miles east of Highway 25."

"This is 385. I'll take that call. I'm on Highway 25."

"Copy, 385. Sending 353 as backup. A man reported seeing a tan SUV Explorer swerving on Wolf Road. It pulled into some bushes near the big gully. They passed him going about eighty then slowed down and stopped, and he passed them."

"Copy. Almost at the scene."

"This is 353, I'm right behind you. Pull off to the right, we can both fit in there and maybe nab the suspect."

I'm glad they dropped the 10 codes and are using clear text nowadays. I could have learned the police codes, but the plain language they adopted after 9-11 to avoid confusion when police from different states worked together simplifies understanding. But what's going to happen now? If they're where I think, they'll pull in right behind my car. She didn't voice her thoughts to the others. What good would it do? She cringed when she realized they were getting close.

Mona pointed to some binoculars on a shelf. "Can I use those?"

"Yes," Eric replied. "They're night-vision binoculars. What are you looking for?"

"Oh, I just want to check on my car." Standing at the window, she raised them to her eyes. At the top of the hill, the two police cars parked side by side. Both policemen got out of their cars. One officer nodded to the other and, with drawn guns, approached her car.

Should she ask Eric let her go back to her car and try to explain why she was there? *They'll take me to the nut house if I tell the truth. Or if they investigate, then what? I could tell them the same story I told everyone else, but they'll still think I'm crazy, wandering in the woods all alone at night just to check on property. It might be best to let them find out what's going on for themselves*. She did nothing, except listen to her police radio and stand by the window to see what transpired.

How in the world am I going to remember all of this? I've got to get₁ it written down. What a story it's developing into. Mona took a deep breath as she pictured herself ascending the stage to receive the Pulitzer Prize.

Chapter Six

The two men wandered around. Then, one returned to his car and used his radio.

"385."

"Go ahead, 385," the operator came back.

He gave the car's make and model. "Looks like it's deserted. Undamaged. Check this license number." He called it out and waited.

"Received, 385."

Oh, God, they're going to find out it's registered to me.

"Copy. We're headed down to see if anyone is hiding in the gully."

Mona whirled around to Eric who was sitting at the ship's console. "The police are headed in our direction. What are you going to do?"

"We're lifting off." He gave the signal.

Mona nodded. She had no way to explain her car being there, so it was important to get away.

They shed the camouflage and went straight up. In an instant, as Mona watched through the night-vision binoculars, the cone-shaped object rose above the trees.

***

Rob reached the scene and retraced his steps, searching for his pen. Voices from two policemen a few yards away prompted him to scoot behind a large oak tree.

"God Almighty!" the red-faced cop exclaimed. "I don't believe this. Now I've seen one myself." He crossed himself. "Did you see that Danny?"

The other policeman shook his head and remained frozen to the spot. He swore as the object disappeared from sight. Both men ran to the bottom of the gully. Rob sneaked behind them as they dug their way through the bushes to a clearing. "Must be the damn spaceship's landing spot, Mahoney." The younger man shined his flashlight around.

Rob jerked his head toward the sky but saw no ship of any kind. *What are they talking about?*

"How in the hell are we going to explain this?" The senior officer scratched his head. "You know what happens when these things are reported, Danny. Nothing. Well, nothing except a lot of questions from the top. And I hate those damn investigations. I'm getting too old for them. I can retire in two months. This cinches it. I'll turn in my papers along with this report."

"I agree with you. They won't pay any attention when we tell them we saw a spaceship, Sarge. But we can't just ignore it. What can we do?"

In the darkness behind them, another spaceship slipped up on them. Rob turned to see it swoop down and head straight for the clearing. The men were caught in the force of it, crushed beneath its weight. Good chance they never knew what hit them. The ship ascended again and was out of sight in seconds.

Rob pressed fists against his cheeks. "Oh, my God!" He sprinted toward the scene but stopped short when he heard the patrol car's radio squealing.

"385 and 353, come in." The operator's voice came loud and clear. "I've dispatched other units to your area, but 350 has just been assigned to this district. He overshot the location."

A new voice spoke. "Car 350. I'm at the location. 332. We're out of the car."

More policemen arrived. Darting behind another tree, Rob peeked out. He recognized Allen Brunson. He'd written a feature story on the man as a new recruit. At twenty-six, Brunson had graduated from the police academy. *I figured him out right away. He's a power-hungry, cocky jerk. Dealing with small-time crooks makes him feel superior. Any ego boost works for him. No telling what will happen here.*

Rob stood back as Brunson and his partner descended the hill. *Damn! I'm trapped. The police are already here. I'll leave the minute I get a chance.*

"Davis, don't be surprised at what we find down below. Might be a whole cache of junkies. You know what a cache is? I learned it in the academy." Brunson chuckled. "I might use it on this report." He punched his partner's arm. "Hey, pay attention. Maybe you'll learn something."

They edged forward. "Okay, Davis," Brunson told his partner, "you take the right, I'll take the left, and we'll see just who is down here."

The men moved apart, guns drawn with one finger on the trigger and another on flashlight switches in the other hand. Rob stayed out of sight as they roamed around through the darkness until they completed a full circle.

"Nothing here, Brunson."

Brunson held up his shoe. "Except dog mess."

Ignoring the remark, Davis walked away. "I'll keep looking."

Rob darted behind tree after tree while following them.

But when Brunson's light fell on a crop of red hair over a mangled bloodstained forehead, he became ill and turned away to vomit.

When he regained his composure, he turned and screamed to his partner, "Come here, quick!"

His partner stood right behind him, white as a sheet.

"I've never seen a decapitated head before," Brunson managed between retches. "Much less one of a fellow officer I knew well." He threw up again.

Davis shined the light full in his face. "Brunson, are you all right?"

Putting a hand on Davis's shoulder, Brunson sucked in his breath. "Hell, no, I'm not all right. Have you ever seen anything like this before?"

Davis shook his head. Then he turned and lost his last meal.

Rob wished he could help, but he didn't want to reveal his presence, so he stayed put.

Then Brunson bumped the light, and it fell from Davis's hands. Its beam spilled out into the bushes where Mahoney had been thrown.

Pieces of the man's body lay strewn all over. An arm, leg, and parts of the torso were scattered about. He cringed, feeling like he'd pass out. Instead, he tightened up his self-control and faced the ungodly sight.

"My God, what could have happened to them?" Davis's mouth hung open.

Brunson shook his head. "I dunno, but we're not safe. Let's get the hell out of here and call for help."

They scrambled up the hill as fast as their legs would take them with Rob close behind.

When they reached their patrol cars, Rob stopped long enough to overhear their report to the operator. Brunson related the gruesome details. However, it surprised Rob he managed to present them in an orderly, matter-of-fact manner. Perhaps the guy had the makings of a good policeman after all. He had remained calm after facing gruesome deaths.

Police cars and ambulances dispatched to the area arrived in droves. Rob had no chance to leave; he'd have been spotted. The police photographer took pictures from every angle before the bodies were removed. The lieutenant in charge surveyed the situation then talked to the officers who were first on scene.

Chewing on the end of a cigar, a man Rob recognized as seasoned police lieutenant, Paul Ramundi, questioned the rookies. Still hidden from sight, Rob could hear every word.

"Look, men, I've got to know what all this is about. Brunson, Davis, one at a time from the beginning, tell me everything that happened. Don't leave out even the most minute detail. Brunson, you go first."

"Well, sir, we were dispatched here on a DUI. But the call was for an SUV Explorer, and it's nowhere to be seen. When we got to this spot"—he pointed to the bushes where the police cars were still parked—"the only car around is the brand-new Camry there. We called in for a registration report, and, while we waited, we radioed we were out of the car and went down the hill to look around."

Ramundi stopped the man. "Don't you know you're supposed to wait for the registration report before proceeding?"

"Yes, sir, Lieutenant." He looked at the ground.

Ramundi glared at him then let it drop. "Go on."

"Well, we walked around but didn't see anything. Then we spotted Sergeant O'Brien...dead." Brunson's voice cracked.

Ramundi shifted from one foot to the other.

Brunson cleared his throat. "Sorry, sir. I feel like I swallowed a golf ball. Next, I saw Mahoney...or what was left of him." He bit his quivering lip. "Most horrible thing I ever came across."

"Did you see anything or anybody else?" Ramundi wrinkled his nose.

"I know an animal had been there. I stepped in some mess. The stinky stuff is still on my shoe. I'd forgotten about it till now. It didn't seem significant."

"In a case like this, everything's significant, Brunson. Hand me your shoe."

Brunson took it off and handed it to the lieutenant "This is from a small animal. Could be a dog." He squinted. "The question is, where did a dog come from? There are no houses nearby." He returned the shoe and Brunson slipped it back on.

"Put it in your report," the lieutenant added. "Finish your story."

"There's not much more. We went back to the car and called for assistance, to let the experts check the area."

Ramundi nodded and turned to Officer Davis. "All right, what can you tell me?"

Their stories matched but Davis added he'd received the report on the Camry, and when he found out Mona Stewart owned it, he recognized her name.

"She's a reporter for *The Daily Times*, sir. Could be out here on assignment."

Brunson looked at his partner. "You should have told me that first."

Ramundi glared at Brunson. It appeared to Rob that Ramundi agreed with him about this new young cop. He didn't seem to like him. Maybe he reminded him of himself as a rookie.

"All right, since you seem to know about her, tell us what she was doing here and where she is now," Ramundi demanded.

"I-I, er, I don't know, sir. But shouldn't her newspaper be able to provide—?"

Ramundi tapped his toe. "Don't try to upstage me. Just do what I say. Go find out."

It seemed to Rob he'd given Brunson confusing instructions on purpose, so whatever he did would be wrong. If he went to the car and called in, Ramundi would tell the rookie, "I meant for you to go to the paper." But if he left and went to the paper, Ramundi would ask Brunson why he left the scene without permission. He shook his head. Even murder didn't stop pettiness.

When the men walked away and turned their backs, Rob saw his chance to escape. On weak legs, he returned to the car he'd successfully hidden and left the area. But the scene remained imprinted in his mind. The gruesomeness of those two violent deaths already haunted him.

***

What will happen next? As the ship Mona was on ascended, she spotted the Torpians' ship readying to descend into the gully. They'd been found out.

Seated at the ship's round table, Eric announced, "Bad news. Torpi contacted me. He bragged they'd killed two policemen and will kill other Earthlings. As your leader," he declared, "I have to act in the best interests of all. We must go back and, if necessary, fight to keep our position." He folded his hands. "I know I am doing an about-face from my previous stand, but by acting like an idealist, I misplaced my trust. The Torpians came to Earth and destroyed human lives. It proves they will stop at nothing to destroy us, and, even more important, they have it in their power to destroy the world as it is today."

He turned to face Mona. "I have not told you, but I suspect if they cannot get us under their control, they will change the past—the time of the atomic explosions—and with the technology available to them, they'll make sure all survivors, except themselves, are obliterated in those atomic blasts."

Mona nodded. "You're saying they'll take the best—or the worst—of both time dimensions' technologies and use them to their own advantage, leaving only members of their own group." She hung her head, deflated.

She was not of this planet or this era, but she had become caught up in the workings of these space creatures' lives. Her interest in their welfare and the welfare of generations to come overshadowed everything else. Unbelievable! Just a week ago, when her boyfriend dumped her, she felt she had nothing to live for. But the wreck changed everything. Finding herself in an interplanetary, interdimensional situation made life for all people, including herself, seem vitally important. She bit the tip of her thumbnail. *And what a story this will make.*

"We cannot hover long." Eric broke into her thoughts. "By tonight, we must go back and replenish our energy source. So, we must decide our course of action. I wonder how many people the Torpians have onboard their ship? I do not believe they would risk using up their energy too fast by carrying many passengers. They may have six, two more than we have. More than six, I doubt."

Mona raised her eyebrows, waiting for his next statement.

36

"I suggest we load the guns Mona brought. We must be prepared to fight. But since we have never used guns on Svar, I cannot promise results. Our bodies have become different. All of us, including the Torpians, may not suffer from bullet wounds. We may be immune to them." After a pregnant pause, he added, "But if Torpi went to the trouble to make weapons with pointed rocks, then he's tested them. He would not be above killing one of his own people to see if those weapons worked. And if wounds of that nature do not heal fast enough, then neither would bullet wounds."

Mona knew Eric had qualified what might happen, and he'd come to the conclusion bullet wounds would be effective. With the guns, they might have an edge over the enemy.

Chapter Seven

At three o'clock in the morning, after a tipster notified him Mona's car had been abandoned and she was nowhere to be found, Frank Dees crawled out of bed and called the police. He was worried. This girl was one of his favorites, but as her boss, he felt it imperative to conceal his fondness. From the time she'd come to work for the paper, he'd taken her under his wing. Every chance he had, he gave her the encouragement necessary to boost a reporter's confidence. Although he did not show favoritism, he would have done anything for Mona.

He had a queasy feeling about her sudden disappearance. In an intuitive moment of hopelessness, he regretted never letting her know, at least in some small way, he had a fatherly feeling toward her. It might be too late.

Hoping he was wrong, he decided to have his best man investigate. He phoned Rob Parker to give him the assignment.

"Rob," Dees apologized. "Sorry to wake you this time of the morning. You didn't answer your landline, but I'm glad I caught you on your cell phone." He explained the latest development, then said, "You're a damn good reporter. Mona's one of us. I don't understand what's happening, but, for God's sake, I hope you can come back with something those dumb police haven't found. You saw Mona's new car, didn't you? Make sure the one they found is it. Get on over to the gully before they tow the car away. Do your best." He hung up.

***

Rob had reached his car and opened the door to get in it when Dees called. Instead, he stayed on the scene. By this time, police swarmed all over. Pretending he'd just arrived, he hunted down

Lieutenant Ramundi and demanded, "What can you tell me about all of this? Are you sure it's Mona Stewart's car?"

Ramundi ground out the remains of his cigar in the dirt and then picked it up and put it in his pocket. Getting a fresh one, he stuck it in his mouth, leaving it unlit. "Don't want to contaminate the scene." He chewed on the cigar. "We don't know much yet, Parker. Just that two of our men are dead. Unusual circumstances, though. Clean cuts like slices, body parts strewn around, and Mahoney's head crushed. We're removing the bodies, but you can see the car for yourself. Take a look at this registration." He handed Rob a slip of paper with Mona's name and address on it. "Since you're here, maybe you can answer some questions." The lieutenant had reversed the situation. "When did you see Mona last? Are you just coworkers, friends, lovers? What was her last assignment?"

After answering all of the questions, Rob cut him off. "If I'm a suspect, I want to be booked. If not, let me do my job."

Pressing no further, Ramundi shrugged. "No, you're not a suspect. Go ahead, get your story." He turned on his heel and left.

Rob walked to the bloody spot where Mahoney's body parts had been. He scrounged around and found a pen stuck in a pile of pine straw. He picked it up and looked for his initials, finding them on the gold top of it. "Yes!" He stuck it in his pocket.

Then he went to the area marked off by yellow tape. They were still cleaning up the mess. Seeing a sliced-up body, he caught his breath. Then, much to his distress, they picked up a part of a hand with a wedding ring still on it. One officer placed it in a plastic evidence bag and then continued to rake around. Rob lowered his head, gagged twice, but managed not to throw up. *God, if they find Mona like this, I'll die, too.* He shuddered and prayed to find her safe and well.

A plainclothes man wearing a badge passed by, and Rob stopped him because he seemed familiar. "Say, aren't you Tony? We were in the same class in high school. Haven't seen you in a while." He held out his hand. "Rob Parker. I'm working for *The Daily Times* as a reporter." *Hmmm, but the names a misnomer; we don't publish daily anymore.*

"Oh, yeah. I remember you. You haven't seen me because I was on the Chicago police force till recently. I moved home, got a big promotion, and I don't have to wear a uniform. Say, didn't this car belong to a female reporter from your paper?" His tone sounded far from friendly.

Chances are good I'm a suspect since I know Mona. Rob grimaced. *And my being chosen as high-school valedictorian over Tony doesn't help. Some people never forget.* "Yeah, Mona Stewart. She's a top-notch reporter." No need to express his concern to this guy. "Tell me, Tony, what do you think could have happened here?"

The wiry guy stiffened and looked him square in the face. "Parker," he sneered, "I thought you already knew everything. Anyhow, if I could answer your questions, I'd already be back at the precinct making my report." He turned and walked away.

Rob had no more information than he had before, and it seemed Tony didn't either. The jealous slur rolled right off his back. Despite Frank telling him to concentrate on finding Mona, everything indicated these two cases were intertwined. His shoulders drooped. So far, the only clue he'd found was the pen.

Staring at the ground, he spotted a square of waxed paper. When it reminded him of Mona's habit of folding taco wrappers that way, he picked it up. When he unfolded it, he discovered a taco wrapper. Since he'd already picked it up, he took a photo of both sides, refolded it, and called a policeman. As he handed it to the officer apologizing, "Sorry, I contaminated this; I wasn't thinking."

The officer shrugged. "It happens." He also photographed it, bagged it, and left.

Rob stood there a moment. *I didn't tell what I know. Mona loved tacos. The wrapper could have contained her last meal.* He didn't know, but he didn't want to get her involved. After checking around a little longer and deciding he'd scouted the area thoroughly, he headed home.

In bed, he tossed and turned, sleeping intermittently. After a few hours, he gave up trying to get some rest, got dressed, and drove to the newspaper office.

When he arrived, the grayness of dawn crept up, causing the streetlights to shut off. Inside, it surprised him to see Dees rummaging through the files. His boss rarely got to work before daylight.

Dees turned, spotting him. "Oh, it's you." His voice sounded hoarse. "What did you find out?"

Rob stared back. "Even a hardened cynic like you wouldn't believe what happened. Dan, the sergeant—what's his last name—oh, hell, he has no last name, he doesn't exist anymore. He's out there in pieces all over the place. His partner's dead, too. God, Frank, it was horrible!" Rob sank onto a chair. "I tell you, I've never seen anything like it."

"My God, man! Who did it? Last I heard, Mahoney and his partner just stepped out of the police car to make a routine check and found Mona's car. You're telling me they're dead? How could all that have happened?"

Rob's mind was awhirl. On the drive to the office, he'd debated how much to reveal. Would his skeptical boss scoff at his report of spaceships? He decided not to take the chance. "All I know is no human could have done it. Couldn't be an animal either. The cuts were too straight. Those guys looked like they'd been caught in a slicing machine—even chops, clean cuts—except Mahoney's head was crushed. I didn't see that." He pressed his hand against his forehead. "He's got a wife and two children." He couldn't bring himself to tell about seeing the wedding ring.

"Could a helicopter be the culprit?"

"No, they checked flight reports. None were in the area." He stood and tried to steady himself by leaning against a desk. "I tell you, there's no explanation. None whatsoever." Nausea overcame him, and he clutched his throat. He yearned to tell somebody the whole truth, but he had no proof. The only two people who had reason to believe him were dead.

Frank Dees handed Rob a cup of lukewarm coffee. "Okay, Rob. Just take it easy. Er, I hate to ask, but how about Mona? Anything on her?"

Rob sipped his coffee. "The car is hers, all right, but there's no sign of her. I haven't been to her apartment yet. I wanted to check with you first and get a recent photograph."

"That's what I just got out of the files. Here's a good print. I'll get copies made for the police." He held it up. "Oh, I also ran copies of Mona's application. Did you know she's all alone in the world? I don't just mean divorced, I mean really alone—no parents, brothers, sisters, or close relatives. I guess that's why they called me. She must've put my name and phone number as the person to notify in case of an accident."

He took a deep breath. "I knew her parents were killed in a plane crash, but I thought she had somebody." He shook his head as he put the photo on top of a stack of papers. "God, how little we know about each other. Who's that boyfriend of hers anyway? Know anything about him? Let's check him out."

"His name's Black, Lee Black, the third. Playboy type. Inherited money awhile back and spent it all fast. I think Mona helped him out, maybe gave him money. He probably spent it on other girls. I met him once or twice. Seemed like a bum to me. I tried to warn Mona off. But she just stopped talking to me about him. Maybe they cut if off, maybe not. I don't know. I'll check, though."

Rob stared at the photograph lying on Dees' desk, an environmental shot taken in front of her apartment on Mobile Bay. Mona leaned against a huge oak. Her dark hair and blue eyes made Rob aware of her nice features and slender figure. He liked her because she was smart and she had a vivacious personality. He knew a lot about her because she was chatty, always talking to people in the office about places she went. But he'd never asked her for a date. She had a boyfriend. Once or twice they'd grabbed a sandwich together at a café down the street after an assignment. It amused him when she took the waxed paper from her sandwich and folded it into a neat square before depositing it into the trash. Otherwise, he'd never paid special attention to her. Until lately. Somehow, in the last few weeks, he'd been more attracted to her and thought about asking her out. Their age difference stopped him. She was six years his junior. Did it matter? Maybe he'd never get the chance to find out.

"Much as I hate to admit it, this isn't going to be an easy case to break, Rob." His boss interrupted his thoughts. "Find out everything Mona's done the past few weeks—who she saw, where she's been." He scratched his head. "Something's screwy about her vacation. I don't know what it is. I got an inkling something was wrong when she avoided talking about it. It wasn't important before. Now, it may be our only clue. This isn't an ordinary case. Don't treat it like one." He pounded the desk with his fist. "Work on it exclusively. I don't want you to do another damn thing until we find Mona's okay. Understand?"

Rob nodded, and when Dees waved his hand in dismissal, he glanced at the clock. Six a.m. Descending the stairs, he was exhausted from being up all night. He sat on the bottom step and closed his eyes. Sometime later, he awoke and rubbed his hands over his face. *I'm too tired to function. This isn't the best way to start an investigation. Oh, God, I can picture Mona hurt somewhere. Perhaps kidnapped. Or even dead. No, that can't be.* The thought made him override self-pity and get on with the job.

Where to start? The most logical place was Mona's apartment. Arriving there, he rang the bell, knowing no one would answer. *Pep. Unless the dog is in the apartment, it's disappeared, too.*

No answer and no bark. No doubt about it, Pep was gone. One day in the café, Mona told him about her pet beagle. "We're buddies. Except when I'm working, Pep's almost never out of my sight. Wherever I go, he goes."

At the apartment complex office, the manager grumbled at being awakened for the second time. "First, somebody knocks on my door in the middle of the night. Now you come banging on it, and it ain't even seven o'clock. Listen"—he shoved uncombed hair out of his eyes—"I can't give you no key. The police have already been here, and they told me not to let anybody inside."

"But I showed you my credentials. I'm a reporter," Rob insisted. "Look, this is very important. We have to have Miss Stewart's copy on a big story to go to press," he lied. "That's all I want. It's on a thumb drive and it won't take me a minute to find it. The police aren't going to bother you about anything like that. They just don't want people nosing around." More lies. "If you don't want to give me a key, just come let me in." He hoped the man wouldn't make the effort to go inside with him.

"Oh, what the hell!" He gave Rob the once over. Squinting, he took a key from a rack. "Okay. Bring this right back to me. Tell you what. Don't wake me up again." He pointed to the door. "Just drop it through the slot." He cocked his head. "This never happened."

People are so unpredictable. Rob was pleased he'd been convincing enough for the manager to trust him. He hurried to the apartment before the man changed his mind.

On his way to the back of the complex, he noticed the whole place was quiet and peaceful. It seemed most of the tenants were still asleep. When Rob got inside Mona's apartment and saw the beautiful view of Mobile Bay, he knew why she chose to live here.

The manager might have second thoughts and interrupt at any moment. He had to act fast. In a quick look around, everything in the one-bedroom apartment seemed in order. Except for a few dog hairs on the braided rug and a frying pan soaking in the sink, the place was neat and clean.

The bed was made. A rosewood chair in front of her dresser had a robe on it and a pair of slippers under it; otherwise, it had no clutter. The bathroom was the same. The brown-and-white ceramic floor tiles appeared to have been recently scrubbed, one hand towel was on a rack by the lavatory, and a matching brown bath towel draped over the glass shower door hung evenly on each side. Rob rubbed his fingers on the floor; it wasn't even damp. Both towels were stone dry, too.

As he wandered around, he found no disorder anywhere. He checked drawers, careful not to disturb anything. In the first one, he found a picture frame face down. When he turned it over, the glass was broken but he could still see the photograph was signed "Lee." *Seems like that romance is over. Looks like Mona threw it down. I wonder why she didn't tear up his picture. Maybe she didn't have time yet.*

How much the split upset Mona, Rob didn't know. Thinking back, she had acted a little strange, edgy, after her vacation. Just different. But not depressed. Did having a new car cheer her up? Maybe a little. He detected something else he couldn't pinpoint, but her whole outlook on life seemed different somehow. Like how a person experiencing an exhilarating episode reacts by operating on nervous energy. Something had changed Mona. *If I could talk to her, maybe I could persuade her to tell me what it was.*

He found nothing else of significance. Before leaving, he closed the closet door and saw a magnetic ad on it saying, "Try Enrico's tacos. A Sauce for Kings and Queens. Call 555-9620."

He laughed. Almost every week, Mona had tacos for lunch and raved about how good they were. Once she told him, "Rob, come along with me one day and try Enrico's for yourself." Somehow, things always interfered and he never made it.

He looked at the magnet. *Has Mona been to the Mexican restaurant in the last week?* Rob needed to find out. Enrico's might be the last place Mona was seen.

After going home for a shave, shower, a bowl of cereal, and a cup of coffee, Rob headed to the restaurant, his notebook and tape recorder in hand.

A dark-haired young man, filling the cash register with change, looked up. "Good morning." He waved toward the back. "Enrico will be with you in a minute."

Rob glanced around the small Mexican place decorated with photos of cowboys with wide-brimmed hats.

"Good morning, good morning." Enrico came from the back wiping his hands on his white apron. "I got four employees on duty most of the time, but I still cook, wait tables, serve, and run the cash register." With a grin, he held out his hand. "So, I know most everybody who frequents my restaurant." His guffaw shook his entire fat body. His long, dark hair, and olive complexion made him look Mexican, but he didn't have an accent. "And I don't think we've met."

Rob shook hands. "I'm Rob Parker." It was just eleven a.m., so Rob asked, "Are you open yet?"

"Yes, sir. We open at ten thirty." He picked up silverware and led his customer to a booth in the corner. "Is this all right? I haven't seen you here before. Welcome." He placed a menu in front of Rob. "I just made a new batch of beef taco sauce. Maybe you'd like to try it."

When Rob nodded, Enrico put a paper napkin enclosing tableware in place.

Rob ordered three tacos and a Coke. Enrico came right back with a tall glass of Coke and one with ice water. Gulping down some water, Rob explained his mission and its possible connection with last night's tragedy. "I suppose you heard the morning news about those two policemen getting killed. Well, you know Mona Stewart, I'm sure. She comes in here every other week."

"Oh, yes. She's a reporter from *The Daily Times*, isn't she? Nice lady. She promised to do a feature story on my place."

"Well, they found her Camry right near the gully where those deputies were killed."

Enrico frowned. "Mona would never hurt anyone."

"Oh, nobody thinks she had anything to do with those deaths," he said in her defense. *Of course, there's a good chance the police have her on their list of suspects.* "But Mona's missing." He did not volunteer any information about the strangeness of the accompanying circumstances. "Anyhow, I just wondered when you last saw her or if you know anything else that might help us find her."

Without further urging, Enrico pulled up a chair. "Mona, she came by in a rush the day before yesterday—late. She bought a dozen tacos. She said her friends, they wanna try 'em out. Then, she looked like she didn't mean to say that, and she left. I don't know. I just don't know." He shook his head. "I hope she's okay. She's always jus' so nice."

When Enrico became quiet, Rob looked at him. "Did she say anything else?"

"No."

Pulling his phone with the photos of the wrapper he'd found in the gully from his pocket, he showed it to the restaurant owner on the off chance some information might be forthcoming.

"That's mine." No hesitation in his answer. "If you jes' look good at it, you'll see how I know." He took an empty taco wrapper from Rob's plate and rubbed the plain waxy paper between his fingers, put it to his nose, and sniffed. "It's a li'l bit thicker than hamburger paper. Tacos are juicier," he bragged. "And you smell it? Is tacos, not hamburger, top quality ground round. Is sauce, not ketchup. Mona loved my tacos. I make 'em good, different." He stiffened with pride.

He leaned across the table and spoke in a confidential, loud whisper. "I can tell you somethin' else, too. I know who ate the taco. Mona. I see the creases and I never saw anybody else fold up a wrapper so neatly. Mona, she always did. Later, she'd put it in the trash." Still holding the phone, in his hands, he deliberated for a moment. "Look right here, in the corner. That's MS, Mona's initials. I always put them on the top taco wrapper."

Rob peered at the tiny initials he believed were printed on the wrapper. Had the police missed them, too?

Then, he handed the phone back to Rob. "Where'd you find the wrapper?"

"Sorry, I'm not at liberty to reveal that information," Rob replied. Until he discovered what Mona was doing in the gully, he did not want to do or say anything that might come back to haunt him by incriminating her.

As Rob drove off, what he'd pieced together about the situation chased round and round in his brain. *Mona was in a car wreck. Suppose she has amnesia...not that I've seen any evidence of it. Okay. So maybe she went back to the scene to try to "find herself," ended up lost in the woods in the middle of the night. Oh God, maybe she was there when the murders occurred. Coincidence? Maybe. But a possibility.* He shook his head. *Maybe she really is planning to buy some property. But when she saw the dead bodies, she got scared and ran? If that's what happened, there's no telling where she went.*

He tapped his fingers on the steering wheel. *No. There're too many holes in that line of thinking. She wouldn't have been there in the middle of the night checking on property. When Mona came back after her vacation, she acted normal. Maybe a little excited about something. Otherwise, she was coherent. Good old Mona. If she'd forgotten who she was, she never would have made it back to the newspaper office.* He'd have to find a more plausible theory. Whatever happened in the gully remained an unexplainable mystery.

Maybe he needed a different tack, sort out what he did know.

Okay, so first of all, Mona's wreck caused her to end up in the gully. Next, she claimed she returned to the area, seeking property to buy. The taco wrapper confirms she was in the gully before the two officers were killed...Enrico explained about the initials on it, how she folded the paper, and exactly when she last bought tacos, and that she'd bought a bunch. He grimaced. *She told Enrico the tacos were for her friends. But what friends? And where?*

Chapter Eight

"Food is not our main consideration. We still have a supply of pills to last quite a while," Eric told Mona as he stood by the ship's round table. "But our energy is getting low. We'll have to land to recharge. And, somewhere down below, I fear our archenemy is waiting."

He tightened the sash on his tunic. "I've heard reports our hiding place on Earth is occupied. Some report other complications brought a bevy of law officers and curious citizens to the gully. But what concerns me most is avoiding a confrontation with the planetary enemy. The Earthlings pose no threat as far as I can tell. I'm the king and I'm responsible for making decisions. I plan on avoiding an encounter with Torpi by choosing a different landing place. Do you have any ideas?"

Mona could not offer much help. She pondered over where they might go as they traveled through space, but each spot she came up with promised no assurance of privacy or even a spot large enough to land in. In her travels as a reporter, she found that farmland she passed one day quite often would have a shopping center being built on it the next. Mobile's population had increased fast. Not too many unoccupied parcels of land still existed. The country was becoming the city. With the many new subdivisions popping up in every outlying section, not many isolated areas were left—unless potential buyers of real estate went way, way out in the country.

But one such place existed, a secluded section around a college where ghosts and strange lights had been reported for years. Mona had once gone there to do a feature story. For two nights, she sat poised with pen in hand, ready to write. She also took photos. No ghosts appeared on them and nothing happened. So, she wrote the story, calling the whole thing a farce, and, instead of ghosts, she ran pictures using shots of the beautiful tree-laden terrain. The story was humorous and interesting, but Mona considered the effort a complete waste of time. Worse yet, when an amateur photographer came up with "documented" photos of an eerie inhabitant lurking near the spot, Dees surprised her by publishing it. Mona was outraged.

Hmmm. I'd forgotten that. Perhaps those efforts weren't a waste of time. Maybe he'll publish my story after all. But I have bigger aspirations for it.

She blinked and forced her thoughts back to the present. After explaining why the location might suit their needs, she told Eric, "But I don't know if I can find the spot."

They risked it anyway, and when they reentered the Earth's atmosphere, Mona tried to direct Eric to the proper area.

As they neared the college, Mona considered it safe for Eric to lower the ship because the stories of a sighting would be taken with reservations. As soon as they came down close, it disappointed her to see it wasn't going to work. From the ship, she read the words aloud on a brand-new brick building. "It says 'National Guard Armory.'"

Eric took command. "We will have to go back to the gully, even if it means a fight. We can no longer stay up here. It is a chance we will have to take."

"Wouldn't we be better off returning to Svar?" Marcus asked, even though nobody else disputed Eric King's judgment.

"Even so," Eric told him, "what good would it do? All we gained would be lost. Torpi would use the opportunity to fulfill his goal of ruling Earth. We may never reach Earth again. Each time we come, we think that trip will be our last, and we will be able to stay long enough to help Earthlings with cures for terminal diseases." Eric rolled his shoulders. "This time, we have to make it or give up."

Marcus opened his mouth, but he did not speak out against Eric's decision.

Another spaceship appeared in front of them. It turned and chased them, forcing them to the outskirts of town. As they reached a spot near the airport, Mona told Eric, "I remember other stories of sightings in the woods. We're speeding so fast, I can hardly tell where they were. But we're not far from the gully. I think we're on the opposite side of it."

Eric slowed and let Torpi's ship pass over them. He dropped

below the level of the trees, and, seeing the area deserted, he landed the ship. The Torpians' ship whirled around and searched for them. It passed over twice before Torpi discovered their landing spot. When he did, he landed his ship right beside them.

Neither ship's occupants got out. For the time being, they had a standoff. Nobody wanted to make the first move. Eric seemed prepared to outwait them. He stood by the radio and gave them the chance to speak first. When they didn't, he turned down the volume.

Mona spoke up. "Would it be all right if I turn the police radio on?" When Eric assented, she set it on the UHF band and listened to see if either spaceship had been spotted.

At first, static prevented their hearing the transmissions. She tuned it and voices began to come across.

"I'm at the site of last night's murders, and I need a replacement to go off-duty."

"Replacement's en route. Is the FBI on the scene yet?"

"I copy. Three of them are here. No report yet."

Giving his number, the dispatcher added, "Move over to channel 230; 301 wants to talk to you."

Mona turned to Eric. "I know 301's the chief of police. I listen to the police radio when I can't sleep. But right now, I'm not interested in something as common as a murder, even two. They happen every night in Mobile. The Torpians are much more threatening."

Eric nodded. The next transmission caused his ears to perk up.

The radio squawked. "Go to where the Camry was parked. Two men, 26 and 30, may be a suspect." He added an expletive that should not have been on the air.

Mona shivered. "A 30 is a missing person. Me. How could I be a suspect? I don't have any kind of a record. Only once in my life have I even gotten a speeding ticket."

"I agree. But what does this mean?" Lydia asked. "How can they possibly suspect you?"

Mona threw up her hands. Sounds of voices came from the ship's radio, and Eric turned up the volume.

"Sounds like the Earthling may be blamed for our misdeeds," Torpi taunted. "Ha, those two men were all chopped up. Our slicers got them on lift off." His voice held no remorse.

Eric lowered his head. "I know what happened. The ship's blades are designed to dig down and grip the surface on which they land, thereby enabling the cone to remain upright. They maimed and killed the two men who got in their path."

"We will get you next." Torpi cut off communication before Eric could reply.

Eric sat in a daze, drumming his fingers on a table.

What will he do about Torpi's plan? Rushing to find out might put him in a precarious position. She glanced at him. *No, Eric is smart. He won't' rush to action. The more time he has, the better he'll be able to handle the situation.*

The others looked downcast, and Mona wrung her hands. Then she turned to Eric. "We're in an awful position. What do you plan to do next?"

"For the time being, you do not need to worry. You are safe in this ship with us. We know the Torpians committed the crime. We know you are innocent. It is more than the Earthlings know, so you are better off with us." He patted Mona on the shoulder and walked over to gaze out the window at the other ship.

"Well, I'm terrified," she told Eric, "but you're right. It's foolish to worry about being accused of murder when I might never leave this ship alive."

First things first. Mona admitted, though she didn't voice her opinion. *If this ship recharges and goes back to Svar, Earth will be left behind. Either way, none of us may ever have to be concerned about anything on Earth again. No more hopes of a Pulitzer Prize.*

Insisting on standing guard, Eric told the others, "As your king, I want to do my share. Get some rest." He didn't have to predict anything to Mona; she knew what would happen. Days and nights *would* blend to the point where no one on the ship would know whether they were tired or not. Even the dates and the days of the week would become difficult to keep track of.

But at this moment, she followed orders; she lay down and fell asleep almost immediately. Pep curled up beside her and slept, too. Appearing warm and comfortable in his ignorant bliss, the little dog showed no concern.

Before long, the ship being tossed from side to side disturbed Mona. She stirred, and then in a half-stupor, she sat up and shook her head. The radio transmission caused her body to jerk. The voice blurted out:

"This is but a sample. We are rocking your ship. How is that for new developments in technology? Does it give you an inkling of the advances we have made on our own? This is not the only thing we have learned to do. Does it frighten you? I hope so." Torpi laughed.

Eric took a deep breath. "As your leader, I must find a way to save you. I am choosing the guns. I'd rather not take this step, but the gases this ship contains could cause an explosion if the rocking causes a combustion. Unlikely, but possible. I cannot take that chance. I have to act now, while I still can."

Without a word or an order, they all followed Eric and loaded guns. Only Mona acted reluctant.

"I understand why you hesitate," Eric said. "You have a right to be indignant because you've been accused of murders you didn't commit—well, practically accused—because you happened to be in the wrong place."

"Yes. Makes me angry as hell." She snatched up a gun and loaded it.

More noises emitted from the police radio. "371, 371. I have a...." Static interfered but the voice sounded urgent.

"Go ahead, 371," replied the operator.

"There's been a UFO sighting four miles past the airport. A man in a car reported it first. Two residents of the area have called in since. The entire neighborhood's buzzing in an uproar. I'm on the scene and need backup."

"371, we got the call on the air. 379 is en route. Wait for backup.
"Copy."

Bad news. She turned to Eric. "What do we do now?"

"We wait."

"Wait? Suppose they come down here and find us?"

"Ah, but if they do not, we would have risked the danger of leaving and running out of energy for nothing. If we wait, we can at least leave with more energy. It is building up every minute. Anyway, what good would running do? We know we have been sighted, and the Torpians are unaware of the fact since we moved the radio out of their range to pick up transmissions. It may give us a chance to escape and leave them here to be caught. One ship would probably satisfy the Earthlings."

Mona conceded. "I suppose you're right. I guess as things stand now, we have a slight advantage, don't we?"

Eric paced the floor like a trapped animal.

Mona frowned. *Is he thinking the same thing I am? If their ship is found, they'll have to contend with the Earthlings as well as the Torpians. Another burden.*

The waiting was unbearable. The do-nothing life of the Svarians made it more tolerable to them than for Mona. If Eric would let her out of the ship just for a few minutes, it might relieve the tension. Of course, that was too risky.

Pep was the only one who left the ship. Mona let him out to take care of his business, and he dutifully returned right away. Nobody else came or went.

After eight hours, the two ships still sat in the brush undetected by humans.

Chapter Nine

Taking time out to sleep and eat, Rob Parker spent three days searching for clues. He interviewed Mona's boyfriend and cut him out of the running as a murder suspect. The only thing Lee Black thought about was himself. Black may have broken Mona's heart and caused her to run and hide, but Rob had no doubt the guy had nothing to do with the deaths in the valley. His alibi of shooting pool at the time proved solid. He had four witnesses. Rob struck him from his list.

After investigating all of his leads, he became disturbed when some things made no sense. For example, Mona just wasn't the type to move out in the country. Many times, she'd bragged, "I'm a city girl." So, why would she consider buying property so far out in the boondocks? She wouldn't. In his quest for more information, he talked to one of the secretaries at the paper and found Mona also frequented a coffee shop near her home. He went there, hoping to uncover something new.

Hopping on a stool at the coffee bar, without giving his name, he managed to get a good bit of information from a petite waitress who looked like a Barbie doll in her red-and-white striped uniform with a skirt barely covering her thighs.

"Hi, there. Haven't seen you here before, have I?" Her squeaky little voice matched her appearance.

"No. First time. I'll have a mocha."

"Coming up."

Rob didn't waste time. "I'm supposed to meet Mona Stewart here. Do you know her?"

Placing her elbows on the counter, she rested her chin in the palms of her hands. "Oh, yes, I know Mona, but I haven't seen her today. She comes in here almost every week. Has one cup of latte and one cinnamon roll. Never a takeout." She wrinkled her nose. "Heh, heh, so I was kinda surprised when she came in the last time and bought a whole bunch of food—like six tacos, six sandwiches, a few bags of chips, and a dozen doughnuts. I asked her if she was havin' a party or what, but she just stared and didn't answer me. Kinda odd, 'cause Mona's always friendly and cheerful."

"When?"

The waitress stood up and pulled on a large silver earring. "Gee, I don't know exactly. Maybe a few days ago. Gosh, she hasn't been back since. I hope I didn't run her off. I didn't mean to be nosey, but you know how it is with chitchat. You can't really talk unless you ask questions." The motor mouth rambled on and on, trying to keep the conversation going, but Rob had enough. He paid the check and walked out the door with the end of a sentence echoing in his ears.

Back at the paper, he reported what he'd discovered to Frank, ending with, "All that mumbo-jumbo wasted my time."

Dees shrugged. "I can't make any sense of it, either. If Mona had visitors, it's odd she didn't mention them to any of us."

Rob shook his head. "No, I'm sure she didn't have company. For one thing, she only has one bed. Oh, somebody could have slept well, er, with her, or in one of the chairs in the living room, but there's no evidence of that. Mona's neat. Her bed was made, and I didn't even find one coffee cup in the sink. Nothing unusual in the trash, either. But she bought too much food for one person. Something strange is going on, Frank. I tell you, that girl would not start buying so many tacos and sandwiches without a reason. I don't know where to turn. Maybe we'd better give this information to the police and see what they can do with it."

Frank banged his fist on the desk so hard Rob thought the wood would split. "No, damn it! If we can't figure it out, they sure as hell can't. They'd bungle the whole thing."

This wasn't the first time Frank had expressed his unflattering opinion of the Mobile Police Department. Every time a case went unsolved, he went into a tirade, claiming they were inefficient.

"They've got two unsolved murders on their hands. Mona's car was on the scene. Some hotshot cop will slap her in jail if they find her, even though they haven't got a shred of real evidence against her. This is a hot issue, and they're looking for a patsy. If we can just find Mona first and let this thing cool off, maybe we can avoid a hassle."

Rob returned to his desk and studied his notes. Mona left all her clothes in her closet. He knew she just had one suitcase because last month at the press convention she'd joked, "I'm the only one here with one rinky-dink bag."

He'd seen the same suitcase sitting on her closet shelf. Wherever she'd gone, she went with the clothes on her back. *Without extra clothing, Mona hadn't planned to stay long...unless someone took her away against her will.*

Rob sighed. The fact remained two men had been murdered in a bizarre fashion. The area had been combed, and no signs of anyone else having been there existed. An autopsy ruled out an animal. Because of the nature of the cuts, the medical examiner had at first said no man or woman could have done it, either. The ME's revised report read: "With the right tools, a surgeon or a butcher might have been the culprit."

No matter how he tried to deny it, Mona was suspect.

He jerked on his jacket and headed out the door. As he passed the newsstand out front, he saw the headlines of his paper: "Sightings Reported in Airport Area." He read it again and frowned. He hadn't paid attention to other news since he'd been on this assignment, not even Hurricane Dennis still swirling in the Gulf of Mexico, undecided about where it wanted to hit land. Did the sighting have any bearing on Mona's disappearance? Speculation ran through his mind. Someone here from outer space might explain the murders. They could have a weapon unknown to man. And if they were frightened—well, they would use whatever they had.

He caught himself. *This is crazy.* Lack of rest and the tension must be getting to him. *Hell, I don't believe in UFOs or little green people. I'd better go get some sleep before I flip out entirely.*

He made it home, and opened his front door.

Ring, ring, ring....

Rob hurried inside and grabbed the landline handset. "Hello?"

"Rob? Frank here. Why didn't you answer your cell phone?"

Reaching in his pocket and finding it empty, he replied, "I guess I left it on my desk."

"Never mind. I know I told you to stay on Mona's story, but something big is about to break. You know those people who spotted the UFO? Well, they're making a huge stink for a thorough investigation. They've built up a group of about twenty, and they've got a little clout. So, get out to 5232 Ink Road right away. That's the address of the man who's heading up this movement, name's...Claude Patterson. Ink Road's about a mile past the airport. Find out whatever you can. Who knows, we might find a tie-in with Mona's disappearance. Hell, it could be just some kooks pulling a stunt, but they still might have committed murder. You can't rule anything out these days."

"Done." Rob ended the call. He grabbed a Coke from the refrigerator, hoping the caffeine would wake him up. Instead, when he popped the lid, it splattered all over him. "Hell. I don't need this."

He slipped on a clean shirt and pants and rushed out the door.

Driving out Airport Boulevard, he explored the possibilities. On the way home, he'd listened to all the details on his car radio. These sightings had been reported to all the proper authorities and no newscasters had tried to persuade any of the callers they'd seen a weather balloon—the standard explanation. *Kind of odd.*

Another unusual thing was the shape of the object they described. None of them called it round or oval. They all reported seeing a cone. They said they saw something very much like a rocket. It disappeared in a wink, indicating a speed potential exceeding all known terrestrial ability.

Get it together, Rob. You're a reporter with an objective, realistic viewpoint. You don't believe all of this. Some crazy stuff happened. Don't let your imagination run away with you. Wait and see, old boy. Hang in there until you hear the report first hand.

A mile and a half past the entrance to the airport, he decided he'd overshot his goal. But he had no place to turn around. The road narrowed from four to two lanes, and, though traffic was light, cars were spaced just right to prevent his attempting a U-turn. Cursing his luck, he traveled farther and farther past his destination. At last, on the right, he saw a road leaving the highway.

"Damn. I've already gone four miles out of my way." In his rearview mirror, he saw a car barreling up behind him. "Okay, buddy, I'm going to make a turn. Slow down or hit me 'cause I've wasted enough time." He wheeled onto the dirt.

Thud.

Rob glanced at into the rearview mirror again. *Did the guy just hit my bumper?* He shook his head. *No. Probably just the drop in the road when I left the highway that caused the noise.*

He drove on the narrow dirt road bordered by tall pine trees around a couple of curves then took a fork to the left, hoping to find a place where he could turn around without getting stuck in the soft dirt. When he did not, he took another turn, this time to the right.

Again, the car gave a heavy bump as he drove uphill. *Great. Either I've got engine problems or a flat tire.* He stopped the car, engaged the emergency brake, and cut off the motor.

Crickets chirping and frogs croaking broke the silence in the pitch-black darkness. Rob whistled to keep himself company. He leaned across the seat and rummaged through the glove compartment, searching for a flashlight, just as the headlights and dome light went out. When he didn't find the flashlight, he got out of the car. Since the road curved enough to take him away from the lights of the highway, he hesitated to start walking in the dark. Something snapped behind him and he jumped. He felt foolish when he saw a limb had cracked off and fallen right at the edge of the road.

He reached inside and fiddled with the switch, but the lights would not come on. *Oh, God. What a place to have a dead battery. I need my flashlight. Maybe it's in my trunk.* Then he slapped his forehead. *Crud. It won't be there. I gave it to the janitor the other day when I asked him to get something out of my trunk and he didn't give it back.* Running his hand around the tire rim, he determined at least the tire wasn't flat.

What to do? Rob got back in the driver's seat and tried the ignition switch again, hoping the battery wasn't the problem. After a couple of *R-rr-rrr*'s, he realized the car wasn't going to start. He reached for his cell phone, and then remembered he'd left it on his desk.

"Damn it all!" he blurted out. "What else can go wrong?"

He had no answer. He got out and slammed the door hard enough to make the car rock. Hoping he wasn't too far from the highway, he picked up the broken branch and used it as a walking stick to help him make his way down the curvy road.

With no moon or stars, Rob couldn't tell which direction he headed in. Listening for noise from the highway to guide him, the only noise was owls hooting and leaves rustling, along with other night sounds of the woods. Branches scratched his arms as he pushed them aside. It had been years since he'd been in the woods at night as a Boy Scout. This reminded him of one of those times.

All of a sudden, he felt so tired and disoriented he leaned against a tree and reminisced. He had been in the Boy Scouts only a year when he was tapped out for the Order of the Arrow. At twelve years old, the scary tales told by those who had already been through the ordeal required to become a member frightened him.

He'd been determined to spend the night in the woods alone, but he had never forgotten the stark terror he felt during that survival test. Never before or since had he been so glad to see daylight come.

Now, here he was again—alone in the woods. This time, though, he expected to be out in just a few minutes. *I've always had a good sense of direction. I ought to be able to get back to civilization.* But after walking quite a ways, except for losing sight of his car, he'd made no progress. He looked at his watch, which glowed in the dark. It provided the sole light around. Eight-fifteen, ten hours till daylight—ten hours he didn't want to waste. *I've got to get out of here.*

He'd gotten so far off track he knew without a doubt he'd strayed into the deep woods. No more path. He had to make his own.

His eyes became accustomed to the dark. In the light of the moon, which appeared from behind a cloud, he noticed a furry object moving toward him.

All I need is a damn skunk! A friendly little tail wagged behind the animal approaching him.

It's a dog. He yelled, "Here, pup. Here, pup. C'mon. You can show me the way out."

The little fellow came closer, and it looked like a terrier or a beagle. But as he stooped to pet the dog, a chill ran up his spine. No wonder the dog had come to him. This was no random mutt. *Pep?*

"How in the hell did you get here, Pep? Tell me, fellow." He stroked the dog's short hair and let him lick his hand. "Where's Mona?"

This was miles from the gully. Even if he'd gone there with his mistress, what was Pep doing way out here near the airport all by himself? No matter, Rob was so grateful to find this smart little canine who could guide him back to civilization he almost forgot his troubles, except finding Mona. Hope surfaced. Maybe Pep would lead him to her.

As if on cue, Pep pulled on Rob's fingers with his teeth, backed off, gave one bark, and moved his head, first in one direction, then in another. Rob understood that meant, "Come on, let's go."

In a sudden bolt, Pep raced ahead and scampered under the bushes. Close behind, encouraged by the prospect of being led out of the woods and hopeful Mona might be at the end of the trail, Rob called out, "Hey, Pep. Don't leave me. I can't get through these shrubs like you can. Wait up."

Pep paused, cocked his head, pranced like a horse, and slowed down a bit. Just as Rob caught up, his jacket snagged on an outstretched limb and he had to stop to free it. He whistled, but Pep kept going. When Rob at last pulled free, the rustling of the bushes stopped. *Which way did Pep go?* He pushed through the brush, but found no sight of the dog. Much to his dismay, Pep had vanished.

An eerie sound like a huge respirator breathing in and out reached his ears. Rob looked at the sky. *Oh, my God.* A tall cone-shaped object towered close to the tops of the pine trees. He started shaking and then froze on the spot. Instinct told him he was not alone. But try as he might to run, he couldn't move a muscle. He felt a force enter his body, and his head began to swim.

Chapter Ten

"Pep, where have you been?" Mona chided as she let the little dog back into the ship. "I've called and called, and you didn't come. Bad boy. Now, don't you do that again." She gave him a pop on the backside. He put his head between his front paws and, crouching down, he crawled under the bed.

Mona wrung her hands. The first time she'd let Pep out he hadn't wandered at all. She hoped he wouldn't run off again. She couldn't chase after him—not here. Satisfied her dog was back safely, she turned her attention to the police radio. Nothing new. She then raised the volume on the ship's radio. She strained to listen but could barely discern Torpi's voice. However, by putting her ear against the speaker, she could tell he called for Eric.

"Eric," Mona called out. "Torpi's trying to reach you."

He shoved to his feet, causing the chair to make a racket when it crashed into the shiny metal wall of the ship's galley. Then he strained to hear Torpi's words.

"Noise doesn't frighten me, Eric," Torpi announced. "I have more important things on my mind. Let's get to business. I must inform you we have the advantage over you. We have something to bargain with. We have captured a man. If you value his life, you will meet our demands. In a moment, I will give you our terms."

"Poor devil," Mona exclaimed. "If they're telling the truth, how did they get him? They haven't left this spot."

"He may have come to them," Eric responded. "I wonder what they are waiting for."

"Because of the medicine we gave him," Torpi said, "the prisoner lost consciousness. We are waiting for him to awaken so he can speak for himself and verify what we are telling you. We already

61

know who he is. We checked his wallet. But we want to make you believe us. His name is Rob Parker, a reporter for *The Daily Times*, and he also has an Associated Press card."

Mona slapped her hand over her mouth. *Rob, oh my God. It's him for sure. He is also a stringer for the AP. This is unreal. We're two reporters from the same paper incarcerated on two enemy spaceships. Impossible!*

"How could they have gathered this information on Rob to use as a threat?" she whispered to Eric. "This is frightening, but they could just have his credentials. I refuse to completely believe they have Rob until I hear his voice."

In the background, she heard Rob's voice, "Pep, where are you, Pep? Where am I?"

"Did you hear that?" Torpi asked.

"Yes." Eric hung his head.

"We're moving Rob away from the microphone"—but not before Mona realized it must have been Pep who'd led Rob to the Torpians' ship.

So Pep must have been with Rob when I let him out. That must be why he was late returning to the ship. She bet Dees sent Rob into the woods to check on the sightings. *If he found them, then somebody else might, too.* Mona couldn't decide whether that was good or bad.

"We have waited long enough," Eric announced, interrupting her speculations. "The Torpians will use your friend, Mona. They will kill him if they have to. They cannot have more than six people on board. I have listened to the voices, and that's all I can detect. We are not totally outnumbered. What we need is the element of surprise to get an advantage. I want each of you to get a gun." His focus moved to her, his gaze serious. "Yes, even you, Mona. We must attack now."

Mona swallowed hard. *How did I get in such a fix, and what can I do about it?*

"It is still dark." Eric turned to her. "We will all leave our ship and try to sneak to their ship without being seen. I have one weapon they do not know about. It is a device to open their door by remote control. But it only works on one of the ships we left behind. I hope the one they are in is the right one. If so, we will enter their ship and start shooting. Then we will find out if bullets hurt them." He took a deep breath. "When Rob sees you, he will come to our side. Since his appearance is different, it will be easy to avoid injuring him.

However, I cannot speak for the actions of the Torpians. I will do the best I can to ensure his safety."

Not much of a promise, but she knew it was the best he could offer.

"If we are successful in overcoming the Torpians and can also avoid attracting the attention of the Earthlings, then we will deal with our next problem—how to remain on Earth. Our bodies are not yet fully adjusted to this atmosphere. My breathing is labored sometimes. But there is still hope. Right now, though, we must confront the enemy. Follow me."

With guns pressed against their bodies, they crawled guerrilla-style on their bellies toward the other ship. As they moved up under the blades dug into the ground, Mona trembled at the thought of what those blades could do to a human body—like they'd done to the two men who had been victims of those powerful weapons. She would be glad to get out of there.

Pep tromped to where they lay. *Oh no! He snuck out when we left*. If he so much as whined or made a wrong move, he'd give them away.

They pushed and shoved at him, but, determined not to leave, he kept following along. Finally, Mona snatched him up under her arm and hoped he wouldn't bark. Besides tensing them all up, carrying the dog made crawling much more difficult for her.

But she didn't have time to dwell on how crazy things were. The entrance to the Torpian's ship lay on the opposite side. She prayed Eric had found it. She moved around until Eric was in her view. He popped his head out from underneath the Torpians' ship, located a button, and pushed it.

Nothing happened.

The respirator, located under the cone, turned on. It's big wheezing noise caused Mona to squeal. Pep yelped.

"Shh." Eric glared at her. "No matter what, you must keep your self-control. And do your best to keep Pep quiet."

Eric pushed the button again.

The ship's door flew open. Mona trembled when she crawled away from the ship and saw a man with a scowl on his face standing full figure at the entrance, protected by a double-door-type shield. Bullets from Marcus's gun did him no harm.

Hands on his hips, he laughed. "Did you think me fool enough to come without protection? I am wise to you, Eric. You cannot harm me. But I can harm you. However, I have an alternate plan. If you agree to it, no one will be hurt."

"What is your plan, Torpi?" Eric snarled through a curled lip.

"As you recall, Eric, we worked together on finding a way to transgress time." His words rang loud and clear. "I know how to do this as well as you. But unlike you, I have no scruples. I can, and I will, use this knowledge to move every living human on Earth into oblivion. If you doubt my ability"—he pulled Rob from behind him—"I can demonstrate with Mr. Parker."

Eric backed away and shook his head.

"You may as well tell me all you know of how to survive on Earth." Torpi grinned. "You have no choice. The safety of all humanity is in your hands. It is your move."

"Give me time," Eric hedged. "I will go back to my ship to think."

Much to Mona's surprise, Torpi agreed to wait twenty-four hours for his answer.

She knew their leader bore a heavy burden. He was in a difficult position. What had happened to all their good intentions in the beginning of this venture? They wanted to meld into human society, not just for their own sakes, but to help all of humanity by providing a cure for cancer. Except, a greedy, selfish group, with self-serving interests, hampered their efforts.

Even if Eric gave his enemy the information, Mona felt sure Torpi would destroy anyone who crossed him. More than once, Eric had said the power-hungry leader's real goal was to rule the world. *No, no matter what the cost, Eric should not budge an inch. Somehow, he must find a way to stop the insane alien.*

They returned to their ship.

"I'm certain Torpi did not want to alert the Earthlings any more than he did, so I don't feel we are in any immediate danger." Eric moistened his lips. "Time is our lever. We must be patient."

"What are we going to do next?" Marcus paced around on the ship.

"For now, nothing. We do not have all the information Torpi seeks. I think they are just taunting us. They have used their maximum force, and it is not strong enough to harm us. Or"—he smiled—"they realize if they kill us they have no hope of getting what they want. As for Torpi and his threats, his knowledge may not be as broad as he claims. We worked together, true, but he did not become involved with all phases of transgressing time. His threat may be hollow."

Whether or not the speculation was wishful thinking on Eric's part, hearing it made Mona feel better.

With her hands folded behind her back, Lydia walked close to her husband and gazed into his eyes. "If we are going to have to make ourselves known anyway, why not just leave? Maybe we could find another landing spot."

Eric shook his head. "The Torpians would follow us. Besides, we would be deserting Rob Parker. I am afraid we are still in for a fight."

For a minute, they were all silent. Eric spoke again. "We must lure them outside somehow. It may be our only chance, but—" His eyes lit up, and Mona anticipated his forthcoming answer. "I know, I know. Why have I not thought of it before? I am amazed at my own stupidity. It is simple."

As Mona and the others listened, he rubbed his chin. "Our ships are different in the way they replenish their energy. The Torpians' requires the use of a respirator. All we have to do is to damage the respirator, and they will have to come out of the ship to fix it. It should be easy. I will go myself. If they do not get suspicious, there will be no trouble. Keep the radio on and attempt to keep them engaged in conversation." He hurried away from the ship.

***

Holding a .22 caliber pistol, the smallest gun he could find, Eric managed to crawl around the ship without being seen. Even if they did not spot him, when he shot at the respirator to disable it, they would hear the gun. Getting away afterward would be the problem. But he would still have his gun. To his knowledge, the only weapons the Torpians had were spears, and they would have to be close enough to him for those to be effective. If Torpi came out without his shield and those bullets worked on the Torpians, he may be able to fell them all before they knew what hit them.

Capture terrified him. No, he would rather die. He readied to fire at the respirator....

Ba-loom!

He dashed back into the bushes to seek cover. *But that sound didn't come from either ship.* He searched for the cause of the sound. Glancing over his shoulder, he stopped short. Next to a huge SUV, with an emblem on the side and blue light flashing on top, a uniformed law officer held a smoking shotgun.

"Cut that out, you damn fool redneck," someone yelled. "You wanna git us kilt? Them could be real Martians in thar. Git on the horn and git us some help out heah."

When he got close enough, he could see the two sheriff's deputies hopping around like frogs. The senior officer stopped, his focus glued on the spaceships. Then his gaze darted from one spot to another. "I tol' you, git some help."

"Ernest," the man replied to his partner, "what in hell you 'spect me to tell 'em? That they's somethin' or somebody out here in spaceships? I want some help, all right, but I don't want to be ridiculed later on."

Both men backed off. The ships remained dormant. Nobody peeked out, and Eric knew the deputies couldn't tell what was inside. When their radio squawked, they both jumped.

"251, 251. What's your location?"

Ernest jerked the mike out of the car. "We're in the woods just off Rollie Lane."

"That's you, isn't it Ernest? I recognize your voice. Take a drunk and disorderly call on Rollie Lane. No numerical address. It's one and a quarter miles from—"

"I know where it is. Been there before." Ernest looked at his partner then at the spaceships. When the deputy nodded, and said, "Let's go, Billy. That drunk will be a sight easier to handle,"

Billy followed right along.

Eric retreated way back in the woods to make sure those deputies did not see him. He wanted no part of a confrontation with the law. Even if the gun blast brought the Torpians out into the open, Eric could not risk a shootout with the police. Besides, he had nothing against them. The Torpians were his target.

For the time being, he abandoned his plan to disable their respirator. He could return to his own ship when the deputies left. Judging by their conversation and apparent inferior intelligence, they would leave shortly. Even if they stayed, he discounted attempting conversation with those two. It would be difficult enough to communicate with any Earthling and make him or her believe what he said. But trying to do so with ignorant, uneducated individuals would be impossible. A better chance would come. At the moment, he just needed a place to hide until coming out was safe.

As he reached the other side of the gully near their former landing spot, almost hidden by the heavy brush and tall pine trees, he saw a small wooden house with a dilapidated outhouse behind it. Even though the walls leaned, the outhouse would serve his purpose. He headed toward it.

When Eric opened the door, a man pulling up his pants let them drop and took a swing at him with a beer bottle. He missed, and Eric took a step backward.

"Who are ya, and what are ya doing here?" The man jerked on his pants again and staggered out on the lawn. He shook his finger. "I'm Tim O'Hara, and thiz is my property."

"I see. Mr. O'Hara, I was lost and saw this building, so—"

O'Hara pressed his index finger to his lips. "Shhh, don't say any more. I've been out on the town. I don't want Mabel to hear." He made an irregular path to the house, and Eric followed. On reaching the wooden porch on the front of the house, he put his left foot on the bottom one and began counting them aloud.

"One, two, free, izzit four, fourah? Sh...can't wake Mabel. She'll kill me. Woo-ooe, is she gonna' be mad." He scratched the stubble on his chin and, with effort, raised his two-hundred-pound bulk over the last step. "That las' pitcher of beer reached my brain." He wagged a finger at Eric. "I'm seein' double." Stumbling and falling forward against the front door, he said in a stage whisper. "Mabel's sure to wake up now."

But silence prevailed. Tim fumbled through his pockets for his key.

"Wisht it wuz back in the good ole days. I could just walk right in. Mabel never locked the door then," he said. "In them days of yore, country people never locked up. But afta an ol' couple wuz murdered in their own home jes a mile down the road last year, Mabel don' take no chances." He waved his hand in a circle. "So, now, I can't git in my own home. Damn it. Tha' keys gotta be on this ring somewheres." He motioned with his head. "Come on' les jes' go 'round back." Finding it, he held up one key. "If it's not one a' those, I'll find a way to get in. But if I'm gonna break in, I gotta go to the back. Sure can't do it here by the window."

He tiptoed back down the steps away from the bedroom where his wife slept.

"Ha, ha." He giggled and pointed to the window. "Tha's Mabel snoring. She's still asleep. You believe that?" He looked at Eric. "You know what? I bet you been drinkin', too. Your nose looks worse than mine." Guffawing, he tapped his finger to his mouth again, saying, "Shhh."

As he staggered around the house, he broke into song. "When Irish eyes were smilin' and my heart was young and gay...." He shook his index finger. "If I can't get in the back door, clear the road. Outhouse, I'm on the way." He repeated those lyrics until he reached his destination.

Eric stood out of sight as O'Hara tried key after key and tugged at the back door knob, but it wouldn't budge. He climbed on a rickety stool and tried unlatching one of the windows. The stool slipped, and Tim crashed to the ground.

He gave up. "I don' care if I nevah get in there," he chanted. "Listen to me. I made a rhyme. I'm a poet and don' know it." He staggered to the outhouse, but he stopped at the door and stared at Eric.

Confident this drunk wouldn't be able to convince anybody of what he had seen, if he remembered meeting him at all, Eric decided to hang around. If O'Hara asked questions, he'd give as little information as possible.

Reeling backward on his heels, Tim squinted as he looked Eric over. "Well, now. I can't figure you out. You're a mite too big to be a leprechaun, aren't ya? And you're not big enough to be a space giant. So what are ya? Could be I know who ya are?" he asked without even pausing for breath. "Could be you're Mr. O'Reilly up to ya tricks again. I told ya after the last one, when ya put on a gorilla head last St. Patrick's Day and sneaked to me window, that ya couldn't fool me, Danny. I knew ya then, too. Now go on with ya before ya wake Mabel, or we'll both need a mask to cover the bruises."

Before Eric could respond, Tim continued, his brogue getting stronger by the minute. "Danny, me boy, there's somethin' I want ya to tell me. Where'd ya get a mask with that funny lookin' pug nose? Oh, ya are original, ya are." He bobbed his head. "Drunk or sober, though, I'd know ya anywhere."

The volume of his voice increased with every word. Before he got the last sentence out, he spoke loud enough to wake the dead.

A woman, who Eric presumed was Mabel, stormed out of the back door with a broomstick in her hand, her flannel nightgown streaming out behind her. Halfway down the porch steps, she lost a slipper and stopped to put it back on.

When she glanced up, her gaze landing on Eric, she dropped the broom to the ground as she ran into the house screaming. "I'm going to call the sheriff!"

Tim O'Hara let out a belly laugh, and then said to Eric, "At least ya fooled somebody," then added, "Wait here while I fetch my wife to let her in on the joke." As Tim stumbled up the steps, he chuckled. "Thiss iz the first time in a long time anybody got the best of Mabel."

When Eric dashed by him, O'Hara made no effort to stop him. "Go on with ya, be a bad sport," he called out. "But don' forgit I caught you at your own game."

Then he yelled to his wife. "Don't bother to call the law, Mabel. That's Danny O'Reilly. He's zup to his ole tricks. I jes ran him off."

***

Rob stared into the face of a man who glared back with his bottom lip poked out. He wriggled his hands that had been cuffed behind his back and tried to loosen the restraints strapping him to a chair. But he had no success. Torpi hovered over him.

"I know you're a snoopy reporter, and you'll try to tell the world what we're doing. Oh," he chuckled, "I'm going to give you your story, but you'll never live to tell it."

He pulled up a chair and turned it backward, sitting within inches of his prisoner. "First off, I'll admit we killed those police officers."

When he sneered, Rob spit right in his eye.

With a hard backhand across Rob's face, Torpi left a bright red mark, but Rob didn't cry out; he wouldn't give Torpi that satisfaction.

Torpi wiped off the spit. "The Svarians have the key to curing fatal diseases and immortality, and we want them. We'll get them at any cost. I have plenty of men to sacrifice. What's human life, anyhow?"

"It's important to us, you fool. We can't live forever, but we do have the good sense to make the best of it while we're alive." He remembered what William Faulkner said in his book *The Old People*, "There's nothing worse than not being alive." No point in trying to make that argument. Torpi wouldn't understand such philosophy.

"Pft. You humans act so superior." Torpi curled his lip. "But the truth is you exploit each other all the time. Your politics are corrupt and even on a one-on-one basis, you treat each other with contempt. Your policy is, 'It's all about me.'"

Leaning his head forward as far as he could, Rob retorted, "And what's your policy, Torpi? Isn't it the same thing? At least we have

69

laws to stop people like you from killing to get what you want."

Torpi got up, pushed Rob's chair over backward, and glared down at him. "It's a 'survival of the fittest' world. The same applies to our planet. We know what we want, and we take what we can. Right now, we want all of Eric's secrets, and we'll get them."

Before Torpi walked out of the room, he jerked Rob's chair to an upright position.

"I got you up this time, but the next time I put you down, it'll be for good."

Chapter Eleven

Frank Dees arrived at the paper and stormed into his office, loosening his tie. On this humid, 95 degree morning toward the end of July, the air conditioner wasn't working properly, one of his reporters was still missing, two policemen had mysteriously been killed, and nobody on his staff had come up with a damn thing. He wiped his brow with his handkerchief and looked at his watch. To top it all, it was nine-thirty a.m. and his ace reporter, Rob Parker, had not shown up for work.

"Hurricane Dennis just took a turn. Now instead of Houston, it's headed our way. What the hell does Parker think we're running around here?" Dees screamed to nobody in particular. He stood up, shoved some papers off of his desk, and kicked a chair out of his way. "Damn it all! Mona's missing. Parker's supposed to be on the story, and he hasn't even come in to make a report on what he's found."

Everybody in hearing distance turned to face the boss. He glared at his crew. "Any of you heard from Parker? Hell, that story can wait. I just want to find out what happened to Mona."

Tall, lanky Morris Olsen walked to where Dees stood. Putting his arm around the editor's shoulders, he gazed at his boss with clear blue eyes. "Don't be upset. Let's call Parker's apartment. He's been going night and day. Maybe he just overslept."

Morris picked up the phone and dialed. "No answer." He returned the receiver to its cradle. "Rob's probably on his way here."

"I'll try his cell phone." Dees dialed the number. No answer. He snatched his coat off of the rack and left the building. "I'm going to look for him," he called over his shoulder.

He returned an hour later and banged his fist against his door.

"No luck. Damn! Now two of our own are missing, and here we sit in a room full of experienced investigators. We should be able to find Mona and Rob. I want some action." He pointed around the room to four of his best reporters. "I want every one of you to drop whatever you've got going. Get on this, and get on it fast. Make sure you don't duplicate each other's efforts." Dees issued orders as fast as he could spout them out. "I mean business."

Reporters scurried out the door and moved off in different directions.

When they were all out of sight, Dees spoke to the air. "I'm coming to look for both of you myself. If this is some kind of a joke, you're both gone forever."

He took a deep breath. He had a gut feeling this was no hoax. His past experience made it easy for him to spot a critical situation. A man who'd seen all he had seldom became fooled. Heavy-hearted, he left to pursue his own course of action. Until his reporters were found, he would not rest.

With a determination to search every square foot of ground around Ink Road, the last place Rob had been sent on assignment, Frank headed in the direction of the airport. Rain splashed on his windshield. The ground out there would be soggy and muddy, and he cursed himself for not wearing his boots, but he didn't go back for them. If he ruined his shoes and got his feet wet, so what? It wouldn't be the first time.

As he approached the airport, the rain ceased, and the sun peeked out from behind a cloud. Maybe it wouldn't be so bad after all. He thanked God for small favors and slowed down so he wouldn't miss the turn on Ink Road. If he hadn't known about where it was, he would never have found it—tall shrubbery all but covered the green-and-white sign. He turned onto the dirt road and, dodging puddles, drove on the red clay for a mile, making a couple of turns along the way. Dense pine trees obscured any houses. Whatever the trees didn't hide, the brush did. Dees pulled to the side and shut off the motor.

His first impulse was to hop out of the car and yell Rob's name; instead, he got out and glanced around, not knowing what he expected to find. "Where do I go from here?"

Far in the distance, a plane approached the nearby airport, but he couldn't see it. He walked a few yards and took a path to the left. It led him to another road where he found a mailbox with "Tim O'Hara" written in big, bold letters on it.

He knocked on the front door. No reply. He walked around back and spotted an outhouse. "Well, I'll be damned. I thought those things were obsolete." He shrugged, walked to the house, and banged on the back door. "Anybody home?"

When he got no answer, he turned around and trudged back down the path toward his car.

***

Eric climbed aboard his spaceship, weary and worried. He had not told his fellow crew members, or Mona, but the food had been consumed, and their pills were running low. Deciding he shouldn't solve this problem alone, he brought it up for discussion. "It's taken more pills than I anticipated to keep us going," he told them. "Our supply is almost depleted. We need to figure out what to do."

"I can go get some real food and bring it back," Mona volunteered. "All along, I knew I could leave and you wouldn't have stopped me. But I've grown to like and respect you." She focused on Eric. "I want to help you of my own free will. I think you like me, too, but I'm the only one who can leave the ship and return with relative safety." She put her hands on her hips. "This is for me, too. I want to get this over with and get my life back."

"Mona, you will run a risk." Lydia challenged her decision. "The Torpians might see you leave."

"No, they won't. I can slip out without being spotted. You forget this isn't the first time I've had to sneak around. Reporting teaches many things." She laughed. "But usually I'm trying to get in some place, not out."

After some discussion and planning, they decided to let her go. "All right," Eric told her, "we didn't want to put you in danger again, but we don't have much choice. You can go, but you need to be very careful."

Eric sighed. "I hope we're making the right decision."

"You are," Mona reassured him. "With luck, I should be able to return before daylight, bringing all the food I can carry."

As soon as it got dark, Mona slipped out, and Pep went with her.

He hoped it would be enough to last a few days and buy them a little time.

Chapter Twelve

Inside the Torpians' ship, Torpi paced. "Our supplies are running low. We must eliminate this man," Rob heard him tell the ship's crew. "We need him as a pawn, but he's using up food we need for own survival. And even without him, I do not know how long we can exist. If any of you have ideas, tell me what they are."

"I have a solution, but I would like to tell you in private," one man offered.

The two left for another part of the ship, out of Rob's hearing. Torpi came back, smiling with his arm around his cohort's shoulder.

"Parker, come with us," he ordered.

Rob didn't move, so two men lifted him and brought him into the other area. They jabbed him in the arm with a needle and as much as he fought it, he fell asleep. For how long, he didn't know. When he awakened, Torpi leaned over him.

"While you slept, we surgically inserted something inside you with the potential to kill you. Whether or not it does is up to you. So, you will go out and bring food back. Get it any way you can. If you do as we say, we will remove the object on your return. If you do not, you will die. Double vision is one of the first symptoms of impending death. If that occurs, it may be too late to save you. Go now and return as quickly as possible. Remember the consequences if you don't follow my orders."

Rob broke out in a cold sweat. Even if he did bring them food, would they let him live?

Torpi and his men took Rob to the door and shoved him out.

"Obey our orders," Torpi admonished.

Rob slogged through the soggy turf and pondered the difference between this and the last time he walked through these same woods.

He'd been lost then. How could he find his way out of the woods this time? He hadn't been able to do it before. At least they'd given him a flashlight.

He needed to find a store, try to act natural while making his purchase, then slip right back into the woods again.

Oh, my God! How can I buy food? I don't have any cash, and I rushed out of my house so fast I left my credit card stuck in my checkbook in my other pants. In his wallet he found two one-dollar bills. He took the loose change in his pocket and counted it. Fifty-two cents. *Two and a half a dollars won't buy enough for one meal. I guess Torpi expects me to steal the food.* He rubbed his forehead. *What am I going to do?* Chewing on his lip, he trudged along, pulling his shirt loose and feeling on his body for scars. There were none. He had no visible marks anywhere. *How can that be? Suppose this is all a ruse. I know they have some strange powers, so maybe they put something in my blood?* Overcome with the fear of the unknown, he searched for an exit from the woods.

***

"Listen, Dees, I know it takes big stuff to bring you over here to my office, but damn it all, man, don't you get on my back, too." Lt. Paul Ramundi threw his cigar nub in the trash and bit the tip off a fresh one. Spitting it out, he drummed his fingers on his desk. "I know two of your reporters are involved. Hell, your whole staff is involved. But has it occurred to you those two might have run off together?" He turned up open palms. "Parker and Stewart's disappearance might not have a damn thing to do with the spaceships or the murders. You have no real tie-in, no connection at all. Could be a coincidence, you know."

Glaring at him, Dees growled. "You know damn good and well those two had no reason—"

"Hold it. I don't know anything except what I read in the papers."

"You know these things fit together. First, Mona has a wreck in a gully. But she keeps going back to the place. God knows what for. Said she wanted to buy some property out there. Anyhow, Rob goes looking for her, and he disappears, too. Something's wrong. It's weird."

"Sounds like you're buying that UFO story, Frank," Ramundi interjected in a friendlier tone.

"I'm buying nothing. I'm reporting facts, you hear? Just facts. But they can't be denied. Mona's gone. Her brand-new car was left deserted on some God-forsaken road, and two men were mysteriously killed, chopped to bits. We have no clues about their murder. Then Parker disappears." He ran his hand through his hair and slumped into a chair. "Something's cockeyed, and, with very little to go on, I came here to get your help. How about filling me in on what you know?"

Ramundi lit his cigar and puffed on it for a minute. "Nothing." He blew out smoke from his mouth and nostrils. "The truth is we've uncovered nothing. Everybody, and I mean everybody, is on our back...people who claimed to see UFOs, the UPI and the AP, every member of the media in the entire city, the county, and my superiors. When John Q. Public gripes, they want results. So far, we haven't turned up as much as a sharp knife." He shook his head. Leaning over the desk he put his hand on Dees' shoulder. "I knew both of those policemen and their families. Helped break Dan in, and Mahoney and I go back a long way. There's nothing I wouldn't do to bring their killers to justice."

Frank nodded. "Yeah, yeah. I know. Sometimes you wonder what it's all about. We're seasoned professionals, why can't we figure it out, Paul? The answer's got to be out there somewhere." He rose to leave. "If by any strange chance my two reporters are pulling some stunt and have left together, God help 'em if I ever get my hands on them. Oh, hell, if that were true, they probably don't know anything at all about all this UFO stuff. Either way, I guess this isn't their fault."

Ramundi pulled on his earlobe. "For their sake and yours, I hope to God they left together. But that's a chance in a million."

Frank took a deep breath before responding, "You're right."

Chapter Thirteen

Rob plodded through the brush and trees. The thought of an unknown object inside his body about to kill him kept inserting itself into his consciousness. *If I can get to a doctor, could he help? But what could I tell a doctor anyhow? "Doc, something dangerous is somewhere inside me?" Ha, I can imagine the response.*

He tromped along, hoping he could make it back to the ship before whatever they put inside him blew him up. First, he had to get food.

Shoplifting shouldn't be so hard. Millions of dollars of merchandise are stolen daily. I'll just have to distract the person at the cash register. I hope I can find a convenience store. They often only have one clerk on duty. I'll ask for something he'll have to get from the cooler, then grab my loot fast. If I can manage to get away, I'll make it. By sneaking off into the woods, I can be long gone before he notices anything's missing.

Rob stopped. *Did I pass a Circle K store while driving down Airport Boulevard?* He shook his head, trying to clear it. *Damn, whatever they gave me or put in me must have messed up my memory.*

The sound of traffic made him think he had to be close to a highway. He hoped it was Airport Boulevard. He proceeded with caution as he hid behind the brush on the roadside. As he neared the sounds of moving automobiles, he realized this couldn't be Airport Boulevard. That city artery would be more heavily traveled. It had to be another road, but which one? *I'm confused and disoriented. I've got to get my bearings.* He stood behind a huge oak tree and listened for noises. *If a plane flies overhead, maybe I can see where it lands and find out where the airport is.*

He didn't have to wait long. In just a few minutes, he heard a plane's roar. For some reason, Rob guessed it prepared for a takeoff, but it was too far away for him to see where exactly. So he headed in the direction of the noise.

On the way, he stumbled upon an old country store. As he reached the entrance, he was relieved to see a dim light still burning inside. For all he knew, the place might have closed at dark. The old man sitting by an old wooden stove in the center of the building seemed engrossed in working on a set of books when Rob climbed the three rickety steps to the door. The idea of taking advantage of a struggling senior citizen who probably made more money for the United States government than he did for himself gave Rob a guilty twinge. He came close to leaving without accomplishing his mission. But the thought of dying overcame his guilt.

The storekeeper peered over the top of his glasses. "Whatcha need, young man? We're closed, but since I'm here anyways, I'll hep ya."

"I'm in a little bit of trouble. My car broke down and my flashlight won't work. If I could just borrow another light, I believe I could fix it. I think it's just a loose battery cable." As a reporter, twisting the truth bothered him. *But I'm telling the truth. My car is broken and my flashlight's not working right.*

The old man grinned. "Well, suh, I don't sell flashlights, but I'll see if Mama can round one up." Picking up the phone, he dialed a number. He held it to his ear long enough for about ten rings. "Damn, she didn't answer." He frowned as he walked to the door and yelled, "Mama, where are you?"

"I'm over here. I been callin' you and you didn't come, you old fool. I slipped on the steps and I can't get up. Come help me."

Without a word, the old man went to his wife's rescue.

Rob searched for what to take, feeling extremely guilty as he stuffed staples and fruit into the biggest brown bags he could find. While he hurried and scurried about, vowing to repay double the worth of these groceries, he found himself taking the least expensive items and only what they'd need to survive. It didn't take long to fill up a couple of bags, which was all he could carry.

He stopped short when the old man came shuffling along, heading back in his direction. He snatched up the bags and hustled out the door.

"Hey! You come back here!" the old man called. "You can't steal my stuff."

Rob darted into the woods. When he reached a safe spot, he sat down on the grass to catch his breath. His head felt a little clearer. Maybe the sedative had worn off and he could remember how to find his way back to the ship.

Guilt made him edgy. *If this is what a life of crime is like, they can have it.*

Chapter Fourteen

Mona made her way through the thicket in the woods, only using the flashlight she'd brought along intermittently. The wind whistled in the trees, animals scampered around, and unidentifiable odd noises left her nerves rattled. She jumped when something darted across her path. Thinking the creature was a rat, she let out a yelp. When she shined her flashlight in its direction, she saw the animal was too large to be a rodent. *A rabbit.*

She looked around. No signs of light or life, so even if anybody heard her scream, they probably weren't close enough to find her.

She had been in many difficult situations as a reporter; she'd even been in one when an angry teenager turned a gun on her. *Thank God he didn't fire it.* But never before had she been alone at night in an area so far removed from other human beings.

"Hey, Pep," She tried to call him back when he ran ahead of her. When he didn't come, she chased after him and became turned around. When she caught up with him, she looked left and right, and then turned in a circle. "Damn it, Pep. Now, I don't know where I am, and these woods are scary."

She shuddered. This was different from the trips bringing food to the spaceship occupants. They watched for her return. But now she was so isolated she felt like she was in a vacuum. This was strange.

Before she walked very far, she became spooked. Imaginary dangers plagued her. Even the name of the nearby road seemed ominous—Wolf Road. Did that mean wolves inhabited the area? Troublesome things crossed her mind. How far away was civilization? Where was the nearest main thoroughfare? How could she find her way? She was so turned around she could be going in circles. Nothing looked familiar. Furthermore, if she reached a populated area, then what?

Pep ran off again.

"Come back here, Pep. Come back."

He didn't obey, but this time she didn't follow him.

"Okay, you'll get lost, and then you'll have to find me."

At least she had enough cash to buy as much as she could carry. Since she'd been buying groceries for the Svarians, she was glad she had a habit of always having a fifty-dollar bill tucked away in her purse. She'd left her pocketbook behind—it too cumbersome to bother with. But she'd placed the bill in her shoe, along with her driver's license. Now, she had to find a place to spend the money. Where would it be?

A long, low howl made her crouch behind a tree. What was it? A wolf? No, it sounded more like a big dog. Mona consoled herself with the hope if it were a dog, it meant people were nearby, too. *But wait. What if he's not on a chain? He sounds fierce.*

Shining the flashlight's beam on her watch, she saw she'd already been wandering around these woods for almost half an hour. She had to find the right track somehow. She'd moved in what she thought should be close to the highway. She still heard owls hooting, scratching sounds and the wind blowing in the trees, nothing else. *Will I ever get out of these woods? What will happen to me? Will Pep come back? Will I ever see him again?* She sat on a log and began to cry.

Mona hung her head between her knees, broke down, and sobbed uncontrollably. This had to be the worst position she'd ever been in. Her whole body started shaking. *No other human in the world can understand what I'm up against. Nobody's suffered through this before.*

Raising her head, she looked in the blackness of the sky. *I'm on my own. I've met challenges before and I've come up with resources I didn't know I had. And I've always been able to work out my problems.* Using her fingers, she rubbed tears from her eyes. *Why am I letting this situation get the best of me? I won't. Problems are things to be solved.*

Mona stood and squared her shoulders. *I'll have to overcome whatever obstacles are in my path.* The future of the world might depend on how she handled this crisis. Rejuvenated, she felt rising to the occasion became more important than her own well-being. She anticipated if she failed, others depending on her would die.

Besides, I still want to write this story and win that Pulitzer Prize. She couldn't let herself fail. She pushed on.

How do you get anywhere? Well, you just keep putting one foot in front of the other and you're bound to go forward. She took her own advice until she found herself at the back of an old house. Peeking around, she saw the name Tim O'Hara on the mailbox.

Mona said a silent prayer of thanks. As she drew closer, loud voices drifted out the bedroom window. Because both a man and a woman were yelling, she couldn't tell what was being said, but there was no mistaking the big fight in progress.

Just as she sneaked up behind the outhouse, Mona flicked on her flashlight and saw a man jump into a pickup truck. He wheeled out, leaving the dust flying behind him.

A woman tore out of the house, leaving the back door flung wide open. "Come back here, Tim O'Hara, you old fool!" she screamed as she hopped in her car and drove off.

Mona took advantage of the lucky break. She looked around to see if the howling dog lived here, but she saw no animal nearby. There was a good chance the couple were the only people in the house because she'd only heard two voices. The argument had been too loud for anyone else to sleep through, even children. Anyway, she had to take a chance.

But as she entered the back door, she had second thoughts. *Suppose someone is inside. What am I going to do?* After shining her flashlight in every room, she found out her concern was totally unnecessary. She was alone with free access to whatever she chose to take. In the kitchen, she crammed canned goods and non-perishable items into plastic bags; no one interfered. They didn't look back. It seemed the O'Haras were too busy racing down the road to care about their house being burglarized.

Loaded down with a bag under each arm, Mona left the house just as she'd found it—except for missing food—with the back door flung open. Since the cupboard was so full, she suspected it might be a while before the theft was discovered. It consoled her to discover she hadn't stolen from anybody in need. *Wait a minute.* She pulled the fifty-dollar bill out of her shoe and put it on the table under a greasy saltshaker. *I can pay for these groceries. I don't need to steal them.*

She sneaked out the door, encouraged to know finding the way back shouldn't be as difficult as the trip there had been. This time, she'd settled down and knew where she was headed and what to look for, and she had paid close attention to the route. She walked due south and hoped her bearings were correct. With a little luck, she expected to be back at the ship shortly.

She shivered. *But it seems like trouble has a way of finding me. No telling what lies ahead.*

Chapter Fifteen

Hearing unfamiliar sounds emitting from the ship's radio, Eric suspected the Torpians of causing interference, but soon he realized the noises were different. These sounds came from far away. Listening closely, he tried to determine what they were. He called Lydia and Marcus, and all three sat around the radio, hoping to receive some clue as to what happened.

"The last time I heard such a transmission was in communication with one of our ships to another from Svar," Marcus said.

Lydia nodded.

"If this is the case," continued Marcus, "we may be in for trouble because it means our other ships have been confiscated and activated by the Torpians. And unless they intend to cause trouble, they would not come to Earth."

"Let's not assume too much," Eric cautioned. "We have been gone from Svar so long these could be sounds we have forgotten or new ones we are just unfamiliar with. We must not be too hasty. That could make a problem where none exists."

"Why would the others come here? They know no way to survive." Lydia turned her palms up.

"Oh, it's not unreasonable to assume they discovered a way to survive just as we did. In fact, they may have found a more effective way than ours. Perhaps they have reversed their bodily appearance, too. If so, they could live here on Earth with no questions asked. If they land and abandon ship, melting into society would be a simple matter."

"You may be right." Lydia lowered her head and her long, blonde hair fell across her shoulders. "I hope so."

Marcus wrinkled his forehead. "We haven't been gone long enough to—"

Eric held up his hand. "If they have been successful, it is true they worked much faster than we did. But if they discovered the hiding place for our scientific experiments, it is possible they worked out the rest of the solution. We were close to it ourselves."

Lydia's pug nose twitched in distaste—she did not like what she heard. She left the radio and went to the galley to count out the pills, sitting in one of the chairs bolted to the floor. Her action reminded him not many were left, and if Mona did not return soon that would pose another problem. He sighed. But if those suppositions about the approaching space vehicles came true, none of them might ever have to worry about anything again.

A loud screeching noise brought Eric to the radio where he turned the knob left to right and back again. More static, no voices. The jumble coming through told him somewhere behind all the static, someone attempted to communicate. At last, the air cleared, and he tuned it; a discernible sound got their attention.

"Hey there, good buddy," a voice with a country twang said. "I'm shore surprised to find anybody out there. 'Cept for a few o' us die-hards, ain't heard nobody on this here CB lately. Guess they all taken to usin' them cell phones. So, what's yoah handle? And what do ya think about this here Hurricane Dennis comin' our way?"

Since the craze on Citizen's Band radios had long since gone out of vogue, and Eric never knew the jargon anyhow, he did not understand what the man wanted to know. Instead of replying, he tuned to a different frequency. The strangeness of the airwaves brought something unexpected—the voice on the air didn't belong to a citizen of Svar.

"Eric," another voice spoke, "if this is your idea of a way to thwart us, you are badly mistaken. Why do you think we would fear a man on your ship with a handle? You are being ridiculous. I must assume this is good news for us. Because if you are deteriorating from lack of adequate nourishment, it means you are running out of pills. You don't know this but we have plenty. You may as well surrender. Agree to give us all of your secrets, and we will do what we can for you."

It was the longest speech Torpi ever made, and it may well have been the most important. Torpi bluffed. Since he mentioned pills, they were on his mind. Eric suspected they were short of food and maybe Torpi lied about having pills.

85

Good, that evens the score. Eric believed his own group had the edge by sending Mona for food. But they claimed they forced Rob to go get supplies. It appeared the groups were in identical positions. Mona had gone willingly, but why did Rob go? Maybe his life was at stake. *But how could they control him if he left the ship?* Despite the difference in motivation, it was probable both would return.

Over in the corner, Lydia stopped working and turned to Eric. "The Torpians exhibited boldness, but do they have any way to back up their threats? Do you believe they would be so brutal as to destroy humanity? Is there a real reason to prophesy doom?"

Eric knew his concern baffled her. All of these people had escaped Earth years ago and banded together to search for another land, including Torpi. Could these peace-loving people change so radically? Difficult to believe. Still, history proved it had happened before.

"I know my doubt of the loyalty of those we left behind on Svar bothers you. I think you detect my fears they might join forces with the Torpians and come to Earth with the intention of overthrowing me." Eric walked over to face his wife. "Our danger is twofold. We may be attacked by the Torpians or by our own cohorts. While we were gone, Torpi may have persuaded our people to join his group."

He took Lydia's hand. "I have not told you this before, but there is a hidden cache of weapons on Svar I think Torpi knows about. By weapons, I do not mean handguns or the like. These are more powerful than any atomic bomb. They were kept to defend Svar should the need ever arise. I will not use them because they have the power to obliterate our society. But if this arsenal falls into the wrong hands, or if anyone, on either side, chooses to use them, all of our efforts to return to Earth will have been in vain."

Marcus remained silent, but Eric knew he'd heard the statement. Eric lowered his head and allowed them time to absorb the full meaning of what he'd said. "So, even if Torpi and his men do not have the technology necessary to destroy humanity, other means are available to them."

He shook his head. "I apologize. I have been so stupid. I do not deserve to be your leader. I brought nothing, not one weapon or even a plan for designing one powerful enough to combat an enemy. All we have are the guns Mona gave us. If we are attacked and destroyed, then I am to blame."

Lydia put her arm around her husband's shoulder. "Eric, oh, Eric, do not blame yourself. Whatever will be is fate. We were all unhappy on Svar. Perfection is not satisfaction. Even death will be better than a dull existence."

The knowledge of so many lives in danger hung over Eric King like a cloud. He could not accept the consolation his wife offered.

"It is strange." Marcus tightened the sash holding his white tunic in place. "Just a short time ago, we were all on another planet, bored and frustrated, even though all our needs were provided for. So, we searched until we found a way—a dangerous way—to escape. In our hope of finding a challenging, rewarding life, we also found the possibility of death." He moistened his lips. "On Svar, when we had no assurance of dying before we became completely decrepit, it seemed desirable. We had no wish to be immortal in the face of a do-nothing existence." He leaned forward. "The Torpians changed their minds about immortality before we did. Now that death threatens us, our will to live resurfaces. Like humans, we want what seems unattainable. Dying has lost its appeal. We must decide what we can do to prevent its happening." He turned to his leader. "Eric, do you have any ideas?"

"Of course, you both realize, although the possibility the arsenal has been discovered is great, we are not certain it has been. However, we must acknowledge whatever weapons the enemy possesses may make us more susceptible to wounds—more so here on Earth than on Svar." He moved away from the round table. "Yes, we are in great danger. Torpi isn't satisfied with ruling his group. His goal is to rule Earth. The only reason he has not attacked us already is because Torpi needs me to do a heart transplant. This is a precarious position to be in. And if Mona does not return soon, we may have to lift off without food."

The gravity of the situation intensified. Problems seemed to be multiplying. If they planned to leave, it would have to be soon.

Another sound blared out of the radio. Once again, the static prevented any clear communication.

Eric wrung his hands. More than ever, that sounded like one of their ships. Something had to be done. To the others, he offered a suggestion. "Assuming this ship—or those ships—are from Svar, we have three alternatives. We must decide immediately what to do, as any delayed action will give Torpi's group just the edge they need. First, we can stay in the ship and hope the newcomers are on our side and they have come to help, not harm, us. Second, we can lift off and try to get back to Svar before them. If our own troops are still siding with us, by now they may have found a way to help. I have many weapons hidden in different places. I may be wrong. Maybe none were found by the Torpians. The last choice is to deplane and try to meld in this earthly society. If we split up and passed ourselves off as freaks of nature, there is a slim chance we would be believed. If so, perhaps someday the change in our appearances we so hope for would come about."

A squawking interrupted their conversation.

"Quit playing, Eric," Torpi shouted. "I have no patience with your infantile attempts to frighten us."

So, Torpi heard the noise on the radio, too. Obviously, Torpi did not know what happened. That meant the other ships could be on either side. It gave some hope. Still, he knew he must not assume anything. Complacency could be fatal.

"Is your shadow frightening you, Torpi?" he countered.

His statement produced the expected results. "Nothing frightens us," Torpi steamed back. "We have the advantage. I told you before we are not scrupulous about using what we have. We will also use our prisoner any way we need to. And we will carry out our other threats, too. Do not underestimate us, Eric. But Parker has brought us food and we have no need to do anything yet." Torpi hastily added. "However, if we do, we will not hesitate."

Already clued in, Eric called the bluff. If Parker had not returned, he needed to know. "Let me talk to Parker. I have a question to ask him."

"He is sleeping. But even if he were awake, I would not let you talk to him. In fact, we may dispose of him as soon as his usefulness ends."

No. My guess is Rob is still away from the ship. But I can't be 100 percent sure. So, no need to jeopardize lives by going out searching for a man who may still be a captive.

Another call came over the radio. He checked connections and discovered the noises they had been hearing were definitely from Svar. The only remaining problem was determining which side the people sending them were on.

Chapter Sixteen

Before Mona could scramble to her feet, she knew she'd lingered a little too long near the roadway. A tan-and-brown County Sheriff's car pulled up beside her. "What are you doing out after dark all by yourself, young lady?" asked the bearded deputy in a husky voice. He leaned his head out the window. "It's not safe."

Mona thought fast. "I jes' came from my cousin's house down the road. The O'Haras." Glad she'd remembered the name on the mailbox, she faked a country accent as best she could.

"Well, it's not safe for a young girl to wander out here in these woods at night. Say, those bags look heavy. Where ya headed?"

"Oh, nowheres, really. I'm spending the weekend there." She pointed to the house, and decided she'd better explain why no cars were there. "They had a fight, and both of 'em drove off. So I jes' stuffed my things in these bags and got outta there." She'd folded the tops of the bags, effectively hiding the groceries in them. "Anyways, if I didn't take my things, they wouldn't think I wuz gone. I'm goin' back. I jes' thought I'd rest a spell, let things cool down. Might scare 'em a little when they come back if they can't find me."

He nodded. "Well, miss, you need to be careful. It's dangerous out here. A hurricane's on its way. You better get back to your cousin's house before you get caught in it." He tipped his hat then pulled away and drove down the road.

As soon as he was out of sight, Mona walked into the woods, vowing to take no more rests until she reached her destination. *That was a close call.*

A owl went, "Who, who." She aimed her flashlight on it and saw huge eyes glaring down at her from a tree. Somehow, the woods didn't seem so formidable any more. She'd become accustomed to the various animal and insect noises.

Everything is relative. A month ago, the prospect of being alone in the woods would have terrified me. Hell, just a few hours ago, it did, too. All I care about is getting back to the spaceship— she laughed at the ludicrousness of the idea—*and saving my friends. My friends? As a matter of fact, they are.*

The whole thing was mind-boggling. Here she was in the middle of nowhere carrying two sacks of stolen groceries and heading for a spaceship. What would happen when she got back to the ship? The supplies she brought would last a few days at best. Then what? They had an enemy ship at their side, one with the potential of destroying all humanity if they found the arsenal with all its weapons. Surely somebody, the police or people like the O'Haras, would discover them sooner or later. What could the Svarians do then? They couldn't just go out into the city. Their features were still too different.

In another wave of despair, Mona almost turned and ran. How had she gotten in this ridiculous, impossible situation? She had no real obligation to Eric, Lydia, or Marcus. In all probability, she could be of little help to them. Temporary help, at best. Her lips and chin trembled. But they'd saved her life, and they wanted to give the world a cure for cancer. Those thoughts nagged at her conscience, making her feel things weren't hopeless. *And all of this can help me achieve my goal. I've got lots more information to write a Pulitzer Prize winning story. I need to keep focusing on that.* Without warning, Frank Dees' words, when he gave her an assignment, reverberated in her ears.

"There's never been a problem that can't be solved, Mona," he'd told her once when she had a difficult assignment. "Sometimes the solutions are not what we hope for; nevertheless, everything has an answer. Hang in there...not just on this but on every assignment. Find out the what, when, where, who, and why and take it from there. You're bright and you're a good investigative reporter, one of my best. You're perceptive and you can figure things out. Never give up. No matter what, never give up."

***

Rob tripped over a fallen tree limb, and one of the brown paper bags in his arms caught on an overhanging branch, ripping it right down the middle. The groceries tumbled all over the ground.

The delay terrified him. He also realized that fall could have been fatal. He still did not know what the insertion into his body was, where it was located, and what it would take to trigger it. If it was in the upper part of his torso, a fall might activate it. *Hell, no matter where it is, I bet it wouldn't take much jolt to set it off.* The Torpians didn't say whether it was an explosive or just a chemical that would eventually cause his body to deteriorate. Lack of information left him at a complete loss as to what to expect.

Rob picked himself up and tried to figure out what to do about the groceries. They wouldn't all fit in one bag. He tried, but the best he could do was to cram some of the larger cans into the bottom of the bag and pile the smaller ones on top. The loaf of bread was squashed into a crushed mass. He scooped some out of the split plastic wrapper and wolfed it down, choking on its dryness, then tossed the rest.

Pulling off his jacket, he tied the sleeves together and made a pouch. Still, it wouldn't hold all of the groceries. What to take and what to leave behind required a big decision. Rob had a limited knowledge of the nutritional value of food. He just guessed what items would be best to leave behind. Deviled ham, he kept. Canned milk, he discarded. Beans, he kept, thinking at least they'd be filling. Other heavier items, he tossed away. One by one, he went through the contents as fast as possible.

Each time Rob turned it on, his flashlight flickered and cut off. When he shook it, it turned back on, but with a dimmer light. "Damn, this could mean big trouble," he grumbled, hoping to complete his journey before it went out altogether. A wave of despair came over him. Would he ever again rejoin other humans? It all seemed improbable. Out in the woods, with some kind of internal detonator in his body or some chemical in his bloodstream, he could only think the worst—he may never live to see daylight again.

A lump formed in his throat. He bemoaned the life he'd lived. *Oh, the days I've wasted. The things I could have done.*

But even now, he held his future in his own hands. Should he continue his attempt to return to the ship and trust the Torpians to remove the object? Or did his chance for survival lie in getting as far away from them as possible and seeking medical help? Neither alternative offered much promise.

Had the Torpians given him any reason to believe they were trustworthy? No. On the other hand, he had no reason to believe any doctor on Earth would give an ounce of credibility to his story. Even if one did, since he had no indication of where the object was hidden in his body or what chemical might be in his blood, what chance was there it could be taken care of? Besides, he was out of time. Caught in the middle, he chose to continue his journey back to the ship and hope for the best.

He plodded along. Looking to the sky, he spotted a flashing white light. How many times before had he seen the tail of a plane in flight and paid no notice? Now, it seemed a contact with humanity. But was it? All of a sudden, he realized it was something more than a plane. He didn't see any motion. This object stood still. He watched for a moment, and it remained immobile. What was it?

Squinting, Rob realized his 20/20 vision did him no good. The object was too far away to tell whether it was a helicopter, a weather balloon, or a ship from outer space. It descended in his direction. He had a sudden inclination to crouch out of its way. Realizing the futility of such a move, he remained standing.

The cone-like object was very similar to the other spaceship. It was much larger than he'd thought. He also couldn't tell whether it was one of the ships in the gully, Eric's or Torpi's. He'd never seen them airborne.

It flashed lights from all sides as if to say, "I'm coming, I'm coming, beware." The indiscretion of such a move astounded him. Wouldn't anyone from outer space want to remain anonymous? Instead, it appeared to flaunt its existence for all the world to see.

But then the ship appeared and disappeared at will. It had gone toward the ground in seconds, but just as it almost touched down, a rapid movement thrust it back toward the sky.

He squinted in an effort to pierce through the darkness. *I wonder if I'm the only human being seeing this.* However, in this remote area, he suspected few, if any, other people were likely to observe this spaceship in action. Maybe the occupants of the ship knew that.

Maybe the ship was Torpi's. What would happen if they'd given up on his returning and left? He took a deep breath. On the other hand, maybe he had nothing to worry about. Perhaps they'd just used the ruse as a fear tactic to force him to get them food. More likely they had stayed put and waited for his return. What would be the purpose in lying to him anyhow? But they had the technology to play this little game. He went back and forth, not knowing what to believe. He banged his fist against a tree then rubbed it where it hurt. Uncertainty was the worst of it all.

The ship disappeared. If it was Torpi's ship, Rob knew he had real cause to worry. He slowed his pace. *Why hurry if I get back to the landing spot and the Torpians are gone? If they are there, as soon as I deliver the food, they could declare me disposable. I might be a dead man.*

In the middle of a dense growth of trees and underbrush, he set the groceries on the ground and sat beside them to rest, as tired as if he'd done two days' manual labor without a break. The crickets called to him, but then a roaring sound echoed through the woods, interrupting them.

What the hell? Lights flashed a few feet from him, just outside the thicket on a narrow path.

The lights and noise racing his way came from a group of dirt bikes. Rob scrambled behind the trunk of a huge pine tree and hoped they'd pass him by. He held his breath. Amid screams and flying dirt, a couple of the off-road vehicles pulled to a halt less than three yards from where he was hiding. Fearing he'd be sighted in their headlights, his heart raced.

Over the sound of idling motors, he heard bikers talking but couldn't distinguish the words. One guy goosed his engine and it sputtered out. The others also cut theirs off. They lit up cigarettes and when the smell of burning rope reached Rob's nostrils, he knew why they'd come into the thicket.

Chapter Seventeen

Tough talk of fights reached Rob's ears. The motorcyclists left their lights on, so Rob peeked out and counted about ten motorcycles.

One hairy-faced guy with tattoos of semi-nude women covering both arms stood with his lip poked out. "Hey, you guys, thanks for the weed," he yelled. "'Preciate you helpin' me out with that damn idiot, too. I was mad as hell when the dude cut me off."

Another man laughed. "Yeah, Bubba. After we made him run off the shoulder of the road and crash and you started beatin' up on him, I think he got the message."

"Well, his face knows it. He ain't gonna be able to eat much for a while, not after I knocked out his ugly yellar teeth. Looked a lot like the damn bozo I floored in Rosie's Bar last week," he bragged. "Y'all remembah?"

"Yeah, he didn't do nothin' to you. Why'd you beat up on him?" The guy speaking was wide as he was tall.

"Wanted to." Bubba cackled. "I jes' didn't like his looks. 'Sides, he deserved it."

Rob's hair stood on end and he shuddered. Leaning a bit to one side to check on the tough gang members puffing on their marijuana cigarettes, he knocked a can of beans out of his bag of groceries. Too frightened to move, he watched it roll down a slight incline right toward the spot where the bikes were parked. When it banged against a rock, one of the cyclists jerked his head in that direction.

Cupping his ears, he whirled around. "What the hell's that noise?"

"Good God, dude. You scared of y'own shadow? Probably just a squirrel crackin' a nut," one of his companions replied as he slapped the air.

"Squirrels don't make that kind o' noise. Squirrels shamper...samper.... Oh, hell, you know what I mean," the cyclist replied, slurring his words. "They go ss-ss-s."

"Who cares? Ain't you got better things to think about, huh?"

But before either of them spoke again, the can came to a stop right at Bubba's feet. He picked it up. "So, it weren't no squirrel," he sneered. "Hey, we got us some beans. Anybody got a can opener? I'm hongory."

They tussled with a beer opener until they got the can open. "We ain't got no spoon. Besides, I ain't hongory enough to eat no cold beans." The speaker dumped the contents on the ground.

Much to Rob's relief, none of them investigated where the can came from. Maybe they were too stoned to wonder. Regardless, he didn't have to deal with it. One long-haired tough revved his motor, preparing to leave, and the others did likewise.

Rob slumped in relief. *I'm safe.*

The group of men hung around a little longer, screaming to each other over the sound of the engines. Then they pointed in his direction.

Rob jolted. *Oh, no!*

Without warning, all of them shut off their engines again. Led by Bubba, they headed in Rob's direction. Bubba held his cigarette to his lips, took one more puff, and then let his arm drop to his side. "If there's anybody in there, we'll get him." His stage whisper sounded like a roar.

Frozen to the spot, Rob stood there shaking. This was worse than facing the devious Torpi. These kooks would kill him in a minute, even though he posed no threat to them. Hell's Angels had nothing on this gang of thugs. They didn't need provocation to strike, and he had no defense against them.

Pain gripped his chest. *Will I last long enough to be their victim?* Cold sweat trickled down his forehead as he felt blood drain out of his head. Weakness overcame him. *Oh, God. I'm going to faint.* He swayed, and his eyesight dimmed.

As he lost consciousness, he saw a bright light in the sky. It, too, headed in his direction.

Rob didn't know how long he was out, but when he awoke, everybody had left. No men, no bikes. Only the track marks made by the bikers' tires showed they'd been there. It baffled him. Hearing a faint noise, he looked upward. Like the reflection of a fish's fin in the water, he saw a glimmer soaring through the sky. He grinned a smug, sideways smile.

Well, if you've taken those thugs, you've got your hands full, whoever you are. He picked up his groceries, stood a minute to steady himself, and then resumed his journey.

All the confusion had caused him to lose his sense of direction. Thinking he might be headed toward the road again, he listened for the sounds from highway traffic or the airport. *Nothing? Maybe I'm heading toward the ship after all.*

The sky remained pitch dark. Exhaustion overcame him. He longed to lie down and go to sleep. Aching feet and scratched arms and legs added to his distress. *What I wouldn't give for a good, hot shower, a hamburger and fries, and a cold beer.* If he could have had anything in the world he wanted, right at that moment, a bed would be at the top of his list—even over a hot shower.

But all of those things were far from his reach. He dare not take a bite of food from the bag. Later, in the spaceship, food might be more necessary for survival than it had been before. Besides, he wasn't starving. He just needed something to salve his frustrations, and food was the only thing he could think of. He resisted the urge and kept moving.

Oh, God, will I ever reach the spaceship again? He trudged forward, glancing at the night sky peeking through the tree branches overhead. *Maybe. Maybe not. I might be doomed.*

Ahead of him, the sound of someone coughing caught his attention. *A female. Out in the woods this late at night?* The high-pitched stifled sound told him without a doubt a woman was somewhere a few yards ahead of him. And somehow, no matter who it was, a female did not seem ominous.

Again it came, more like a throat clearing this time. Pushing through the underbrush, he hustled along, trying to catch up to her. Whatever the outcome, he couldn't allow her to escape. He needed to talk to another human being.

The dim light from his flashlight offered little assistance. It had almost completely gone out. Up ahead, another light flickered through the trees, and he debated whether to call out. All he could see was the outline of a slight figure. Her light shifted from side to side. *Wait. What is that in her arms?* Packages, but he couldn't tell what they held. She moved fast. He had to hurry.

Leaving his groceries behind, he jumped over fallen tree limbs and made it close enough to the woman for her to hear his approach.

Turning, she dropped her bags on the ground and flashed the light full in his face. "Who's there?"

He blinked. Before he regained his composure, two arms flung around his neck.

"Rob, oh, Rob." She backed off. "It's really you. I was afraid you were gone forever." She pulled him close. Mona's arms encircled his neck again. "Ah, this is the best feeling in the world. Am I hallucinating? This is too good to be true."

Rob held Mona at arm's length. "I can't believe this."

"Neither can I." She reached up and moved a strand of hair off his forehead. "You won't believe what's happened to me."

Rob stared straight into her eyes. "I think I will, considering what's happened to me."

They stood there, recounting the past week's events for a few minutes. After comparing notes, they came to the present time.

"This all seems like a dream, a nightmare." Mona blinked. "But it's wonderful to have someone who understands and believes me."

"Same here," Rob agreed. "I guess we just have to accept the reality of the problem and try to figure out the solution."

"Yeah. At least we have each other."

Rob sighed. "But we need more. We need a plan."

"Listen, I've grown close to Eric, Lydia, and Marcus. I want to return to the ships. I don't want to leave them stranded."

Rob grimaced. *Good to know all aliens aren't bad.* "Well, since I need Torpi to eliminate this object from my body or to give me something to counteract what they may have put in my blood, I have to return to his ship. I have no choice."

He still had the gnawing feeling he might be a goner no matter what he did. He and Mona retrieved their groceries and made their way back to the ships.

On the way, he stopped and held onto her arm. "You know, I've been thinking. We shouldn't discount other possibilities. Eric could be in charge by now, or Torpi could have overcome Eric's ship and be waiting for us to return." He shrugged. "And I don't know about the spaceship I saw—the one I told you must have taken those bikers."

Too many unanswered questions. In an effort to put it all out of his mind for a while, Rob changed the subject.

"What about Pep? Is he still in the ship? It's not fair for an innocent little dog to be caught up in all of this."

"He got loose, and I don't know where he went. But dogs have good instincts. If none of us survive, there's a good chance Pep will." Her shoulders shook. "If that happens, somebody will find him and take care of him. I hope." She sniffled. "I can just picture Pep trekking through the woods with the little bell I found and attached to his collar jingling to the rhythm of his trot."

Rob sucked in his cheek. *Yes, unaware of inner and outer space, Pep would go merrily on his way, searching for his mistress. Perhaps his nose will instinctively lead him to his home, her apartment.*

Rob released Mona's arm, and they resumed their walk.

"We've got to make some quick decisions," he told her, thinking without a precedent to go by the difficult situation presented almost insurmountable problems.

Solutions, even ideas, seemed to lack clarity. Every answer they came up with seemed either wrong or ridiculous. They had only one thing in their favor.

Mona grabbed Rob's elbow. "I recognize this area. I came through here before. We're just on the other side of the gully. I know the way back. It's not far."

"Okay." Rob patted her hand. "We need to be careful."

"We could try to get close enough to check things out." She turned in the direction she'd indicated. "But we won't be able to see inside of the ships, so seeing the outside of the ships won't tell us anything conclusive."

Rob mentioned a possibility. "Torpi may have left. If he did, I don't know what my chances are. Hell, I don't know if Eric has the knowledge to help me. Will he even know what the insertion or the chemical in the blood is?"

The prospect wasn't good. But Rob knew they couldn't just stay in those woods. Time could be a crucial factor regarding saving his life. When they finally spotted one ship, they stuck close together and headed straight for it.

Chapter Eighteen

In outer space, Eric no longer had any doubt as to what happened. All the remaining spaceships left on Svar had been activated. He still did not know whether a friend or foe was responsible. Despite using all available electronic equipment, he could not establish contact. Static and squawking sounds filled the airwaves. Torpi broke in with wild threats, threats he had no way of carrying out. To compound the problem, interference came from United States planes near the area.

"A spaceship is out there," one pilot reported in a higher-pitched voice. "No, wait. I see more than one. Three are advancing. They appear and disappear at will." He then gave his location and requested other planes be sent to the area.

The planes didn't concern Eric or his crew. He wanted to communicate with the other ships so they could find out their loyalties and their intentions. If they were friendly, he would solicit their help. If not, well, he would have to deal with them in another manner. *Time to make a move.*

He advised his crew of his actions. "Before they veer too close to Earth and into more crowded airways, I think we should lift off. Perhaps then we can make contact with them."

Lydia and Marcus nodded. Eric regretted leaving Mona behind, but he couldn't wait any longer. They prepared for lift off, and, in minutes, they were up and on their way. As they neared the other ships, Eric glanced back. The Torpian's ship followed them.

"It might complicate matters for both ships to be in the air. It worries me because they're identical, and I don't know how the arriving ships can tell them apart." Eric wrinkled his pug nose.

Marcus shook his head. "Torpi is smart. He knows even if the oncoming ships are on our side, unless we establish communication with them, they can be of little use to us. Torpi lifted off knowing full well our ships are identical. How can the other ships take sides? We must make our presence known as Svarians. Then, if those ships want to support us, they will know who to help. If not, we have no hope."

Exerting all the expertise he possessed, Eric adjusted the radio controls. Noises came forth but no clear words. He tried again with no results. Torpi must also have been having trouble. Either he stayed off of the air, or he could not get through.

Even if he established contact, he only had a fifty-fifty chance of help. After all, when he left Svar, Torpi had plenty of time to convince the Svarians their leader had abandoned them. For all he knew, Torpi might have become their new leader. Without communications, he had no way to vindicate himself. It was in fate's hands.

***

Rob and Mona approached the clearing where the spaceships landed, and she swallowed hard.

"I wish I were with Pep. I wish you and I both were. Wherever my little dog is, he's safer than he'd be here. How did we ever get into this, anyhow? We're going back to the spaceships willingly. Nobody even knows we're still alive much less that we're caught up in such an impossible, unbelievable situation. How can anyone help us?" She grabbed his elbow. "I'm scared." Her voice quivered.

He put his arm around Mona and squeezed her to him. "If it's any help, I'm scared as hell, too. But it'll all work out. Somehow, someway, we're going to get back to civilization safe and sound. One day, we'll laugh about all of this."

Unconvinced, Mona shrugged. But shame overcame her because Rob was worse off. *He doesn't even know what they put in him. He could die at any moment and here I am complaining. I should be trying to make him forget his problem. Instead, I'm making things worse.* In an effort to compensate, she rose onto her tiptoes and kissed him on the cheek.

He gave her a crooked smile. Despite the seriousness of the situation, she snuggled close to Rob. Her heartbeat picked up, tapping a quick rhythm against her ribs. *Rob's really my kind of guy. When we get back—*

"Look over there," he said all of a sudden. "It's the landing spot. We're here. Good God, the ships are all gone! What the hell is going on?"

A roaring sound drew Mona's attention to the sky. She gasped.

Flashes of light almost blinded her. The most elaborate display of fireworks any Fourth of July professional show could produce filled the heavens. Spaceships appeared everywhere. They fought each other, but it was impossible to discern what type of weapons they were using or who was who; all the ships were identical. She couldn't determine which ship belonged to Eric or the Torpians. The ships annihilated each other.

"Good Lord!" she screamed. "I bet nothing like this battle has ever been seen from Earth before!"

She and Rob froze in their tracks, heads bent as far back as they would go to view the action above.

When a huge explosion came, it rocked the ground beneath Mona and Rob's feet. The force shook them, the impact like a category four hurricane, causing Mona to duck even though she wasn't in their path. Groceries they'd dropped on the ground scattered in the winds. Cans shot out of bags like balls from a cannon. The need for food or pills had disappeared for one spaceship's occupants. From all appearances, Svarians were no longer immortal.

With Rob's arms encircling her, Mona grieved. "Oh, Rob, I'm afraid my friends may have perished. Somehow, I just know they're gone." She had not known them long, but she knew them well. They'd formed a bond, and their relationship may have been brief, but strong. In her lifetime, she could never hope to find others quite like those Svarians. How strange to have developed close-knit ties with beings from a different planet. She could never explain this to anyone, not even Rob. Deep in her soul, a loss unlike any she'd felt before overwhelmed her. She broke into uncontrollable tears.

Patting her back, Rob pulled her close. "I know. I understand. But remember you had an experience no one on Earth has ever had. You lived with people from another planet and from a time far in the future. You had a chance to know them, even if only for a little while. Maybe someday you'll share this experience, write a story about it to convince others it's true."

She didn't accept his appraisal of the situation. Even writing about this seemed impossible. *But that's the only way to get the Pulitzer Prize. I wish I could talk to somebody about this, but Rob doesn't understand. His experience with the Torpians, the enemy, was different from mine.* Still, she appreciated his efforts to console her. It helped ease the pain. Little by little, Mona regained her self-control.

She pulled away from Rob. "We've got to go."

He nodded, and they left the scene.

Soon, they reached a path leading to the highway "Listen to that noise." Rob cocked his head. "Those are sirens."

"Maybe they came for a different reason. The O'Haras are probably fighting again and somebody called the police. I bet they don't even know about the spaceships."

He wrinkled his nose. "Who are the O'Haras?"

She took his hand and smiled. "Long story. I'll explain later."

As they walked along in silence, Mona mulled over the events of the past week in minute detail as she struggled with conflicting ideas ping-ponging in her brain. Although inclined to blame herself for Rob's predicament because she'd let Pep out and Pep had led Rob to the ship, after careful consideration, she decided she had little to feel guilty about. If Rob was destined to get to the ship and be taken prisoner by Torpi, he'd have gotten there without Pep's help. *Poor Pep. Where in the world is he? I hope he's okay.* She wrung her hands. *I can't do anything for you now, boy, but I'll be looking for you as soon as this mess is over.*

"What will be, shall be," she told Rob. Her old bespectacled English teacher with horn-rimmed glasses slipping down on her nose came back to offer words of comfort with her quote. "Fate, or God's will, or whatever else it can be called, has more power than I do."

"To be out of a tight corner satisfies me. I could beat myself up, but I don't need personal recriminations. Fate's given me a reprieve. If I can just discover what, if anything, the Torpians put in my body"—he cocked his head—"maybe I can find a way to safely get it out."

***

The sky brightened, and the sun came up. The long, hard night was over, and the gray light of dawn allayed some of the mysterious, unexplainable foreboding of darkness. But with it came a need for judgments. Nothing had been settled. Until Rob found out what to do to be saved, everything else was left hanging.

"You know, it'll be hard to find a doctor who'll take me seriously." He shook his head and shrugged. "I mean, how can I possibly find out what the Torpians did to me? No doctor or hospital will believe my story. I wouldn't believe it myself if I hadn't experienced it. What's the use of looking for a doctor anyway? Sure, they'd examine me. If they didn't find anything, they'd write me off as a kook. I've got the feeling whatever they put inside me is well hidden." He glanced at the pastel sky, pinks and purples announcing a new day. He committed it to memory. Who knew how many sunrises he had left? "I've proved to myself the Torpians did something to me," he told Mona. "The more I think about it, the more I realize the odds are against the Torpians just making threats."

He patted all over his body again in the hope of finding a clue. Nothing.

"I know something caused me to pass out a while ago and it wasn't just fear." He searched his pockets. "I sure could use a cigarette right now." He took his hands out of his pockets. "No luck. You don't smoke, do you, Mona?"

"Nope. Never have. Sorry, I can't help you there."

"That's okay. I quit a year ago, but I usually keep one in my pocket in a plastic case with my credit cards to prove I won't give in to temptation. Right now, I've got the urge to smoke and my cigarette's gone. Just as well."

"Oh, look, Rob. This sunrise is too beautiful to miss. Isn't it magnificent?" She pointed to the east.

The arc of the orange sun rising on the horizon presented a gorgeous work of nature. It was a sign of a return to humanity. From a practical point of view, it showed which way east was, too. Mona smiled. "There is a God. The sun let us know which way east is. Knowing we're headed in the right direction sure is encouraging."

"Listen, Mona," Rob said. "I hear cars."

At the sound of automobiles whizzing down the highway, he grabbed her wrist and gave it a tug. Together, they broke into a run, ignoring the branches slapping and scratching their bodies. One of Mona's shoes slipped off, and she paused long enough to shove it back on her foot.

No sight could have been more welcoming than the early morning traffic flowing down the highway. In a moment of jubilation, Rob and Mona stood at the edge of the road, waving at cars passing by. He sat, flopping on the dew-soaked grass covering the embankment bordering the road.

"Gee, it's great to be back," Mona told Rob. "Cars never looked so good to me before. What a wonderful feeling to be free again—free and out of the wilderness." She jumped up and ran around in a circle with outstretched arms flapping like a bird's wings, unconcerned with what passers-by might think.

Rob laughed. "You look so cute doing that."

Mona plopped on the ground again.

It was so relaxing to be away from the pressures of recent hours he could not even worry about the future. Rob pulled her to him and gave her a passionate kiss.

Separating, he gazed into her eyes. He felt her gentle touch when she ran her fingers through his hair. Neither spoke, but he realized a new relationship had begun, and it would not end with episode one. But they had to deal with his ordeal before taking time for romance. And that wouldn't be over until his problem was solved.

Rob smoothed Mona's hair back from her face. He whistled a slow tune, breaking the silence, then shook his head. "Unfortunately, we've got to get back to the matter at hand." He rubbed his hand over the stubble on his chin. "But where do we go from here?" He pulled her to her feet.

Mona shrugged. "I don't lack compassion, nor do I intend to be frivolous. I guess I just need a little breathing space." She looked into Rob's eyes. "I don't know where we go from here." She rubbed the dimple in his chin. "But I'll follow you anywhere."

He chuckled. Her reply gave him a much-needed sense of normality. Back at the paper, they had to rely on their sense of humor often to keep their sanity when dealing with the seamy side of life. The little jokes they told in the newsroom kept them from going crazy.

Mona backed away, saying, "This'll just have to wait. Rob, your life's in jeopardy. We need to act. What are we going to do?"

"I know." Rob squeezed her hand, sorry that the brief romantic moment had to end. "We've got to do something fast." With a sigh, he became serious again. "Okay, it's obvious we can't stay in the Mobile area. Too many people know us here. If I go to any hospital in town, my name will be on the news in fifteen minutes. What do you think about hitching to Pensacola? They have a good hospital and a lot of qualified doctors. I can give them an assumed name."

Mona frowned. "Do we have time to make it there?"

"I don't know. I guess we'll just have to take a chance. I'm afraid I won't get the proper treatment if I stay here, especially if they know who I am. They might think I'm just making this up to get a scoop on a sensational story." He rubbed his chin again. "With this growth of beard, I'm sure I'll look like an indigent...and I could get admitted to a hospital without presenting an insurance card or a credit card because they have to take emergency cases nowadays."

"Okay, that might work." Mona rubbed her temples.

"I can pay them later." He moistened his lips. "But the problem is how to tell them what's wrong."

Mona plopped down on the grass again and cupped her face in her hands. She had nothing to offer.

Stooping beside her, Rob kept talking. "One thing's certain: what happened must be kept a secret. Regardless of the fact sightings will be all over the Mobile paper, we can't break our story. We may have to tell a doctor, but, for the present, nobody else should know what happened to us."

Mona flicked a gaze upward. "You're right." *But as long as everything's a secret, I'll never get back to find Pep. I miss him so much.* Reality took over. *If the news broke, the media would be out in force. Other reporters would be right on our backs, hounding us to death.* She knew just how those things worked in the trade. It wouldn't make a whit of difference they were in the same profession. To a good newsman, a story is a story no matter who gets stepped on. It wouldn't even matter that their interference might cause Rob's death. They'd get their story, whatever the expense. *Yeah, but I'm saving this one for myself. And my story's going to get me that Pulitzer Prize.*

They could allow no leaks. This had to be her exclusive. Besides, if they did have a leak, Rob might not have a chance to get treatment he needed. They wouldn't know until after they determined whether his injection or blood tampering was real or fake.

Rob gave Mona a hand up.

Looking straight in his eyes, she said, "Let's go for it."

Together, they stepped right out to the edge of the highway and held thumbs up. In five minutes, a rickety old pickup truck pulled to the shoulder of the road.

The driver stuck his head out the window and yelled back at them, "C'mon. Hop in."

Mona climbed in the middle next to the driver, and Rob squeezed in next to her, slamming the door. It creaked on its hinges and didn't close all the way. *Can this broken-down truck get us as far as downtown Mobile, much less any farther?*

"Old Jenny'll get us there, miss. Don't you worry," the driver said in a coarse voice as he patted the steering wheel.

A rusty old fellow with a ruddy complexion, he looked like someone who'd spent most of his life in the sun. His red eyes, and breath reeking of whiskey, made Mona wonder if her fears had been misplaced. Perhaps the driver, not the truck, should be her concern. He drove slowly and the traffic had thinned out, but she did not feel very safe. The shorter the distance he took them, the better she'd like it.

"How far can you take us?" She hoped he'd say he soon had to turn off.

"Depends on where you wanna go. I'm stopping at Pensacola. If you're headed in a different direction, jes' let me know where to let you out." He sped up, jerked the wheel, and swerved around the car in front of him, missing its back bumper by inches.

Gritting her teeth, she tried to think of what to say next. She had to reply quickly before Rob accepted. Did Rob realize this old codger was stoned to the gills? They'd already been through too much to end up a statistic in highway fatalities. Mona wanted out of this truck.

Facing Rob, she stammered out words, slurring syllables on purpose, hoping he'd get the hint. "Glad for the shride, mis-stuh. But all we need is to get to the bushtop—ha, ha, I mean the bus stop." She winked her right eye at Rob, hoping he caught on.

"Yessuh," he added to her ruse. "Thas all we need, a ride to a buzzstop."

At those words, the inebriated driver glared at them. "Hey, you two, I thought you wuz okay, even though you look shoddy as hell." His voice sounded as if he were shocked sober. "What the devil are you on? I ain't giving you two druggies a ride no farther. Get out." He motioned with his head. "I ain't giving you no chance to rob me."

Pulling into a grocery store parking lot, the old man leaned over both of them and opened the passenger side door. Without a word, he jerked back a thumb and motioned them out of the car.

"Get out!"

When they did, he pulled away as fast as the old truck would allow.

Mona glanced at Rob. "Whew! The feeling's mutual between the driver and us. We're all glad to be rid of each other."

Across the street, a sign read Mobile Transportation Department. Right behind it sat a McDonalds. The traffic light changed and they crossed the street.

The scent of food cooking prompted Mona to say, "Gee, I'm famished. You hungry, Rob?"

"Yeah. I could sure use some food." He rubbed his stomach.

"Hey, I've got some money." But when Mona pulled off her shoe, the bill she'd put there was gone. "Damn. I guess I lost it when my shoe fell off." She slapped her hand against her cheek. "Oh, no. I left the money at the O'Haras to pay for the groceries I took. How're we going to buy something to eat without any cash? I don't have a credit card, do you?"

Rob shook his head. "Just a little change."

Her dry throat and parched lips begged for relief.

Rob dug in his pocket and pulled out two dollars and fifty-two cents. "We won't get much for this."

At the counter, the smell of freshly brewed coffee reached their nostrils, and a whiff of it caused Mona to say, "Smells like heaven."

"Coffee's just a quarter for senior citizens. I'll say I'm old enough to qualify." Rob read a sign advertising a special and added up the tab. "I think I've got enough for a couple of sausage biscuits, too." He shook his head. "I don't have enough for sales tax. Do you have a nickel or four pennies?"

Before Mona could answer, an overall-clad male standing in line behind them tapped Rob on the shoulder and handed him a nickel.

Rob's face broke into a broad grin. "Thanks, man. I really appreciate it. You saved my life."

The server who took their order gave Rob a hard look, but she still sold him the coffee for a quarter. Three minutes later, Rob and Mona sat in a booth and gobbled their food.

"Look at these people." Rob pointed to the morning trade coming and going. "They don't even see us. They're oblivious to the fact we were captives on spaceships until just a few hours ago. Like most of the citizenry of Mobile, Alabama, and the world, they know nothing of outer space activities that could change the course of humanity. Of course, neither did we, till recently. Oh well, maybe it doesn't matter. How important space activities are, future generations will determine. Time will tell. Only time will tell."

***

After the explosion in the sky, Marcus and Eric crawled out of a ditch, battered and bruised. Marcus fell to the ground. "Let me help you." Eric stopped and tried to help him up. But he couldn't budge him.

"What's wrong, Marcus?" When Marcus did not respond, he knelt beside his friend and raised his eyes to heaven: "No immortality for us." Then he took Marcus' pulse and felt his weak heartbeat. "You know I don't give up easily, but I don't think I have a choice this time. I'll be joining you soon, my friend."

He let his head rest on Marcus's chest and waited. *Will anyone ever find us?*

Chapter Nineteen

When they finished eating, Mona sighed. "Mmmm, very good. I feel refreshed." Rob squirmed in his chair. "What's wrong? Didn't the sausage agree with you?"

He shook his head. "No, it's not that. I just keep going hot and cold worrying about the implant." He drummed his fingers. "Hell, there's no point in trying to find a doctor. It's useless. We're just kidding ourselves. No doctor's—"

Putting her finger to his lips, she stopped his negative outburst. With an uncanny, unexplainable wave of communication between them, they let the moment pass without another word.

"Okay." She scooted her chair out and stood. "We'd better be on our way."

As they left McDonald's, an idea formed in Mona's mind as to how they could get at least part of the way to Pensacola. The long-haired youth who'd given them the nickel stood near the exit, chatting with a girl and another couple. And they didn't act drunk.

With her special knack for being able to engage people in conversation, especially oddballs, she quickened her pace to catch up with them before they left the premises. In this case, she decided a direct approach would be the most effective. She didn't have time to let Rob in on the act, so she moved ahead while he trailed behind.

Catching up with the foursome, she held the door open for them. The tall bleached-blonde looked over her shoulder and eyed Mona. "I bet she wants something," she mumbled.

"Say, is there any chance you're going our way...toward Pensacola?" She pointed at the girl's male companion. "He knows we're broke. He lent us a nickel so we could get breakfast. We don't have any wheels. So, if you're going in that direction, we sure could use a ride…even part of the way. Who wants to get stuck here in this dead city?" She waited for a reaction, and when none was forthcoming, she decided to take a different tack. Maybe they liked Mobile. She'd better take back her criticism. "I mean, there's nothing wrong with Mobile, but there's more action in Pensy."

Her jivey talk made a hit. Long Hair cracked a smile, and the others followed suit. He seemed to be the leader of the group. As if on cue, they all laughed, even the somber blonde. She turned to the brown-haired leader, who had holes in the knees and backside of his jeans. "Hey, Mr. D, she's cool."

Mona put her hand on Rob's shoulder. "This is…." She faked a cough long enough to think of a name. The first thing coming to mind was a comic strip character named Slingo. "Sorry, my drink must have gone down the wrong way. My friend here is Slingo."

She pointed to her chest. "And I'm Peppy." She used the first name that popped into her head, and she didn't mind having the same name as her dog at all. *Gosh I miss him. I sure hope he's okay.*

The tall blonde held out her hand. "I'm Ta." She pointed to the girl next to her wearing a halter and cut-off jeans. "She's Shawn." Then she reached over and rumpled the curly hair of a chubby round-faced teenager who looked like he didn't belong with the rest of them. "He's Bubba. You've already met Mr. D, right?"

Rapport had been established. Ta tightened the band around her ponytail. "Say, Mr. D, we can go to P'Cola, can't we? Let's take them along. They're with it, and we've got room. We could use some new blood. How 'bout it?" She put an arm around his lanky shoulders and batted mascara-covered eyelashes in his direction.

Mr. D. winked at her. "Why not?"

Mona and Rob followed them to their old van, and the six set out together on Eastbound I-10. When they reached the van, Shawn slumped in the seat. "Nobody's told me where we're going. First, y'all talked about New Orleans; now, looks like we're taking these two to Florida." She pointed a thumb in Mona and Rob's direction as they squeezed into the car's back seat.

"Let's go down to the boats and play a few slots first," Bubba suggested.

Mona pressed her hand against her cheek. *What boats is he referring to? Could he be talking about Biloxi? How crazy. That's the opposite direction.*

"Naw," Ta objected, much to Mona's relief. "We're not going to Mississippi. We gotta take our friends here to Pensacola."

Mr. D tapped his chest. "Listen up. I'm the one who's driving, and I'll say where we're going." But he didn't. His attitude bothered Mona, so did what Ta might have meant about needing "new blood." By their kooky actions, she figured this group they'd hooked up with could be druggies. Under normal circumstances, she would have shied away from such people, but nothing about her current circumstances was normal. However, she'd done many things out of the ordinary lately. Nothing surprised her. Not even the unpredictability of her companions. She just hoped they'd get her and Rob to Pensacola without incident. They didn't need a confrontation with the police.

From the tone and tempo of their conversation, Mona wasn't sure they even knew what they were going to do next. It seemed they'd just met up with each other and nobody knew what was what.

"I jes' met Mr. D this morning. Seems like he's the impulsive type." Ta confirmed Mona's speculations. "And here we are...on our way to P'Cola." She snuggled closer to Mr. D. and leaned her head on his shoulder. "Ouch!" She jumped and rubbed her upper arm as she glared up at him. "What'd I say? Why'd you pinch me?"

"Don't mouth off," he replied. "I told you I'd decide where we're going."

His admonishment didn't stop Ta from chatting away. She climbed over the seat and plopped herself between Mona and Rob in the back. The conversation went from disconnected sentences to Ta's expounding on the benefits of modern psychology. She spouted vulgarities and expletives that would make a sailor blush.

Nobody tried to hush her, but, after Mr. D passed around some little red pills and she took one, her talking ceased. Instead, she leaned against Rob's shoulder and fell asleep. Mona managed to spit out the pills and hide them in her pocket along with those Rob handed her.

Mr. D took his turn talking. Even though he'd pretended he had impulsively decided to go to Pensacola, Mona discerned from his erratic conversation he had been headed there all along. He also revealed they were all high on a new hallucinogenic drug unknown to any but the heaviest users.

"I got a dealer who supplies me with all the drugs I want and some big bucks," he bragged. "Ain't no big deal. All I gotta do is deliver drugs to ships leaving the Port of Mobile. Easy." He motioned to the others who were dozing. "They don't know it but the back of my van's loaded. I'm on my way to furnish a supplier in

Pensacola some to take to the Keys. Dunno where they go from there. To ports unknown, I guess."

Mona made a face. Once again, she wanted out, but this time she couldn't find a way to escape the situation. Pensacola was less than thirty miles from here. She crossed her fingers and decided to just take a chance on not getting pulled over by the police.

Mr. D glanced back at Mona and Rob. "Hey, you guys must really be into this if those pills didn't knock you out." He chuckled. "Those wimps are blown away already. They don't know nothin' 'bout what I jus' tole you." He turned and glared at them. "You better keep your mouth shut, too."

The car veered right onto the shoulder. He got back on the road just in time to swerve back into his own lane and miss an eighteen-wheeler headed straight for them.

"I don' know much, neither. Jes' who my contact is. But it's all I need to know. Okay?" He checked in the rearview mirror. "You guys want in on the ground floor, jes' say the word."

Mona found Mr. D's trusting two strangers unexplainable. Though he didn't insist on an answer, it would be wise to give one.

"Naw, man. We got other contacts, and they don't like double-dippin' o' no kind. Have to pass."

Mr. D nodded and didn't question her. The others stirred, and he quit talking. The six of them traveled together the rest of the way as if they'd been lifelong friends.

When they reached downtown Pensacola, Rob said, "Can you let us out here?"

Mr. D pulled over. As soon as they were out of the vehicle, he reached out the window and held out his hand.

"Hold on." He kept a very straight face. "That'll be twenty each."

Rob paled, and Mona caught her breath. But before she had time to get too upset, Mr. D let out a big horse-laugh.

"Har, har. I know you two ain't got no money. But I gotcha, didn't I?"

He and his companions wheeled off, leaving Rob and Mona standing on the curb.

Rob puffed out his breath. "Those were some strange characters."

"Yeah." Mona pulled on her ear. "But you know what? I've got some neighbors in the apartment across from me who are almost that bad."

Rob laughed, but he stopped when a car ran a traffic light and he had to jump back on the curb to dodge it.

So much had happened. Mona shook her head. "I can't believe we're on Palafox Street." Yet, here she was, four blocks from Rosie O'Grady's, a place she'd always had fun, with a yesterday nobody would believe, a today that was unpredictable, and a tomorrow nobody could anticipate. The glance into the past from Seville Square—the Bourbon Street of Pensacola minus exotic dancers, the place she and Lee frequented often—reminded her those times with Lee Black were gone forever. *Thank God.*

But being here boggled her mind. It surprised Mona to find a fun city could exist amidst the confusion in her head. Many times she had visited the quaint section noted for its cheap drinks and talented piano players. Memories. Silent movies and jazz songs played by retired engineers, pros at the art of capturing the interest of their fans. *Does Rosie O'Grady's and all the other interesting restaurants and bars truly occupy the city's old quarter? Or is it an alleyway I imagined, an unreal place dreamed up to satisfy my yearning for a spot of history and a love affair preserved?* At the present time, everything seemed like a fabrication of her imagination.

Mona gritted her teeth. *Am I losing my grip? No.* Like the space people and the druggies who got them here, Seville Square and Rosie O'Grady's were real. So were Mr. D and Ta. What would happen to them?

"Mona, Mona. Come in, Mona." Rob tugged on her arm. "Where are you?"

His words brought her back to reality. "Rob, oh Rob, everything that's happened is getting to me. Memories cropped up and then I kind of worried about Mr. D." She shook her head. "Sounds crazy, but I hope he doesn't get caught. I know he's a drug dealer and the others are users, but they're also human beings with problems and fears. We have different views of life, but maybe we should have tried to help them."

Rob took her hand. "I guess this affected you, a female, more than it has me. You're empathetic, aren't you? But I don't know what we could have done. Besides, we don't have time to be bleeding hearts. We have our own difficulties to deal with."

"I guess you're right. Maybe we couldn't help them." Mona sucked in her cheek. The past was past, and they'd do well to forget it. Solving humanity's problems was out of their realm. Facing their own problems was difficult enough. Time was moving on—with or without their progress. They needed to move on, too.

The midmorning traffic on the city's thoroughfare was light. Mona glanced around but didn't see anyone she knew, still a little apprehensive about being on a public street. However, she realized they were less likely to be recognized in Pensacola than they would have been in their hometown. It seemed ironic. At this time of year, people flocked to Mobile to visit the battleship *USS Alabama* or to see beautiful Bellingrath Gardens with its thousands of plants, some always in bloom. Yet, she and Rob left for the safety of a Florida city.

"You know what? I just remembered one of Frank's idiosyncrasies about the South." Deepening her voice, she quoted him. "'Mona, I do not care what the English books say or what the professors at the University of Alabama may have told you. When you refer to the Azalea Trail in Mobile, spell South with a capital S.'"

She laughed. "I don't know why this came up. Homesick, I guess. Frank has his rules, and if you want to keep your job you don't violate them, do you?"

Rob put his arm around her, but she shied away. "We've got to concentrate on locating a doctor for you. Let's find a pay phone."

He patted his pockets then shook his head. "I don't even have a quarter left."

"Oh, I just want to check the yellow pages."

Since cell phones had replaced many pay phones, they had to walk a couple of blocks, but they found one on a corner by a long-deserted hotel. Rob thumbed through the directory. "Do you think we should try a hospital or a doctor?" Before she answered, he showed her a listing. "Wait. Here's a general practitioner, right on the street we just passed. Might be an omen. Maybe he's just what I need."

She nodded. "Let's try him. What have we got to lose? By the way, what do you plan to claim is wrong with you?"

Rob wrinkled his nose. "I don't know. I'll think of something."

Chapter Twenty

When they reached the street where the doctor's office was, Rob grumbled, "Damn. Look at that low number. We'll have to walk a mile."

Mona bit her lip. "And the doctor might be out to lunch when we get there." Bushed, she felt she couldn't take one more step. Her feet dragged. Since complaining would do no good, she took a deep breath and forced herself to keep trudging along. A young man across the street passed with a beagle on a leash and Mona shivered. *I wonder where Pep is now?*

In a few blocks, the street curved. Mona clapped. "Hot damn! The numbers jumped. We don't have far to go after all, Rob. We'll be there in a couple of minutes."

Close to their destination, she considered the next step of their plan. "You need to decide what your complaint is going to be."

Rob shrugged.

"It needs to be something requiring lots of testing of your whole body. We're almost there. Hurry up and make up your mind. Whatever you trump up has to sound authentic."

"I'm doing the best I can," he barked at her. "It's my body. Let me figure it out."

Clasping her hands together so tightly the whites of her knuckles showed, Mona tried to keep from crying. Exhausted, dirty, and tired of all of this, his outburst both hurt and angered her. But Rob was at his wits end, too. She knew she couldn't afford to indulge in either emotion, so she ignored the insult, blinked back tears, and let Rob do the talking.

Rob leaned over and gave her a little peck on the cheek. "Sorry. I think I'll say we're both on drugs. He should have no trouble believing that story."

Rob's unkempt clothes reminded Mona of her own appearance. She winced as she ran her hand over her oily hair. She couldn't agree more. Once the doctor saw the two of them in their present condition, he'd believe it all right. They could pass for a couple of bedraggled users anywhere.

Was their story feasible? A great deal depended on the doctor's reaction. But a doctor might refuse to treat Rob. They needed a better excuse. "On second thought, a doctor will do tests. He'd find out in a hurry we aren't users. Can you come up with something else?"

Rob rubbed his temples. "Okay. I could tell him I have a headache...and it's the truth. They told me this would happen. I wonder if it's a symptom or just brought on by the power of suggestion?"

As they approached the street number they sought, her pulse quickened. On an old house on the right, she saw a sign. In worn-off paint it read: Nicholas P. Romano, MD.

"Oh, God," Rob blurted. "I just remembered something. The other day I ran into a guy I knew in high school. Hadn't seen him in years. He worked in Chicago on their police force. Tony's a plainclothes man on the Mobile force now. I couldn't think of his last name at the time, but it hit me the minute I saw the sign. It's Romano. You don't suppose this doctor's related to him, do you?"

"Rob," Mona chided, "you're getting paranoid. Even if those two are related, what's the chance of this doctor making a connection to you?" She tugged on his sleeve. "I'm getting edgier by the minute. Let's go inside."

One topic they'd avoided discussing was money. Finding a doctor who might locate the problem and fix it would be a miracle. But expecting a physician to treat a dead-broke transient was reaching for the moon. Mona knew ignoring their inability to pay wouldn't deny its existence, but it had taken the problem off her mind. "What do you plan to do about his fee?"

"I'm pretty adept at the art of negotiating. I think I can get past the nurse by convincing her this is an emergency. I'll make an excuse about an insurance screw-up and persuade her to let me discuss finances with the doctor." He pointed to a sign with the doctor's name on it. "Oh, there's his office. Let's get this over with."

The dingy reception room's outdated Venetian blinds were closed, and the sixty-watt bulb in the table lamp didn't provide much light. However, the Early American furniture had been dusted and the bookshelves on the wall were well stocked. No dust gathered there, either. Mona suspected somebody in this office was an avid reader.

When Rob and Mona entered, the nurse glanced up from the newspaper she held. She looked as old as the building. With gray hair askew, she peered over thick glasses. "May I help you?" Her cracked voice showed slight suspicion and irritation at the interruption, rather than concern.

"Yes, ma'am." Rob stepped closer to the reception window. "I've been having these God-awful headaches. I'm sorry to bother you, but we're just traveling through, and I don't know where to go. I've reached the point where I've got to have some relief. We were searching for a hospital when I saw your sign." He pressed the palms of his hands to his temples and turned aside. "My head feels like it's going to explode," he mumbled to Mona. "It may be my imagination, but the throbbing is awful."

The nurse adjusted the glasses perched on her nose. Mona surmised she was deciding whether to take pity on them or not. She bet the nurse wondered where these two swamp rats came from. Their tattered clothes and grubby hands were in direct contrast with the crisp, old-fashioned white uniform and manicured nails that contributed to the nurse's neat appearance. Except for those few stray hairs, she was the picture of efficiency.

Enough judgment time had passed. Mona had taken all the nurse's scrutiny she could stand. She opened her mouth, but before she got a chance to speak, the woman pushed her chair back. She looked Rob right in the eye and told him in a calm voice, "If you'll just have a seat, Mr..... I don't believe you gave your name."

"It's Slingo, Ray Slingo."

"All right, Mr. Slingo, please wait here and I'll find out if the doctor can see you."

Mona detected a little doubt in the nurse's voice as she repeated the name. She wished Rob had used a better one. But on the spur of the moment, the pseudonym she'd dubbed him with may have been the only one he could think of.

Except for the two of them, the waiting room was empty. While they waited for the nurse to return, Mona read the titles of some of the large variety of books on the shelves. Most of the medical books were old, but the others ranged from *War and Peace* to novels by Tom Clancy, John Grisham, and some on science fiction—those tweaked her interest. She held one up and whispered, "How about this, Rob?"

She also surmised the doctor must have plenty of time to read. He sure didn't seem swamped with patients. Nobody had come in, and the phone hadn't rung since they'd been there. Doctor Romano's appearance in the doorway of his office told her why.

With his first words of greeting, "Come, er, come on back. You two, the two of you," she could tell the very old man was drunk. One whiff of his breath verified it. The hand he held on the door frame slipped and he almost toppled forward. It was difficult to ascertain whether his age or his condition caused his feebleness. She suspected it was a combination of both. How did she and Rob manage to come into contact with so many addicts in one day? Thinking they'd get no help here, she turned to leave. But she stopped when she noticed Rob didn't follow her lead.

"Excuse me a minute, Doctor." Rob reached Mona's side out of the physician's hearing. "I know what you're thinking," he whispered. "I can see this guy's condition, but I want to give him a try. I think I can control the situation, and it might take a drunk to hear me out. Besides, a weak-willed degenerate hungry for patients is a lot more likely to help me than a prosperous physician with a thriving practice."

Mona frowned. "I don't know, Rob."

"I don't have much choice. Besides, who can say a man like this can't rise above his personal imperfections to dispense proper treatment?" Rob pulled Mona back. "This may be my only chance. This doctor still has his shingle out. Young or old, drunk or sober, he's a doctor. You saw his license on the wall for the current year." He folded his arms. "I'm not leaving. It might take a drunk to accept as truth any, or all, of the story I have to tell." He returned inside.

With a finger twisted by arthritis, the elderly man motioned Rob into his office. Mona sat in the waiting room. Expecting Rob's visit to take some time, she picked up a dog-eared magazine with last year's date and flipped its pages. Noticing a gold-starred story marked as a prizewinner, she bemoaned the fact with all the drama, she'd just about forgotten her goal to join that writer's ranks.

Chapter Twenty-One

In the inner office, putting on a pair of thick glasses, Dr. Romano peered deep into Rob's eyes. He then took Rob's blood pressure and checked his pulse.

The man moved papers on his desk aside then sat straight up in the ancient tall-backed swivel chair. "Your vitals aren't bad. Pressures a little high, but pain causes that. How often are you having these headaches, young man?"

With the coming of a patient, Rob noticed the old man had changed miraculously. His posture suggested an air of authority— no, more, professionalism. He wasn't the same man who had come to the door. Even some of the redness in his eyes had disappeared. He couldn't remove the undesirable odor from his breath, however. The mints he'd popped into his mouth couldn't disguise it. But he no longer sounded drunk.

"A couple of weeks." Rob shifted in his chair. His advantage over an inebriated man had vanished. He felt like a first-grader faking illness to skip school and having his bluff called by being taken to the doctor by his mother. He also couldn't think straight. His head ached constantly. The uncomfortable pounding turned into a full-fledged, blinding headache. Gritting his teeth, he grabbed the edges of the desk and squeezed with both hands, hoping it would help him bear the intense discomfort.

"You really are in pain, aren't you, son?" Reaching into his desk, the doctor produced a couple of tablets and handed them to Rob. "Don't take these if you're on anything." He squinted. "But you aren't, are you? You look like an addict, but you don't act like one." He stared into space. "In Vietnam, I had to set a man's leg on the hood of a Jeep once, and he was so stoned he didn't even feel it." He turned back to Rob. "But you're sick. I can tell by your eyes."

Rob washed the tablets down with a glass of water the doctor had the nurse bring in. He studied the man who sat facing him, thinking how remarkable human beings can be. Here was a man, a doctor, still at least under the influence, old, debilitated. Yet, at a glance, he'd sized up a patient accurately. Many a specialist wouldn't have done as well.

With a sigh, he stared straight at the doctor. Convincing him of what happened would be a challenge. "Doctor, I'm going to tell you the whole truth because I must have your help if I'm going to have a chance for survival. Whether or not you believe me will determine my fate. I hope I can convince you. Anyway, here goes."

Rob held the doctor's attention throughout the entire narration. When he finished, Dr. Romano puffed on a cigar he'd lit during the first sentence. It had burned down to a nub, but a tiny flame still peeked from its tip. Snuffing it out in an ashtray, he summoned the nurse and told her, "Send the young lady into my office."

When Mona entered, Dr. Romano listened while she first told what happened to her and then verified Rob's story.

Leaning back in the creaky old chair, the doctor pulled on his chin. In a few seconds, he leaned forward. "All right, I like you two, and it seems like we're going to be around each other for a while, so call me Nick or Doc." He folded his arms. "You've come to the right person. Let me tell you about my own experience with an unidentified flying object about five years ago."

He told first about how he became an alcoholic. He lowered his head. "After the UFO incident, my, er, drinking problem, which started with a decline in my practice, got worse. With each passing day, it took a little more whiskey to inebriate me." He admitted being up to a fifth every twenty-four hours. "Still, I kept feeling justified in drowning my sorrows."

The medication had helped reduce the pain of Rob's headache. His head still ached but not as much as before, so he could focus on Nick's story.

Continuing his life story, Nick Romano told about delivering "almost an entire generation of babies in the Pensacola area." Then came the experts, the specialists who stepped into his territory and took over. With their fancy methods and persuasive smooth talk, they convinced most of his young patients they needed an obstetrician for prenatal care. Even some of his older lifelong patients and friends sought medical aid from the new specialists in all areas of medicine who'd come to town fresh from their internships.

"My practice fell off to nothing."

His words caused Rob to speculate on how this sensitive, dedicated, and loyal doctor treated many elderly patients long after they lost the ability to pay. He cringed a little when the doctor added, "I even lost my patients on Medicare and Medicaid."

Nick sighed and closed his eyes for a second. "What kept me going for a while was the love and attention of my wife, Ellen. She was a nurse, and we worked together right here in this office. We were married forty-six years." He took a deep breath, and the lines in his face deepened. "She took great care of me. We wanted children of our own, and I think I took it harder than she did when all three of ours were stillborn."

Stiffening, he added, "I thought it was the worst time of my life. I'd delivered all those healthy babies, but I couldn't do anything to keep my own children alive. It was awful, but the worst was yet to come."

Rob shifted in his chair. *When will he get to the UFO sighting?* But he didn't think rushing this man would help. He might even clam up altogether, so he acted attentive.

"You see, one day Ellen found a lump in her breast. Oh, she had a mastectomy right away, but too late." He curled the corner of his mouth. "All the Johnny-come-lately experts I consulted couldn't do anything for her. I watched her go down, down, down until she was so weak and helpless I prayed for her death. When it came after all those long days and nights of agony, I just couldn't cope. I broke down completely and turned to the bottle to salve my intense bitterness at the inadequacy of the science of medical care."

Rob massaged the nape of his neck. *Is he finally coming to the UFOs?*

"Ellen's gone but she's stayed with me." Nicholas Romano rambled on. "I talk with her during the day and on rarer and rarer occasions when I'm lucky enough to have a patient, I consult with her regarding the diagnosis—just as I did when she was alive."

Half closing his eyes, he admitted his failings. "By nightfall, when I've consumed most of a fifth of whiskey, I drive out to the graveyard where she's buried. I tell her how much I miss and need her. On one of those nights, close to midnight, I saw the UFO. But in my, er, condition, I thought sure my eyes were deceiving me...at first. I sobered up enough to know it was real, though." He made a cone with his fingers and thumbs, holding it up. "That huge cone-shaped thing appeared in the sky again. I watched it come and go at will. Once, on its descent, it looked like it was going to land right on top of my head. In a nanosecond, it changed course and moved away. Left me blinking in disbelief, I can tell you."

Romano scratched the snow-white hair behind his ear. "It's so strange. Somehow, I wasn't afraid. And I've seen a lot and been frightened by a whole lot less in my lifetime. But this, well, somehow it seemed almost like a reassurance a Superior Being existed. I guess I took it as a sign there is a God and a heaven above.

"Oh, I know you're going to think I'm crazy when I tell you this." He leaned forward. "But I went right back and said to that marble headstone, 'Ellen, nobody'll ever believe a drunken fool like me. So I won't tell a soul what I saw. But I saw it. Somehow it makes me think I'll be with you soon.' It brought a peace to my soul I hadn't felt in a long time."

The doctor seemed far away and absorbed in his story. Rob leaned forward to get his attention. "Doctor, er, Doc, do you mean you believe us? Do you understand we saw the same thing?"

"Yes, yes. I do." Romano emphasized the words. "I believe you. Our stories are similar, but you experienced even more. You actually talked with the outer space beings. I didn't. I never mentioned this to other people. Up until now, the only person I ever told was Miss Croft, my nurse. I'm not sure she was convinced. In fact, she once told me if that really happened, it would've made me stop drinking. Since it didn't"—he shrugged—"I guess it just gave me another reason to escape into the bottle.

"Well," the doctor abruptly shifted the course of the conversation, "since I've qualified my reasons for treating you, let's get back to your case. Except for the headaches, have you had any other symptoms?"

Rob shook his head. "So far, I haven't had any sign anything, physical or mental, is wrong."

"All right. Get on the table."

"Miss Croft," the doctor called to the nurse. "Please come in here. I want to do a complete physical. Also run blood tests. I paid a small fortune for a new X-ray machine. I'll finally get to use it. We'll do a complete set."

Rob could sense Romano's elation at the opportunity to use the treasured X-ray machine. When the doctor left the room, chatting with Mona, the nurse prepped him.

"Doctor Romano's right. He did pay a small fortune for the machine, hoping to compete with other physicians in Pensacola who had all the latest technology. At first, it did seem to renew his patients' confidence, but gradually they drifted away again."

Rob filled in the blanks. He figured when the doctor's overindulgence in alcohol became known, his practice dwindled.

"I've been with Dr. Romano since I was seventeen years old. He hired me even though I didn't have much training, and he knows I run my mouth too much. Never did get over the habit. For a while, he could barely pay my meager salary, but he'd treated me like family and I wasn't going to desert him." She shrugged. "I get Social Security. I'm content. Being needed satisfies me. I'm not married, and I live alone, so I enjoy having a job. I keep the office open nine a.m. to five p.m. And today"—she straightened her shoulders—"for the first time in quite a while, I have important work to do."

"Mr. Slingo," the doctor grinned, "except for headaches, you're in excellent health. But this case intrigues me. It's beyond those my colleagues or any of the specialists have ever encountered, I'm sure. I'd know about those." He twiddled his thumbs. "Since I don't know anyone I believe can help you, I'm determined to keep your case all to myself. Why don't you stay and have a bit of lunch. We can talk some more, and maybe I can figure out this enigma."

Over a cup of coffee and BLT sandwiches Jane Croft prepared, Dr. Romano made a suggestion.

"I understand you two can't go back to Mobile. And you can't wander around the streets of Pensacola without anything to eat or a place to stay. Besides, I'm sure you know Hurricane Dennis may hit here, too." He rubbed his right ear. "So, why don't you stay right here with me? I've got plenty of room...there are four bedrooms, and I can't use but one. The menu may not be exotic, but it's good wholesome fare." He smiled. "Miss Croft does my cooking, too. You can stay inside the house as much as possible, but if anyone sees you and asks who you are, I can pass you off as cousins. Quite frankly, I'm intrigued with your case because I believe every word you say."

"Very generous of you, Doctor. I'm thrilled." Mona smiled at Rob, and he nodded back at her. "The best we'd hoped for was a doctor lucking up on something in a routine examination. This is marvelous—a place to stay and an interested physician who can relate exceed my wildest expectations."

Rob raised his brows.

"We'll stay, won't we Rob?"

"Fine with me."

The doctor cleared his throat. "You are two very astute young people, so I'm sure you're concerned about"—his face turned redder than usual—"er, my condition. However, rest assured it will not be a problem. This case will occupy me body and soul. I'll have no need for a crutch."

He took a bottle out of the buffet and went to the kitchen adjoining the dining room. With the door wide open, he poured the contents down the drain in full view of Mona and Rob. He returned to his chair and folded his arms. "Rob, how about going over the details of the encounter again. Somewhere, there's got to be a clue," he stated with confidence.

But Rob's rehashing of the incident uncovered nothing new. They still didn't know if he had anything inside him that could cause his death. They were as far from the solution as they'd been when Rob opened the reception room door. Although the doctor determined the blood was clear, Rob told him, "It looks like finding where an implant could be hidden in my body is an impossible task."

"Don't give up. This has been a long day." Mona set her hand on his arm. "You're feeling the entire impact and the amplified suspense."

Rob yawned. "I guess I am. I'm worn out. Could I take a shower and freshen up?"

"Bathroom's on the right with towels in the cabinet and the guest bedrooms are on the left. I know this ordeal has gotten to you. But don't get discouraged. The good thing is I don't see any immediate danger. A rest would do you good. Besides, I do have a couple of patients to see. I'm the only doctor in town who still makes house calls. So, I'll make my rounds while you two take a nap." He slipped into his coat and picked up an old-fashioned black bag. Whistling a cheerful tune, he went to his car.

Chapter Twenty-Two

Returning just before dark, Dr. Romano found Miss Croft still at the office.

"It's so exciting, Doctor. I had to stay around. I just couldn't leave till you got back."

Elated to have someone to share his enthusiasm for the case, the doctor replied, "It's a challenge, Jane, a real challenge."

"Oh, Nick, I'm sure you'll meet it." She covered her mouth with her hand.

Romano smiled. Rarely did the nurse dispense with the formality of addressing him as "Doctor," although he frequently called her by her first name. He patted her arm. "How many times have I asked you to call me Nick? I know, we're both from the old school and we feel strongly about the importance of respect and dignity in a professional relationship." He nodded. "We've had few disagreements. But we're friends, Jane." No need to tell her she didn't have to "keep her place."

"You're a good cook, and since you prepared a huge dinner, I'd like you to stay and eat with us. Since you know the details of the case, you'll be interested in any pertinent conversation held while we dine." He cocked his head. "Another ear might detect something new, something to help diagnose what's wrong with Rob."

Jane stayed and served the meal before joining the others. As they savored pot roast and mashed potatoes covered with thick brown gravy, Romano listened as Mona and Rob recalled things they'd forgotten before. While much of it was inconsequential, anything they said occurred during the episode held his interest.

"Surprisingly," Rob concluded with a smile, "when I awoke, my headache was better, Doc. It's crazy. But the pain has moved to my jaw. It's just a dull ache now." He rubbed a spot in front of his earlobe and swallowed. "Mmm, this pot roast is delicious." He pointed to Jane. My compliments to the chef." Then he sighed. "All this seems like one big, crazy dream. Sometimes I find myself wondering if I did go inside a spaceship. Oh, hell, I know it happened, but it all seems so weird."

Mona sighed. "It is hard to believe. Here I am, thanks to Miss Croft—who washed and dried our clothes while we took a nap—all cleaned up. I feel as normal as anybody, yet I've been through an experience nobody will believe." She studied each of the others one by one. "Present company excepted. And the only aftereffect concerning me is finding out about Rob's condition." She lowered her gaze. "I hope my little dog Pep is safe, too." She patted Rob's knee. "But maybe nothing's wrong, huh?"

"Sorry to put a damper on your hopes, Mona," the doctor interjected. "But I'm fairly well convinced Rob's headaches indicate the Torpians were telling the truth. He has no history of headaches, so this isn't normal for him—even following a trauma. So far, I can't justify dubbing his headache as an emotional reaction." He shook his head and switched positions in his chair. "No, I'm afraid Rob's own words deny that. All indications are we'll have to find and remove the implant to save Rob."

"Your news doesn't shatter me. I've lived with the unsettling probability so far. I can face whatever comes next." Rob leaned forward. "You can do any necessary tests tonight, Doc. Honestly, I feel up to it. You and I both know how important time can be. Let's get on with it." He shoved his chair away from the table. "No matter what the consequences, I'm determined to face reality with action."

Romano cast his gaze to the floor. Was Rob kidding himself, or had he accepted how grim his reality could be?

Chapter Twenty-Three

"We're being invaded," newspaper editor Frank Dees said when The Associated Press, United Press International, Columbia Broadcasting System, and National Broadcasting System, plus many other media representatives, arrived in Mobile, Alabama, trying to dig out all they could about spaceship sightings and explosions, especially one explosion, which was reported right before dawn.

They swarmed all over the city and its outskirts with crews of reporters and cameramen and women, disrupting its order and creating a chaos all their own. Dees wasn't pushed aside; he stayed right in the middle of it. He started by interviewing the person who claimed to be first to witness the unusual event.

Shirttail sticking out and hair uncombed, Tim O'Hara answered the door. "Ah, you must be Mr. Dees, *The Daily Times* editor who called me." He opened the door wide. "Come in." He pointed to a rickety wicker chair, and Dees sat in it.

Tim sat opposite him and leaned forward. "I know what you're here for. So, if ya like, I'll tell ya my story. The explosion happened when most people were still asleep, but"—he straightened his shoulders—"I had the advantage of being first to see the unusual event." He grinned. "I, er, came in late and me wife locked me out." He raised his brows. "Ya won't believe me, but I saw a spaceship, hangin' up there, right above my house." He paused and cocked his head. "Do you believe me?"

Dees nodded. "I'm listening. Keep talking."

"Okay. I went around back and banged on the door and tried to get inside, but I couldn't. I guess me wife didn't hear me."

The beer on his breath made Dees want to back away but he couldn't, so he stretched his shoulders and leaned back in the chair.

"Before I could wake up Kathleen, a loud explosion reached my ears." Tim banged a table beside him and Dees jolted. "Terrified me, it did." Tim made the sign of the cross. "I slammed a chair against the back door. The lock gave way, and I dashed into the kitchen, and switched on the light. Me wife, wide-awake then, yelled from the bedroom, 'O'Hara, damn you! What in the hell are you up to?'"

Tim laughed. "I ignored her. I just got the telephone book and called the police, and then I called your paper and the TV and radio stations." He chuckled. "Had to make those calls with me wife hangin' over my shoulder. She started rattlin' off, 'You're crazy' when she heard me say to the operator, 'I want to report a sighting. Two spaceships were in the sky right over my house. They've exploded, and pieces may be falling all over me backyard.'"

Dees knew the rest of the story. He was familiar with Tim's reputation and could tell the man he was talking to was sober. He'd heard enough. He studied his notes while Tim rambled on about a friend of his who'd dressed like an alien trying to fool him.

"Source may not be reliable," he'd written. "Comes from Tim O'Hara. Check it out anyway." He also knew the police hadn't rushed to the scene because they expected to find the usual domestic trouble.

Tim's wife came in the room and sloughed the incident off, slapping him upside the head with a newspaper. "You're a crazy drunk, O'Hara. Go sleep it off and forget all this foolishness." She turned to Dees. "Don't pay no attention to my husband. I know him, when he started his ranting and raving, I didn't even look out the window. I did follow him down the road later, though."

"You think I'm making this up?" Her husband curled his lip "I know what I saw." He shook his finger at her back as she walked out of the room. "You just wait till you see what's on TV."

Dees left with many doubts about Tim's statements, but he had to admit one thing: Tim's report of sighting spaceships wasn't the only one they received. Other calls had the paper's phones ringing off of their hooks.

When the news broke, it was convincing enough to bring media people to the South as fast as planes and cars could carry them. By breakfast time in the port city, representatives of all the major networks were on Bates Field landing strips, eager to get the story first.

Dees agreed to cooperate. He had already determined neither he nor his paper could handle this alone. The big leaguers had arrived. Maybe they could even find his two reporters.

He went to the airport to meet his old friend, Loren Brady, an anchorman for *CBS Evening News*. He and Loren attended the University of Alabama together, and, though they had lived in different states, they were in the same line of work. Loren had become nationally known, and Frank hadn't. Occasionally, their paths would cross, giving them a chance to renew their friendship.

Frank was glad to hear CBS had given his friend this assignment. If anybody could find the real truth, it would be Loren. Besides, the two men worked well together. In Loren's quiet way, he complemented Frank's blustering personality. Together, they should be able to solve this mystery.

God knows, somebody has to do it.

As they drove toward the place where the last sighting occurred, Frank brought Loren up to date, giving his friend an edge over other reporters coming to the scene cold. Most of them knew only what had come in over the wire. Firsthand information, such as what Frank provided, saved Loren time and energy. It also clued him in regarding the missing man and woman.

"The worst part as far as I'm concerned is two of my reporters are missing," Dees concluded after telling the story of Mona's car wreck and Rob's disappearance. "I sure hope you can help me find them."

"I'll do my best, old buddy, I'll do my best," Loren promised.

"I know you will," he replied with a smile.

Someone to talk with bolstered Frank's spirits. Maybe with an expert to help, he could locate Mona and Rob, as well as prove or disprove the sightings. His situation lost a bit of its desperation. Support of a colleague gave Frank the courage to believe. Another perk was he could transfer some of the responsibility to a person of higher authority. Yes, for many reasons, to have Loren Brady on the job made Dees happy.

"You're a good friend, Frank. Not many editors let you in like this."

Frank cocked his head. "Old buddy, it's good to know I can count on you. I do appreciate your help."

In a familiar gesture Frank remembered from years gone by, Loren leaned over and squeezed his shoulder. "The old saying, 'There's no friend like an old friend' sure applies to you." Clasping his hands behind his head, Loren put the seat back, stretched to a relaxing position, and closed his eyes.

When they reached the turnoff from Airport Boulevard to Ink Road, Frank wondered how many more times he'd have to come out here. Maybe many. Loren gave him credit for more information than he had, maybe just to be polite. As a seasoned newsman, Loren was bound to know this was just the beginning of the story. Filling in the spaces was an understatement. Much more investigating remained to be done.

At a roped-off area, a policeman stopped the car. "Can I see your identification, please?" He held out his hand.

Both men flashed press cards and were motioned through. Alive with members of the media, the clearing appeared to have just been invaded. Few spots were unoccupied. Evidently, the three policemen and one policewoman still there had finished conducting their own search and weren't preventing others from taking a peek. Perhaps they'd find something the police missed. Many took photos of everything and anything. Some were down on their hands and knees searching for bits and pieces of evidence. Others worked the ground with metal detectors. A few nearby residents had escaped the watchful eyes of the guards and sneaked through the woods to see what they could find. They hampered the efforts of reporters who had the authority to be there, but with so many people about, it was almost impossible to police the entire area.

"Damn," Frank said. "I bet these woods never had so many people roaming around in them. Look over there." He pointed to his left. "We're among the few supposed to be here, but even some kids got through."

A deputy parked next to them spoke on his car radio. "We need backup." He hung up muttering to his partner, "They had a four-car wreck on the other side of the county tying up the other deputies. When they cleared it up, two cars got lost on the way here. I hope they'll get here soon. We need reinforcement."

"It's good for us they can't get more deputies," Frank told his friend. "Cuts down on restrictions as to what we can do."

They glanced around, hoping to find something to add to their knowledge. After half an hour of searching, Loren turned his palms up, "No luck. So far, even with so many people searching, it seems like nothing has been found. It appears to me, if any spaceships exploded around here, they were far enough away to burn up before hitting Earth."

Still, like every other reporter, Dees wanted to be sure. After checking the clearing, he decided to venture beyond where others had gone. *The best clues aren't always found right at the scene of the crime.* On a hunch, Frank motioned to his friend. "Come on."

Loren followed him as they wandered off into the woods. A few yards away, they found broken branches.

"What do you make of this?" Frank held up a branch. "'Course some of these curiosity seekers hurrying through the woods could have broken them, but"—he stared ahead—"it's obvious this path leads deeper into the woods. Puzzling. There aren't many houses around here, but that's away from any of them as far as I can tell."

"Let's go a little farther. Maybe we can get some clues as to who broke those branches," Loren urged, leading the way. A few yards later, he paused. "Look at this. Tire tracks." He stooped down and put his fingers in the ruts. "By the size of these tracks they were made by dirt bikes. Four or five." He glanced up. "Do you think there's any chance these riders are still around?" He took out his cell phone and snapped a few shots.

Frank took a few shots with his phone, too, getting some different angles.

"I didn't see any bikes when we came in, did you?"

Loren furrowed his brow. "No, and I didn't hear any, either. They haven't been gone long, though. These ruts are too well defined. There's not a mark disturbing them. It's muddy, too. I think it sprinkled here this morning. Feel the dirt?"

Frank touched the places where the tires had been. "You're right. That moisture's a little more than morning dew. So it seems those cycles were here just a few hours ago." Noticing the confused expression on Loren's face, Frank asked, "What's the matter?"

"Something's funny here. These tracks stop dead. They don't go anywhere. How could that be?" He pointed to a spot. "See, they came in over there. But how did they leave? The tracks just stop. If the rain didn't wash these away, it couldn't have washed any others away, either."

It's a real mystery. Along with Loren, he felt the ground again and checked in every direction to see if they'd missed a clue. Still, they found no tire tracks or footprints past that one point. "Whatever the explanation is, it's beyond me. Where do we go from here?"

"Damned if I know." Loren shook his head. "I suppose we should tell whoever is in charge what we found. I've seen some unexplainable things in this business, but this is one of the craziest."

Frank shrugged. "I know what you mean. If I didn't know

better, I'd think the world stops here." He scratched his head. "Sound nutty?"

"My friend, right now nothing sounds crazy to me."

What they'd just seen defied explanation, but, as a skeptical newsman, Frank didn't accept oddities without question. Neither would Loren. Although they required documented facts, what better documentation could they have than to be on the scene and see things with their own eyes? Much as it baffled him, he had to acknowledge the tracks were there, but the bikes and the riders had disappeared into thin air.

After poking around for fifteen minutes and finding nothing else, in order not to arouse too much curiosity, they slipped back in the clearing the same way they'd gone out. All the other newspeople were intent on their own searching. When Loren and Frank rejoined them, nobody noticed where they came from.

It started pouring rain, and Frank shook his head. "This'll wash away those tracks. You think there's any need to mention them to the authorities?"

Loren scratched his neck. "Nope. We can't prove anything right now, can we?" He patted his pocket. "At least we took photos."

The shower passed. After scrounging around for another hour and talking with other newspeople who didn't know as much as Frank did, they discovered none of them knew anything about Rob and Mona.

A plainclothes man leaving the scene stopped Frank on his way out. "I hear you're searching for one of your reporters. What's his name? Is it that guy who thinks he's a hotshot—Rob Parker?"

Frank glared at him. "Yes, it's Rob. But I've never heard.... Never mind. Do you know anything about him?"

Tony Romano shooed away a mosquito. "Not much. I saw him out here yesterday. He recognized me and spoke. Like all reporters, he tried to pick my brain about this case."

"Did he say anything about where he was going from here?"

"No." Gritting his teeth, he added, "I'm telling you, that's all I know." He turned on his heel and left.

Frank looked at Loren. "So much for that." He glanced at his watch. "Damn. I've got to get back to town. It's almost noon, and I've got a stack of stories on my desk to be edited before the three o'clock deadline. You want to stay out here a little longer, Loren? I can find somebody to give you a ride back to town."

"No, if I haven't found any clues yet, I don't expect one to pop up after you leave." He shook his head, and together they walked back to the car.

They rode to town in silence. Absorbed in his own thoughts, Frank switched on the radio and listened to the threats of a hurricane coming in their direction.

"Hurricane Dennis should reach Mobile Bay by Sunday. Its winds have reached 145 miles an hour. Take any necessary precautions immediately," the announcer added, giving the latitude and longitude coordinates.

"Oh, listen. I know it's a real threat, but they hyped Hurricane Arlene to the point of overkill. And nothing of significance happened. I wonder how much attention people will pay to the warnings this time."

"The governor has ordered complete evacuation of Mobile County," the voice on the radio continued, adding "I65 North will have both north and southbound lanes going north only."

Frank slammed his fist on the steering wheel. "It's crazy. It's impossible. He should never give an order that can't be carried out."

"Evacuation is mandatory for people living south of I10," the next announcement said.

"What is going on here?" The editor looked at his companion.

Loren didn't get an answer because, by then, they'd reached the newspaper's offices.

"Well, we made good time." Frank snapped his fingers. "If this storm doesn't throw too much copy my way, I may make my deadline after all."

While he worked, Frank let Loren borrow his car. Loren wanted to talk to some witnesses, and Frank had so much to do he wouldn't need any transportation until late in the evening. Grabbing up the top story, he dug in.

Before he scanned one page, his telephone rang. Picking it up, he barked, "Frank Dees."

"Mr. Dees, this is Al Fairchild of Navarre Beach Hotel. I'm sorry to have to tell you this, but I'm afraid I have some bad news."

Frank gripped the phone hard, hoping for news of Rob.

"You see, we found somebody, a young man with the name Frank Morgan on his driver's license and an identification card saying to notify you in case of accident."

Stunned speechless, Frank could not answer. This was his namesake, his deceased sister's son. From the way the man spoke, he felt sure the boy was dead.

"Mr. Dees, Mr. Dees—"

"Yes, I hear you. It's...it's my nephew. What happened?" He struggled to get the words out.

"We're not sure. He's...he is dead. I'm sorry. And I hate to ask, but we must have some positive identification on the body. Could you come to Navarre and ID him?"

Frank wanted to ask a thousand questions, but he restrained himself. Better to wait until they could talk face-to-face. "I'll leave right away. Thank you for calling."

He'd have plenty of time to get the details after he got there. He told his secretary who to get to finish his work, gave her a message for Loren, took the newspaper's car, and left on the grim mission.

Winds from Hurricane Dennis picked up. As soon as Frank got on the road, he realized this drive wouldn't be easy, even though 99 percent of the traffic headed in opposite directions—north or west—and he traveled south. His car swayed back and forth, and once, it almost blew him across the median into the long line of traffic evacuating. Tightening his grip on the steering wheel, he managed to swing back into the other lane. Before he got out of the city, a police car blocked his path and directed him off the interstate.

"Can't go any farther, mister," the officer told him. "The hurricane's headed this way. Interstate traffic is all reversed. North only."

Frank took a deep breath. "What can I do? I have to get to Pensacola." He explained about his nephew's death.

The officer shook his head. "Well, you may be going right into the path of the hurricane."

"I realize that. But I have to identify the body."

"All right." He motioned with his thumb. "Pass on through. You can still get on Interstate 10. Might be best, though, to go down Government Street through Bankhead Tunnel and take the Causeway. Stay on Highway 98. On that route, if the weather gets worse, it's easier to pull off. Good luck."

Luck. He'd need it to make it to Navarre. No telling what this hurricane would bring. Florida had been hit with four storms in recent years, and one of those, Hurricane Ivan, a late storm in September, wreaked havoc on repairs made on property previous hurricanes had damaged. Hurricane Arlene hadn't helped, and this storm would add destruction to the most vulnerable structures already weakened. Tarps still on roofs would blow off, and wind and water would take their toll. An awful prospect.

Frank took the policeman's advice. During the fifty-plus mile trip on Highway 98, he recalled passing many buildings and homes not yet repaired after Ivan. They'd lost the blue-tarps on their roofs, and with them, all protection from the elements. He knew the story well—his paper covered it all. The aftermath of the storm devastated home and business owners. They had little hope of help. Although contractors came from all over the US, they needed more. Unless they made repairs themselves, people had to wait in line to get their property in livable shape again.

Frank's thoughts were filled with all the hard luck his nephew had in life. He'd been orphaned by a car wreck, only thirteen years old at the time. Guardians sent him to a military school he hated. He'd entered a junior college in Pensacola but discovered he was not college material. *Or maybe he just wasn't ambitious or mature enough to apply himself.* Regardless, he then moved in with a friend, took out a loan to attend trade school, and, in the interim, stopped writing. Later, he'd finished college and worked his way up through the ranks of the newspaper until he became editor.

With the pressures of the paper, Frank let the communication gap widen with his nephew until they lost touch. He should have kept up with the boy, tried to help him out. *Too late.*

Frank sighed. At least, he was doing his duty now. He vowed to find out exactly what happened. It sounded like an accident. But if foul play was involved, he'd make sure the criminal, or criminals, were brought to justice.

Remorse tugged at him. For the time being, Mona, Rob, and the spaceship sightings moved back a notch in his thoughts.

Chapter Twenty-Four

On the following day, Rob awoke with more than a headache. He opened his eyes, blinking when he saw two mirrors overlapping each other on the dresser. As the Torpians predicted, he'd had double vision. Shaking his head didn't alleviate the problem. He got up, felt his way along as he left the bedroom, and banged on the doctor's door.

"Doc! Doc, I need you!"

It was barely daylight, but rousing the doctor took less than a minute. Pajama-clad, he opened the door.

"What is it, Rob?"

"I've got it, Doc, the double vision. Do something quick!"

"All right. Calm down. Let's check it first and see. Come into the office."

"What's all the commotion?" Mona came out of her room, rubbing her eyes.

Rob blurted, "I can't see straight."

"Okay, Doc will take care of you." Wearing a robe a couple of sizes too large she'd found in the closet, she stopped in the reception room. "I'll wait here."

Fifteen minutes later, the two men came out and without a word. Doc went in the kitchen and put on the coffee pot.

Rob felt his way to a chair and sat holding his head in his hands. "Mona, Doc can't find anything. He's been honest with me. He just can't tell what's wrong. I have double vision just as they predicted. I'm afraid my days are numbered. I don't know what to do." He looked up at her. "Hell, Doc doesn't know what to do either."

Lowering his head again, Rob sobbed.

Mona put her arms around him. "Nothing's hopeless. I'm sure

Dr. Romano will come up with something. He'll figure it out. It'll be all right. I'm sure it will."

He nodded, but, as convincing as her words sounded, he had doubts.

Doc brought the coffee in. With blurred vision, Rob raised his head and accepted the cup Mona placed in his hands. He sipped his coffee, relishing the taste and thinking it might be the last cup he'd ever drink.

"If I could get my hands on Torpi," he said between clenched teeth, "I'd pull out his fingernails, break his legs, and then strangle him." His voice mellowed. "I have to deal with this. But let's find a bright side. Now I see two of you instead of one. And that's a real treat."

Doc smiled. "Your little joke's a good sign. As long as you can laugh, you're not in complete despair. Any condition can be worsened by a negative attitude. Staying optimistic helps."

Doc paced around the room. "Rob," he said in a calm voice, "you and Mona may have forgotten something. I know it's tiring, but why don't you run through this again? Tell me one more time all that happened."

"Okay." Rob folded his arms. "But I don't know anything to add."

The three of them went through the whole routine once more. Rob and Mona told the story—repeating incidents and details, hoping something new would evolve. Doc asked questions, drilling them to dig out more details. When they were exhausted and nothing new came to the surface, Doc resorted to his books. He searched and searched, pulling down text after text and spreading them out on his desk. Nothing turned up.

His files were next. "I don't have any files on double vision, since so few cases have come to my attention, and most of those were from other doctors. But I'm checking for any related illnesses and trying to recall conditions surrounding cases. I'll be honest with you. I've only seen one or two patients with double vision. Most people with that malady consult an ophthalmologist, not a general practitioner, so my records are limited."

The doctor pulled out a file, and his eyes widened as he opened it. "Aha! This is a similar case. My connection with the patient didn't start with treatment for double vision, though. A man in his fifties came to me as an emergency—a car wreck victim with a broken arm and a head injury. Six weeks after the patient's release, he returned complaining of double vision. Befuddled me. He had minor head injury, with no evidence of permanent damage. It had been so slight it didn't even break the skin, and X-rays gave no indication of concussion. I didn't understand it at all. I repeated all the tests and X-rays. Still, nothing showed up. But just before they called in a specialist, the man kept a routine dental appointment."

Romano shook his head. "The dentist discovered a badly infected tooth. The patient had been told before to have the tooth pulled, but because it did not hurt, he was reluctant to lose a molar. Then the job had to be done. And, oddly enough, as soon as the tooth came out, the double vision disappeared."

The doctor gripped Rob's shoulder and shouted, "I think I've got it. Your problem could very well be a tooth, too."

Rob hugged Mona. *Hope.* Maybe he could be helped after all. He blinked, and then backed away. "Well, Doc, discovering what the problem might be takes us halfway; we'll have to decide what to do about it and how." He clicked his tongue. "This isn't as simple as your other case. I can't just go to a dentist and be treated. We'll have to find a very special dentist—and to help me, he has to be a believer."

Who would believe what they were up against, not ask too many questions, and keep the matter a secret?

"I'm wracking my brain, and I've drawn a blank. I just don't know anyone," Doc Romano admitted. He put his hand to his mouth and tapped his lips. "Wait a minute. A name just popped into my mind. But he's 350 miles away, in Huntsville." He stood. "Wait a minute. No, he isn't. I got a letter from him a couple of weeks ago saying he'd planned a trip here." His eyes lit up. "Come to think of it, Joe McNally may be in the area right now." He rushed to a drawer, dug through it, and pulled out a letter. Holding it up, he read it aloud:

Dear Nick, It's been a long time since we've seen each other, and I thought since I'm taking a vacation down there, we might get together. I'll be there the week of July 15 at the Navarre Beach Hotel. Give me a call and we'll have lunch or dinner together.

"Good. The hotel's phone number and his cell phone number are on the bottom of the page."

Doc set the letter on the desk. "When it arrived, I was, er, in a despondent mood, and I didn't follow up with a call. But today is July 16. He should be at Navarre Beach, and it's less than thirty minutes away." He rushed to the phone and dialed the hotel's number. "I guess they've already evacuated." He shrugged. "No answer. I'll try his cell phone."

It seemed like hours, but, in seconds, Doc's eyes lit up, and Rob knew Joe McNally had answered the phone. "Listen, Joe. I'll come right to the point. I need your help." He told his friend the situation—vague high spots with enough information to hopefully whet Joe's curiosity.

***

While waiting for a reply, thoughts drifted through Nick's mind. Though he and Joe were the same age, his cohort had lived a healthier life. Also, his friend's round face and thick, brown hair made him appear younger. When Joe smiled, it covered almost all of his broad face and lent a youthfulness to his lean countenance.

He could imagine the questions Joe asked himself. Was this real or just a figment of a drunk's imagination? Joe was well aware of his weakness, had been for years. But he never denied friendship because Nick became addicted to alcohol. Maybe that was because Nick never asked for repayment of the two thousand dollars he'd loaned Joe when he got a girl in trouble as a teenager. Nobody knew about that but the two of them. Besides, though his story might be odd, today Nick was cold sober. He hoped he'd convinced Joe this was no hallucination and he needed a dentist.

"Nick," Joe replied after a long pause. "Lots of problems. They've boarded up the hotel and told us to leave. I'm in my car, headed to a shelter. Okay, I'll come there instead and do what I can. But I don't have my equipment here, of course."

Why didn't I think of that? Nick groaned. He didn't need another problem. "Wait. It's Saturday. Dentists won't be working. Do you know in this area who might let you use their office? Think fast. Time is imperative." As he spoke, Nick wished he could tell his friend why time was so important, but he didn't feel comfortable revealing any more information than he had to. In fact, telling lies about Rob having a toothache gave him a twinge of guilt, and more fabrications would just complicate matters.

"Matter of fact, I do have a college fraternity brother who practices in this area. I know you pledged with another group, but maybe you remember him being in an English Lit class with both of us. You know, the one the skinny lady we called Stick Woman taught. His name's Marvin Lucas."

"Marvin? The guy who never brought his book to class and always borrowed paper?"

"Right."

Nick flipped through the phone book. "Okay. His office isn't far from where you are. It's on the other side of Santa Rosa Island." He called out the address.

"What's his phone number? I haven't figured out yet how I'll explain this, but I'll give him a call. From what you've told me, Nick, I think that man's tooth's going to have to come out."

***

Joe McNally frowned. Dr. Marvin Lucas was not in his office. The squeaky-voiced assistant offered more information than an answering service would have. "Oh, I'm sorry," she told him. "We're closed."

After swearing to himself, he thought fast. "This is Dr. McNally, and I'm also a dentist. Dr. Lucas is a very good friend of mine." Implying he was local, he made up things. "I have a patient with an emergency—it'll require some special instruments I don't own, some Dr. Lucas told me he recently purchased. I'd like bring my patient there and use them, if I may."

"Oh, I'm sorry, Dr. McNally," she replied, "but I don't have the authority to agree to any arrangement like that. I never heard of anything like this happening. I-I, errrr...."

She sounded flustered. Joe took advantage of the pause. Her insecure hesitation gave him an opening to use his most authoritative voice. "Oh, it's quite all right. By the way, what's your name?"

"Danielle."

"Well, Danielle," his deep voice held a chatty tone, "we often share our facilities in situations like this. It's kind of an experimental case," he lied. "I'm surprised you don't know about it. How long have you been working for Dr. Lucas?"

"Oh, um...just three weeks. Dr. Lucas is on vacation until August first. The burglar alarm went off and when they couldn't get him, they called me. I checked. It's just the storm, I guess. I was just leaving."

Joe knew how to get what he wanted. He took charge. "That explains it. All right, I can meet my patient there in thirty minutes. Rest assured there'll be no repercussions. By the way, Danielle, are you a dental assistant?"

"Yes, I just got my associate's degree in May." Her voice steadied. "This is my first job."

"Great. This shouldn't take more than an hour. If you can stay and help me, I'll pay you a hundred dollars."

A gasp came from the other end of the phone. "Oh, yes, sir. One hour? Okay, I'll do that."

He hung up and dialed another number. "Everything's all set."

Nick's heavy sigh of relief came over the line.

"I'll meet you back at the hotel." Joe glanced in the rearview mirror. He'd gotten up early to answer the phone. Then they'd begun the evacuation. He needed a shave and shower. *Maybe I can sneak in and shave, at least.* "No need to take two cars in this weather. How long will it take you to get there?" he asked Nick.

"We'll be there in half an hour."

Chapter Twenty-Five

In five minutes, the doctor, Mona, and Rob were on their way.

As they crossed the bridge to Santa Rosa Island, the whipping wind pounded waves against the shore. Hurricane Dennis showed his stuff, worsening by the minute. Rob squinted, unable to see clearly because of his distorted vision. He wished they'd get to their destination soon.

"You having trouble seeing, Rob?" Mona patted his knee. "Anything I can do?"

"No, I'm okay, and I can see twice as much as you," he joked. However, behind it all, he was worried sick about his condition. If the diagnosis determined a tooth had to be pulled, several things could happen. The most formidable prognosis was, with the tugging on the tooth, an implant containing explosive material could be activated. It could be the end of him. He hoped if it was, he would not take others with him. But the risk was real. If there was an implant, nobody knew what was inside it, or the power it held.

On the picture's brighter side, there was a remote chance if a tooth was removed, the double vision might reverse. The object could be nonexistent, or it could be removed with no ill results. No object was the most desirable, but the least likely, scenario.

"Just five more miles," Nick announced.

So, good or bad, we'll soon know my fate.

At the hotel, Nick got out of the car and slammed the door. "Hell, I didn't write down Joe's room number."

While he went to the desk to check on it and waited behind a large group of college students arguing with the clerk about having to leave and saying, "Our fraternity paid for rooms and we're staying. We've got a party planned," Mona and Rob walked around the back of the building. Since Navarre was close enough to Mobile to be frequented by Port City citizens, they'd decided to keep out of sight.

Halfway guiding Rob down a covered walkway and still being pelted by wind-driven rain, Mona took his arm and led him to the Gulf side of the hotel. "You know what," she told him, "we should relax. With this hurricane coming, most people have evacuated. It's highly unlikely we'll see anyone we know."

"Yeah." Rob nodded. "But some people, like those fraternity guys, refuse to leave no matter what the danger. They're hell-bent on having their hurricane party, but they may not survive it. Crazy!"

As they reached the side of the building, Mona grabbed him, pulled him into an alcove, and shocked him by engaging him in a passionate embrace. She pressed her lips to his.

Then a familiar voice boomed nearby, and he knew why. Frank Dees strode down the covered walkway, the hotel manager and a policeman trailing him. "Suicide! He showed signs of depression in the past, but I didn't expect this. He was just a kid who had a hard life. My poor sister. I'm glad she's not here to see this. Of course, I don't suppose it would have happened if she'd lived to raise him. Never know, though."

When Mona relaxed her grip but still kept him close, out of the corner of his eye, Rob saw Dees look at his two escorts. "God, I should have done more myself. Always too busy, you know. I guess we put emphasis on the wrong things until it's too late."

To a clap of thunder, Dees walked away staring into space, passing Mona and Rob with his hands pressed against his forehead, ignoring the water dripping from his clothing. He never glanced in their direction.

When Frank moved out of sight, Mona released Rob—who was in no hurry to end the embrace—and they gazed into each other's eyes, oblivious to the world around them. For one brief moment, he'd tasted ecstasy.

Mona backed off asking, "God, how horrible! Did you know Frank had a nephew, Rob? He's our boss. You think we ought to do something?"

Rob shook his head. "There's nothing we can do. Anyway, we can't let him know we're here."

"Well, what a hell of an irony. Frank's looking for us; he's dragged to Pensacola with a storm brewing; and we're put right in his path, but he doesn't see us."

Doc's approach interrupted their conversation. Rob explained what happened. Then, the trio hastened back to the car where Joe McNally awaited. It had been a very close call.

***

On the way to Dr. Lucas's office, Mona said, "Dr. McNally needs to know everything, so he can diagnose properly."

Nick looked at Joe. "You're right. Besides, we can't ask a man to risk his life without forewarning." So, he gave a full account of the episode with space beings and the rest of the situation, finishing just as they reached the dental office, where the wind was whipping and howling around the building and pounding on the roof. Mona entered the small dental exam room last, her wet shoes making indentations on the carpet. She stopped at the door while McNally introduced himself, her, and the others to Danielle, a blonde woman of about twenty with a petite figure, a round face, and eyes like Elizabeth Taylor.

After a "Pleased to meet you," Danielle busied herself putting fresh towels and tools on the tray beside the dental chair. "Oh, Dr. McNally, I forgot to tell you our X-ray machine isn't working. They're supposed to fix it while Dr. Lucas is gone."

McNally removed his coat and water dripped on the carpet as he hung it on the back of a chair. He shook his head. "Tough luck. We'll just have to do the best we can without it. I'll see what I can find."

Mona leaned against a wall to watch the procedure. After Danielle draped a protective towel around Rob's neck, McNally slipped on a mask and surgical gloves and went straight to work. He probed Rob's mouth without comment. Romano kept silent.

He checked tooth after tooth, asking, "Does that hurt?" and received negative answers each time.

Doc shifted from one foot to the other, and Mona fidgeted, too. Yet, she felt encouraged. If he hadn't found anything yet, maybe no implant existed after all.

The dentist stopped probing. "Wash out your mouth."

Danielle handed him a cup of water.

"Do you remember anything at all when you were asleep? Did you have pain anywhere when you awoke?" McNally asked.

"No, I don't remember anything, and nothing hurt."

Did Dr. McNally believe them? He seemed convinced, nodding while we shared our story. She'd floundered about keeping this encounter with outer space creatures a secret. Reporters need to report. People have a right to know what's happening in the world, even on other planets. If she could convince the doctor, perhaps others would believe her story, too. The Pulitzer Prize could be hers. Even though the thought made her feel better, it didn't compensate for the fact the dentist had found nothing so far. Rob remained in danger.

When his questions provided no additional information, the dentist resumed his examination. As he probed deeper, Rob let out a squeal. Although Mona sympathized with his pain, she bet, for the first time in his life, Rob was glad to feel a tooth hurt. *Maybe this is a good sign.*

The doctor dug a little deeper. "Aha, I see a small cavity in the rear molar, not visible from the front. I sure could use an X-ray machine." He motioned for Danielle to turn the light more in one direction. "I see it—a tiny speck of something. Wait a minute, wait a minute. I see something here." His voice was muffled by the mask.

Mona moved closer, staying out of the dentist's way. "What is it?"

McNally gingerly touched the object. "I've discovered a gelatin-like substance. I don't know if it will explode if punctured. Stand back. I know little about explosives. This could be triggered by a wire somewhere else in Rob's mouth." He searched. "But I don't see one. The only thing to do is to try to remove this object intact. If I have to, I'll pull the tooth. No need to take a chance on puncturing the vial. Even if it doesn't explode, it might release poison into Rob's blood stream."

When he paused for a second, Mona asked, "Can you tell what it is, Doctor?"

"No." He took a deep breath. "With all the unknown factors, I'm going to have to extract the tooth. Nobody knows when the time is up." Reaching for the anesthetic, he went through the routine procedure of swabbing the area around Rob's molar with cotton before injecting a needle several times.

Mona noticed he did not reassure the patient by saying, "This won't hurt a bit," as was the custom. For all any of them knew, it could blow them all to hell.

While waiting for the anesthetic to take effect, the dentist arranged his instruments in the order in which they'd be used. He mumbled, "I'm checking further."

The sweat on his brow made her wonder if he was hiding something. Maybe he thought nothing would be gained by frightening them. Making his companions aware of the danger of the next few minutes wouldn't help matters any, nor would raising false hopes. Besides, delaying things by explaining would serve no purpose.

Poking at Rob's lip, the dentist leaned closer. "Feel like it's dead yet?"

Rob nodded.

"Open wide," McNally said.

Danielle handed the dentist each tool he requested. Nick kept silent, but he studied McNally's every mood. Like her, he must have realized the guy had not picked up the instrument used to pull teeth for nothing. He was going to do an extraction. But, much to her surprise, the dentist hesitated. Then he set down the tool and picked up a pair of tweezers.

"I'll try to extract it." Cautiously, he inserted the tweezers into the space where the foreign object lay.

Mona clenched her teeth. *It must be tiny, something only a specialist would attempt to remove.* She worried about McNally's competence.

As he worked, seconds dragged into minutes. Right in the middle of the most crucial part, a knock came at the door.

"Damn," the dentist frowned. "I don't need an interruption."

"Security," the voice on the other side called out.

Pausing, Dr. McNally motioned Danielle to respond.

When she came back she giggled. "That was the guard. I cracked the door open but I blocked it with my body so he couldn't see inside. He got a burglar alarm call just like I did and came to check on it. He didn't even ask about the car out front. He just told me I better go on home fast as I can."

McNally nodded but kept working. "It's oval shaped and filled with liquid, smaller than a Jelly Belly," he announced without looking up. "Most likely deadly if it escapes from its container."

He directed his next remark to Nick. "Time's a factor. The anesthetic won't last forever, and I don't want to give Rob another shot if I can help it. No telling what effect it will have on his body, especially if any of the liquid escapes from the vial. I considered not using sedation at all, but I discounted that option because the patient has to be absolutely immobile." He adjusted the light again and, with a little maneuvering, got it around to the back of Rob's tooth. "Now I can see what I'm doing."

Mouth set, he said, "I'm easing it out. I don't see any wires, thank God."

When the dentist placed the minute capsule on a soft towel on a tray, Mona breathed a sigh.

Rob had made no attempt to ask questions, even when the dentist's hand was not in his mouth. "I'm still groggy," he told Mona. "I feel like this is happening to somebody else. It's like none of this concerns me at all." Between his emotional state and the anesthetic, she could see how this whole thing might have taken on a surreal quality.

As the dentist told Danielle to mix a temporary filling, which he placed in Rob's tooth, Mona wondered about Nick Romano. It seemed he'd done a little soul searching. Dr. McNally had found and removed the implant the Torpians had put in Rob's mouth. Nick had known the object might have been an explosive, yet, like her, he'd stayed there and faced death without searching for a drink. After so many years of hard drinking, that was unbelievable, but in these last few days, it appeared liquor had been totally off his mind. His actions spoke volumes about his character. She was impressed. Perhaps the mundane existence he'd been living was the biggest disservice he could do to himself.

Knowing she might die did not bother her as much as she'd expected. To her surprise, her own safety hadn't been her primary concern. She looked at Rob and her heart fluttered. She'd wanted to be sure he would be all right. If she could give her own life for his, she would gladly do so. Impossible, of course, but the thought both surprised and consoled her. *How could all of this have come about in just a couple of days? Do I love Rob? Giving your life is the ultimate sacrifice.*

"This is it," Joe McNally announced as he pointed to an object so tiny it fit between the tongs of the tweezers. Mona took a step forward, and he shook his head. "Don't get too close."

Rob craned his neck to look at the object. "How could such a little thing create so much havoc?" His eyes brightened as he touched his jaw. "I bet it has the potential to cause problems." He yawned. "Anyhow, I'm relieved to have it out of my mouth. I'm also glad I didn't lose a tooth." He blinked. "My head isn't throbbing as much, either."

As Mona and Nick strained to inspect the object, McNally cautioned, "Don't be fooled by its size. The thing is still potentially dangerous. It could explode on its own. We're not dealing with a known substance. Anything could be contained in that little vial."

Chapter Twenty-Six

So far, Danielle had stood by without saying a word. But now she asked, "Would you people please tell me what you're talking about?" Danielle, who'd been quiet since the guard left, put her hands on her hips. "I'm not stupid, you know. What is this dumb pill?" She reached out.

Dr. McNally grabbed her wrist. "Don't touch that."

Danielle's eyes widened as she stepped back.

"We're done here," the doctor told the girl. "Go make some coffee."

When she left, Mona looked at McNally. "I hope we're not going to have a problem with her. We've got enough to deal with." Mona stared at the object in the pan, her heart beating so hard she could barely catch her breath. "What are we going to do with it? I think we should to throw it into the Gulf of Mexico."

"We agreed to make this public." Nick walked close to McNally. "Why don't we take it to the police station and let the bomb squad handle it?"

McNally scratched his ear. "How about seeing if a hospital laboratory can analyze it?" He snapped his fingers. "No. It could jeopardize many people's safety. And they'd make us report it to the police first."

Rob looked at Mona. "I don't care what you do with it. It's out of my mouth, and, praise God, I just realized my vision has cleared up—that's all that matters to me."

Although Mona remained reluctant, the rest agreed nobody would give credence to space creatures. McNally stood with his hands on his hips. "We don't have a clue how this might affect ocean life. It could possibly destroy all of humanity in the process. It may be like mercury poisoning and have a chain reaction."

Nick laid a hand on his shoulder. "You're right. This is alien technology. None of us know how it might affect the Earth's ecosystem." He dropped his hand, stepped back, and stretched his shoulders. "But we've explored our choices and, unsavory as it is, this seems to be the best one."

In the end, they concurred with her idea of tossing the capsule in Gulf waters. The hurricane had run boats out of the waters and swimmers off the beaches, and this pill would, no doubt, sink or wash away in the storm. If they could just get it to the Gulf without incident, they should be able to dispose of this little object, hopefully, without repercussions. With luck, maybe nobody would be endangered.

But Mona brought up another problem. "Danielle knows a lot. We need to make sure she keeps quiet." She turned to Nick. "You've done so much for us already, I hate to ask you this, Doc, but do you have some cash with you?"

Nick reached into his pocket and pulled out five one hundred dollar bills. "I planned to spend these at the dog track." He curled the corner of his lip. "But this is putting it to better use, I guess."

"Danielle," Mona called out. "Could you come in here, please?"

"You need me?" The young dental assistant stopped in the doorway. Turning to her, Mona handed her the money. "The less you know, the better off you are. You just get everything here back in shape and never mention this to anyone. You hear?"

"You mean not even Dr. Lucas?"

"Not even him."

"Well...." She fanned the money in her hands, looked at it for a moment, and then pocketed it. "You sure Dr. Lucas won't find out? I don't want to lose my job over this."

"I promise you he won't. You know none of us will tell. And you won't lose your job."

"How about the security guard?" Danielle's squeaky voice got higher pitched. "He might say something."

Oh, damn. The guard. How can we take care of him?

Nick gestured with his hand, indicating the waiting room out front. "What did you tell him when you went to the door?"

"I said Dr. McNally came to use the X-ray machine." Danielle shrugged. "I didn't tell him it wasn't working."

"Good. I'll catch up with him and reinforce what you said. That'll take care of it," McNally added.

She poked out her bottom lip. "What if Dr. Lucas asks questions?"

"Don't worry about it." McNally waved it away. "If I know Dr. Lucas, all he'll be thinking about when he returns is getting back to business."

"Okay, if you say so." She shook her finger at him. "But you better back me up if I need it." She busied herself putting things back in order, waited till they left, then locked the door behind her.

"You know, Nick," McNally chuckled as the four of them headed for the car, "you probably just threw away your five hundred dollars. It's very likely nobody will believe Rob, Mona, or even you. Why in the world did we consider they'd believe Danielle?"

They got in the car and left together with Nick driving. About five minutes later, Nick pulled into a deserted area and the foursome got out. Strong winds and rain slowed them down as they walked along the beach, the mysterious object wrapped in the double thickness of a towel. As Mona carried it tightly in her grip so the wind wouldn't whisk it away, Frank Dees came to mind. She hoped he wouldn't up show up around here. *What a fluke that would be.* However, when they reached the water's edge, the beach was deserted.

McNally had taken the biggest bottle he could find in Lucas's office. It had a wide mouth, one the small towel could be stuffed into to protect the capsule. But in order to give it some weight to carry it out to sea, it needed something heavy inside.

"We need some rocks," Mona told the others who helped her look around, but the only things they saw were seashells of various size, shape, and color. "I'll fill it with sand. That ought to make it heavy enough."

As she leaned over and picked up a handful, lightning struck, and she jumped and dropped the towel. Before the wind whipped it away down the beach or the others saw what happened, she grabbed it up, slipped the capsule into a handful of tissues, and stuffed it in her purse with shaky fingers. *I may not keep my part of the bargain not to tell. The world has a right to know.* She knew the chance she was taking, but they'd all been in danger in the dentist's office. This was risky, but the possibility of the Pulitzer Prize overrode her fear.

"Give me the towel, Mona." McNally held out his hand.

She handed it to him, and he packed it into the bottle. He added as much sand as he could fit in and popped a screw cap on top.

"It's not going very far, but I guess this will have to do." McNally frowned at the lightning striking all around them while the wind blew heavy rain into their faces. "We've got to get rid of this and get out of here."

Rob agreed. "Yeah. Or we won't need to worry about the bottle. The hurricane will be the thing that'll do us in."

But who has the best arm to throw the bottle into the water? Not Doc Romano. Mona couldn't throw far, either, and Rob still seemed too groggy from the anesthetic. *McNally.*

The dentist raised his arm. "I wish this were heavier. I've got to get rid of this damn thing." With the pitch, he let out a sigh. "This is an experience I never want to repeat as long as I live...if I live."

Mona tightened her grip on her purse, and a chill ran up and down her spine.

The bottle hit the water not far from the shore, making a small splash.

"Well, it didn't explode." Joe sighed. "I guess destroying the world wasn't the Torpians goal. Wait just a minute." He frowned at the bottle at the water's edge. He walked over and picked it up and the sand trickled out. When he retrieved the towel, no capsule fell out of it.

"Where did it go? God, did it just fall out?"

Mona sobbed out loud and he whirled around and screamed at her. "Did you drop the towel on the way?"

She swallowed hard and, from quivering lips, uttered a weak, "Yes." *He caught me off-guard. Why didn't I just deny it?*

"Oh my God." He grabbed her shoulders and shook her. "Where?"

She pointed behind her. "There...I think."

After scrounging around in the sand for fifteen minutes, they found nothing. The weather got worse and worse. It interfered, but despite the wind whipping all around them and the rain soaking their clothes and pounding their heads with icy fat drops, they kept searching. Mona hoped they'd decide the capsule would get washed away in the storm and would never hurt anyone. She made the excuse to herself she had to risk taking it because she was obligated to let the public know about the spaceships. *And, without that capsule, I have no tangible proof of my experience, and no Pulitzer Prize.*

When they finally gave up their search, Mona asked, "What now?"

McNally motioned them to come to the car. "We need to get out of this weather before we get struck by lightning. Let's go to my hotel room."

With his hair soaked and drops of water on his face, Rob slept on part of the short drive, but McNally turned on the heater, hoping to dry out some. Then he sat quietly, staring straight ahead. *Odd.* Even when he unlocked his hotel room door, he didn't say a word. He closed and locked the storm outside behind them.

"Damn." He whirled around, his gaze landing on her, and Mona flinched. "You tricked me, made a fool of me." He clenched his teeth. "This is all one big farce, and I can't let you get away with it. You lost that capsule on purpose."

She shook with the fear. *God, what if he discovers the truth?* She clutched her purse close. "How in the world can you say that? You think I'd just drop it in the sand and take the chance of somebody, maybe a child, stepping on it and blowing themselves to pieces?"

"Yes." He grimaced. "Or maybe it wasn't dangerous at all."

"Wait just a minute." Rob stepped toward the man. "You have no right—"

"Listen, Joe." Nick moved between the two guys. "I know you're upset, but you're wrong. Mona wouldn't—"

"Nick," Joe growled. "I know what you've been through in the last few years. And I understand this is just a form of excitement for you. You believe this cock and bull story because it's what you want to believe."

As Nick attempted to speak, Joe held up his hand. "Actually, this has been good for you. You're sober for the first time in a long time. But you can't let yourself fall for this. It's a fake. Oh, I'll admit they even had me fooled for a while." He pointed his finger at Mona and Rob. "But those two haven't seen any outer space beings. It's a publicity stunt."

Mona frowned. "Not true." She pulled on her wet sleeve. "If you think we'd go through all of this just for a story, you're crazy!"

"You listen to me, young lady." McNally shook his finger at her. "I know you news people. You'll do anything for a story. I'm going to tell you what I think you're up to and let you fill in the blanks." He caught his breath. "After your wreck, Mona, you two decided this would make a good copy. But for it to stick, you had to have evidence. So, you put that object into your boyfriend's mouth. You had something explosive inserted into the capsule so you could prove it was dangerous when it was removed. I'm sure whoever mixed up this concoction told you it was harmless as long as it was in Rob's mouth." His voice was as harsh as a growling lion.

"Wait a minute. I bet you had some shyster dentist insert it in a tooth that probably already had a cavity or had lost its filling. And I'm sure you had a plan to remove it safely. Then it boomeranged. I think it was nitroglycerin mixed with another chemical. Whoever gave it to you discovered it was dangerous. And they let you know. I bet Rob's tooth started hurting, and when the dentist couldn't get the capsule out of it, you panicked and searched for a sucker who'd sympathize with you. You found one, and, through him, you just plain lucked out getting to me." He folded his arms across his chest. "You didn't think I'd see through your scheme, but I did."

"I can punch holes in your theory." Mona shook a finger at him. "With so much danger, why do you think we'd come all the way to Pensacola—"

"Oh, you may have already been on your way over here, maybe to cover the storm. Somebody probably gave you Nick's name. Or maybe you looked for a dentist first and couldn't find one. Who knows?" He waved her away, not giving her a chance for another rebuttal. "But your little ruse didn't work. I felt obligated to save Rob if I could, but the more I thought about it, the less I believed your story. Do you realize what a foolish trick you pulled? You could have both been killed. Think of the lives you could have endangered. And now, you've conveniently lost the explosive."

The dentist finished his spiel. Mona rubbed her forehead. *He doesn't believe us. What a bummer. Well, it's a relief he doesn't know the whole truth. And I'm not going to tell him.*

Rob and Nick protested in unison, but Nick spoke the loudest.

"I'm sorely disappointed, Joe. I didn't think you were so cynical." He pointed the finger this time. "You're the one who's wrong. Dead wrong. This couple has been telling the truth. I believe them because I've seen a UFO myself." Nick's voice cracked, but he kept talking. "Call me what you like, but don't question my ability to make judgments of people. That's my job. I know what I'm doing. All my life has been dedicated to deciding what's good for people. I'm good at it—drunk or sober." He pulled out his checkbook and a pen and made out a check to Dr. Joseph McNally for five hundred dollars. "This should take care of your fee and don't worry, my check's good."

Shoving the slip in Joe's hand, he refused to take it back. Mona knew none of them would be able to convince McNally their report of seeing spaceships was factual. He wouldn't listen to his friend.

"Just remember when you cash that, everything I told you is true," Nick insisted. "I know what I saw."

"Hell, Nick, in the shape you were in, you could've seen most anything, even spaceships." Joe made a half-hearted attempt to patch things up with his old friend, but the man's patronizing manner did not sit too well with the doc.

Rob stepped in. "Look, I'm grateful to you for saving my life, Dr. McNally, and I'm sorry you don't believe us. We're not getting anywhere, and this storm's getting worse."

He walked to the door, set his hand on the knob. "Come on, Mona, Doc. Let's go."

As they left, rain blew right in Mona's face. She was disappointed. Dr. McNally hadn't believed one single part of their story. How deflating. If he didn't believe it, would anyone else, like the judges of the Pulitzer Prize? *Why write it if that's the case?*

But she admitted they had several good results—the object had been removed from Rob's mouth, his double vision and headache had disappeared, and she hoped they'd broken their last tie with the space people. Still, instead of finality, she knew, like her, Rob and Doc considered the job incomplete. She'd never be satisfied until they convinced others of the existence of the outer space beings they'd seen with their own eyes.

And my poor Pep. Her heart ached with the thought of her cute canine companion. *None of this will truly be over until I find him and bring him home again.*

Her head kept swimming but Rob got her attention when he asked, "What next, Doc?"

"You're asking the wrong person." He yawned. "I'm too weary to think, and I can feel every one of my years." Doc shook his head. "I don't have any idea what to do next, except find safe harbor from the storm. So, I guess I'll head for the safest place I know, straight back to my own home."

Chapter Twenty-Seven

Frank Dees tried to forget current events complicating his job and his life. His sad mission of mercy, which had taken him away from the city of Mobile to attend to his nephew's funeral arrangements, didn't take his mind off his two missing reporters for long. In addition, reports of big news had to be attended to. Not only was Hurricane Dennis on its way with a force stronger than any in Alabama since Hurricane Frederick in 1979, but the spaceship sightings were still being investigated with no visible results. *Thank God Loren Brady's in Mobile. He'll pursue the story of explosions in my absence, and he'll keep me up to date.*

He planned to stay in Navarre until funeral arrangements were complete. Cremation wouldn't take but one day. Perhaps having time to think would give him a better perspective.

At six p.m., Frank went down to the poolside solarium area carrying a flask of Maker's Mark to have his first drink of the day. The bar would be closed, but he brought his own glass. He'd always made it his policy never to drink during working hours. Many, many times his luncheon companions had tried to persuade him to "have a drink with us," but their pleas always failed. Today had been depressing, and he felt tempted to break his rule of not imbibing before six p.m. He'd have a stiff drink, though, when the magic hour came.

***

Dr. Joseph McNally had changed clothes, so it annoyed him to get wet again as he walked along the open walkway to get to the main building. He was on edge. The disagreeable exchange with his old friend, Nick, hadn't helped matters a bit. *Those reported spaceship sightings are part of a contrived fallacy. Those two reporters worked out this crazy scheme to attract attention. Well, they succeeded. National news media is sprawled all over the city of Mobile investigating a space oddity.*

He could see how Nick might believe them since he'd had a sighting of his own. They'd timed this well-planned farce very effectively. Whatever they did and however they did it didn't matter. At least, he'd seen through it. Maybe he'd cash Nick's check, and maybe he wouldn't.

Question now is whether to tell anybody. If so, whom? Preoccupied as he entered the hotel bar, he bumped right into a bulky form.

"Oh, I beg your pardon." Joe looked the man square in the face. With a double take, he exclaimed, "Why you're Frank, Frank Dees. It's good to see you. I'm Joe McNally. Remember me?"

When Dees just stared back, McNally said, "We go back a ways. When I first finished dental school, I bought a house in Mobile, hoping to use it for my office as well as my home. I sunk every dime I had into it. To complicate matters, I had zoning problems. You came to my rescue. After you did a feature story on it, it was rezoned to commercial."

Dees's eyes widened. "God, man. I've haven't seen you since then."

"Yes, but if it hadn't been for you, I might still be trying to start a practice. As it is, a few years later, I sold my place in Mobile and moved to Memphis. Worked out fine. Business is thriving. Come on." He held up his bottle. "Let me buy you a drink for old times' sake."

Frank followed him to the foliage-covered area and sat surrounded by plants in the solarium-type section of the hotel. They had the entire area to themselves. Joe went behind the counter of the bar facing the pool, found a glass and poured two fingers into it and his own glass. He held it up. "To us." They clicked glass and each one took a swig.

"Guess the storm's run everyone else away," Joe commented. "Kind of dark in here with the windows covered. Say, how come you're still here?"

Frank sighed. "I'm on a sad mission." He told the story about his nephew's suicide. "Since the boy's parents died in a car wreck, I'm the only blood relative. I've got to stick around till everything's settled. Sure is a bad time, though, with this storm—"

Thunder shook the building.

"This sure sounds like a big one." Joe glanced toward the boarded-over windows. "Maybe I'd better leave. I'm here on vacation...a long weekend. Some vacation." He decided fate might be with him, if Frank still worked for *The Daily Times*. "Are you still at the paper?"

"Yes, I'm the editor now."

"Well, I knew you'd be successful. You've always had it in you." He squinted. "It's a real coincidence meeting you here." He took a sip of his drink. "By the way, I met a couple of other people you know." His cell phone vibrated.

"I need to take this call. Wait here." He walked across the room to another area with a small uncovered window. "I'll be back in a minute to finish my story." Pushing his chair back, he left the table.

"Dr. McNally," a breathless Nick Romano said when Joe picked up the phone, "thank God I caught you. No matter what you believe, you've got to help us. Rob is hemorrhaging from that tooth. I can't stop it. I've tried. We've packed it. The bleeding just won't stop. Under the circumstances, you're the only one I can call."

"Try 911."

"Hell, I already did. They don't think they can make it here with the hurricane so close." His voice quavered. "Please help."

Joe watched the trees bending in half in the wind. "What makes you think I can get there? Damn, man."

"Please, at least try," Nick replied.

With no further argument, Joe hung up and bolted out of the door. His personal feelings didn't matter. When duty called, he answered. Why the hell couldn't Nick, a medical doctor, stop the bleeding? If he couldn't, how could a dentist?

He stepped out into the driving rain. *Whatever had been in the cavity could have set up an infection. The man might need to go to a hospital. How can he get there? Could it be possible they were telling the truth about the extraterrestrials?* He had serious doubts.

Missing his chance to query Dees about the space incident nagged at him, but it wasn't a priority. Right now, he needed to attend to his patient, even if he had to face a hurricane to do so.

As soon as he turned the key in his car's ignition, he saw the gas gauge registered empty. *Damn it. I'll have to stop for gas.*

He pulled out of the parking lot and turned on the car radio to hear weather conditions. All bad news. "Most people have evacuated the panhandle of Florida after Alabama's governor issued a mandatory evacuation targeted at the area south of I-10. They know Florida's governor will soon follow suit," the reporter announced. "Many service stations are out of gasoline. So, if you haven't filled your tank, you may have difficulty."

What next? Picking up his cell phone, Joe dialed Nick's number.

"Hello?" Mona answered.

"This is Dr. McNally. I'm trying to get there, but my gas tank's empty and I just heard most stations are closed. How's Rob?"

"Still bleeding, but it's slowed down a little."

"Hold on." Water on the road almost caused the car to hydroplane. "Okay. Keep doing what you can. I don't know if I can be of any help, but I'll get there as soon—"

The phone clicked off.

In water splashing against his car door, Joe slowed down and tried to make it through. His radio told him the storm would probably hit in the next few hours. His car spluttered, and then flooded out. He could not make it move.

***

Rob sat in a chair in Nick's house with Mona pressing a blood-soaked towel against his mouth. Extremely pale and only half-conscious, sweat ran down both cheeks. Mona held his free hand. Nick prepared a shot. "Hemophiliacs take this injection of the clotting factor missing from their blood. I don't know if it'll work with Rob, but it's all I can offer."

"Rob," Mona said. "We've tried, but 911 has stopped taking calls. I think the bleeding has slowed down a little. Doc's getting you a shot, and McNally should be here soon. The storm's worse, though, and we're going to have to move into the hall. I'm scared."

Doc just managed to give Rob the shot before the lights went out. He brought in an oil lamp and a huge flashlight along with candles. He and Mona maneuvered Rob into the hall, laid him on some thick sofa cushions, and sat down beside him.

In a few minutes, Mona looked outside. Shutters flapped in the wind and trees blew to and fro, some bent almost in half. The thunder and lightning subsided, but the howling wind kept blowing. Mona walked back into the hall and sat shivering while Rob dozed, the effect of a sedative the doctor had given him earlier.

Minutes later, a loud snap caused her to jerk.

"There goes the pine tree in the front yard." The doctor blew out his breath.

"How do you know?"

"Oh, I've been through quite a few hurricanes, including one last year." He got up, went to the end of the hall, and stared out the living room window. Mona moved to stand beside him. He leaned over and whispered in her ear. "This weather's too bad. Joe's not going to make it here."

Rob moaned, and Mona went back to him. She took a soiled towel off his mouth and replaced it with a clean one. "Look." She held up the one she'd removed. "Maybe your shot worked. I think the bleeding's stopped."

The blood on the towel had almost dried and no more oozed out of his mouth. Just then, though, a loud crash sent Doc rushing into the living room. "Oh, my God, a red oak smashed through the roof and water's pouring in!"

Mona stood at the exit from the hall and exclaimed, "Good Lord, what are we going to do?"

When the whole house shook, it didn't result in the explosion of the implant object still in her purse. Despite her relief, Mona bemoaned the fact she hadn't disposed of it, even at a lot of risk to others.

She gritted her teeth. How could anything else go wrong? It gave her a desolate feeling to know the living room would soon be flooded, and they could do nothing about it, and they had no one to call for help. She shuddered. *My God! The whole bottom floor could flood, too.*

"Come on." Nick grabbed Rob's left arm. "Help me. Get his other arm. We've got to get upstairs while we can."

With much effort, they dragged Rob upstairs one step at a time. He'd fallen asleep and didn't awaken. Mona feared he had lost so much blood he'd become unconscious. When they got him to the top and into a bedroom on the back of the house, Doc took his pulse.

"He'll be all right. Don't worry."

But worry plagued Mona. *How long is this storm going to last? We won't be able to get any help until after it subsides, maybe not then. If Rob needs blood and can't get it, will he die? Oh, God, how terrible!*

She and Doc managed to lift Rob onto a bed, and then Doc went to another room and got blankets and pillows. Mona thought about the capsule. Evidently, it wasn't as shock sensitive as she'd anticipated. However, even though the tree's falling hadn't caused it to explode, if another fell, they might not be so lucky. To protect it as best she could, she found a couple of extra pillows, put her purse with the vial in it between them, leaving it in the tissues, and hoped for the best.

The wind whistled louder, but no more trees fell. In less than an hour, the horrible sounds of the hurricane ceased. Still no electricity, and neither the house phone nor the cells phones worked. Doc stayed close to Rob and kept piling on blankets to help prevent Rob from going into shock. He also checked his patient's pulse at regular intervals.

Mona tried to sleep, but she couldn't close her eyes. She just lay there, watching the dim candlelight flickering against the wall and praying all would be well.

Chapter Twenty-Eight

Dr. Joe McNally prayed his way through the storm in his car, reciting some he hadn't said since childhood. His biggest fear, his car floating away into the Gulf of Mexico. It had moved down the road quite a ways, but a tree blocked its path. Except for rocking, it remained in place.

When the storm had done its worst and Joe felt a little safer, he left his car and waded back to the hotel, not knowing what he'd find. It was much closer than he'd anticipated. Despite having to duck under limbs hanging from trees and climb over debris, the trek only took about twenty minutes.

His wet cell phone had quit. As he'd expected, no clerk was on duty at the desk. When Joe tried the phone there, he couldn't get a dial tone. Navarre Beach had become a ghost town. If he could find Frank, maybe his phone would work. He could also tell him the rest of the bizarre story. Maybe he'd get an objective opinion on the real deal regarding the spaceship sightings.

Somehow the power had been restored, so Joe had no trouble checking the lobby, the solarium, and even the area around the inside pool, but Frank was nowhere to be found. Evidently, he'd risked returning to Mobile.

Too tired to look any farther and too keyed-up to sleep, he went to the upstairs lounge to indulge with whatever liquor was left in his flask. He was shocked to find a bartender on duty and to hear loud music—old Jimmy Buffett songs.

"Say," Joe called out above the chords of "Margaritaville." "How'd you manage to keep electricity?"

"We lost power, but we got three generators working in the kitchen, the lobby, and a couple of other areas. What'll you have?"

"A double bourbon and water. Maker's Mark." He held up his flask. "I'll save mine for later. Keep 'em coming. I've had a rough night."

"We all have," the barkeep barked. He stuck a pen in his shirt pocket with *Jimbo* embroidered on it. He made the drink, and when he placed it on the bar, he brushed Joe's sleeve. "Say, you're all wet."

"Yeah. My car flooded out. I had to walk back in deep water and drizzling rain."

"Man, you're lucky to be alive. Are you staying here?"

Joe nodded.

"Maybe you ought to go to your room and get on some dry clothes and shoes."

Joe looked at his pants' legs. "I guess I should. I will after a couple of drinks. By the way, I'm a doctor"—he deliberately did not say dentist—"and I need to check on a patient. It's a serious case. Are any of your phones working?"

"Nope. Not even cell phones. I tried mine. Towers must be damaged or down. Sorry." He wiped off the damp bar. "Can't help you there. No telling how long they'll be out either."

Dejected, Joe sat and gulped down two drinks. "What's the damage?"

He paid the tab along with a generous tip and left. By the time he reached his room, he was ready for a shower and a good night's sleep.

The next morning, Joe McNally packed and was ready to leave by eight a.m. He couldn't stay at Navarre another minute. *Some vacation—all work and no play.* However, if he could find a working phone before he left, he'd call Nick and check on Rob. He pulled out his cell phone, glad to find it had dried out. No signal. Just as he reached for the bedside phone, it rang.

"It's good to hear your voice, Joe," Nick said when Joe answered. "How'd you make it through the storm?"

Not feeling like going into a long diatribe about his ordeal, Joe replied, "Well, I got stuck on the way to your house just a few blocks from here, but, after things settled down, I made it back to the hotel." By the tone of Nick's voice, McNally could tell there were no hard feelings. "How did you folks do? Did you manage to stop Rob's bleeding?"

"Yes, thank God. The patient's doing fine. He should be okay now. Er, look, I had a long last night to think this over. You get kind of serious when a tree crashes through your roof." A wry chuckle sounded over the line. "We had to go upstairs to get out of the water. Had a lot of time to think. Anyhow, I, er...well, I understand why you don't believe all this. If I hadn't seen those spaceships myself, I'd probably feel the same way you do. Just wanted to let you know. Oh, wait a minute. Rob wants to talk to you."

"Dr. McNally, I didn't mean to seem ungrateful. I do appreciate all you did for me. You saved my life. And I know you did it even though you didn't believe our story. Thanks."

"Well, I have to admit I've never been in that kind of position before, Rob. But since I was put there, I had to do my job." *God, I have a lot of mixed emotions about this.* He didn't apologize for not making it back to help. It was nature's fault, not his.

"Well, okay. I wish I could convince you to believe us, but I guess you have to trust your own judgment. Doesn't lessen my gratitude. I feel like I owe my life to your skill. Hold on, Mona wants to talk to you."

"Doctor," she said, "you probably saved all of our lives. Nick has your e-mail address. I'll get it and send you mine. If there's ever anything we can do for you, please let us know. I mean it."

When Nick got back on the line, Joe said, "Hope you can get your house repaired soon, my old friend. Get busy working again. It's good for you. Keeps your life interesting."

"Yeah, it'll keep me on the wagon. No kidding, I'm through being an alcoholic."

"Looks like this incident fulfilled a purpose. I'm glad it did some good." *But it definitely spoiled my vacation.* "At least we're all alive."

***

At Nick's house, the mood had lightened. After the conversation with Dr. McNally cleared the air, Mona cheered up. "If you don't mind, Doc, I'll go find us something to eat."

He waved her off. "Make yourself at home. I can use some help in the kitchen. Jane had to go check on her sister. She's older and alone and she gets frantic about hurricanes."

Rob followed her into the undamaged kitchen. She found a box of pancake mix, dug a whisk out of the drawer, and whipped up a batch. "Good thing he's got a gas stove."

As she stirred the batter, she noticed Rob's soulful eyes.

"I wish I could eat some of those," he said, "but I'm afraid to chew."

While Mona and Doc ate several pancakes each, Rob drank a glass of milk for breakfast. "I'm starved." He rubbed his jaw. "But I'd rather go hungry than to risk a repeat of last night's frightening performance. I'll survive on a liquid diet until I'm sure the bleeding won't start again."

Mona promised, "I'll fix you a big steak and potatoes tonight. Doc says you should be able to eat by then. Oh, I hope you don't mind us confiscating your food, Doc."

Nick nodded. "No problem at all." He got up, went to the freezer, took out three large tenderloin steaks, and stuck them in the refrigerator to defrost. "These will be good for dinner. You don't need to ask permission. Use whatever you need."

Mona put her hands flat on the tabletop. "It's amazing how fast friendships and strong bonds can form in the few days of trauma we've shared." She narrowed her eyes and focused on Romano. "I think you feel it, too, Doc."

However, while they sat like one happy family enjoying a meal together, Mona faced a reality. She looked first at Rob and then at Nick. "It makes me sad all this will soon end." She took Rob's hand. "I hope you and I will stay together, but"—she turned back to Nick— "we know you'll remain in Pensacola."

Even if they kept in touch, the familiarity of this moment and the knot tying the three of them together would be loosened. Most likely, it would come completely untied. Things would never be the same again.

Mona stared at the piece of pancake on her fork but didn't lift it to her mouth. "You know, Rob, here we are, safe and sound, enjoying good food. I can't help but think about the Svarians and the Torpians. It seems almost certain they all perished in a space war. I wonder what would have happened if they hadn't been destroyed. Maybe the Torpians would have blown us to pieces. Or, maybe the Svarians would be sharing our meal."

Rob chuckled. "If they were, they probably wouldn't appreciate our food. They're so used to a diet of pills; this might not appeal to them at all."

Mona looked at him. "You're right. Anyhow, I don't feel sorry for the Torpians. Their motivation was all wrong and selfish. They deserved to die." Her eyes blurred with tears. "But, how I wish Eric could have survived! He lived up to his name. He was a great king. With his altruistic attitude, he could have done a lot for humanity."

"Don't worry, Mona." Rob squeezed her hand. "God has his ways. Someday he'll send someone to finish the job."

Mona cut her eyes to the ceiling. *But when and where will that happen?*

Chapter Twenty-Nine

Frank Dees answered his cell phone in his hotel room. "Mr. Dees, this is Kaitlin Conner. I'm one of your new reporters. I went to the Stewart woman's apartment complex, and the manager said her dog had come back. Mr. Swift, the newspaper carrier, discovered the dog waiting on the doorstep and alerted the manager to its presence. I saw the little bedraggled pup, and he looked as if he'd been traveling for a couple of days."

Pep must have been with Mona and they got separated somehow. I need to check on him—maybe it'll give me some clues about what's happened to Mona.

Frank changed his plans and decided to return to Mobile. He'd ridden out the storm in a Navarre Beach hotel, but he needed to see about his house and how things were at the paper. He could do nothing more for his nephew. Plans would be disrupted anyway. They'd just have to make new ones. Maybe have a gravesite memorial service. Things could wait. Right now, he needed to get home and back to business.

On the drive to Mobile, Frank speculated about what Pep's return meant. He was a smart little dog, maybe smart enough to find his way home no matter how far. Not unreasonable. Dogs have homing instincts. They've been known to make their way home even when they have to travel across country.

But considering the entire matter, he realized how much time had passed since Mona first disappeared. Pep got some food somehow, or he wouldn't be alive. If Mona was with him, she'd have fed him. Why would he leave her side? If Mona wasn't around, maybe Pep could have been tied up somewhere and later released or perhaps broken loose from his bonds. So many possibilities and no certainties. And nobody to ask except the dog, who couldn't talk.

Frank first went to the paper to discuss things with Loren Brady who waited in his office.

When he walked in the door, Loren stood. "I heard the dog's in Mona's apartment. Is there any way I can help?"

"Thanks," Frank replied. "I came back to investigate. You've sure got the experience to know how to do that, and, as they say, two heads are better than one. Let's go to her apartment and see what we can find out."

When the two men arrived, the apartment manager reiterated his story, but he didn't add much. He pulled on his pencil-thin moustache. "All I know is early this morning when Mr. Swift delivered the newspaper, he saw Pep scratching at Mona's door. When she didn't let him in, he began to run up and down the hall barking. Swift called me before five a.m. None of them mind waking me up," the old man grumbled. But then there was a twinkle in his eye. "Course, I'm sure glad Pep showed up. I worried about the little fellow. Kept him for Mona once when she had to go out of town on assignment. Good little pup." He shrugged. "I didn't know what to do with him, so I put him in her apartment. He's still there."

Dees reassured him. "You did the right thing. After all, he does belong to Mona, and she rents the apartment. Say," he added, using an excuse to get inside, "if you want to give us the key, we'll let him out to do his business."

"I don't reckon there's no harm in that. It'll keep me from havin' to do it." He handed it to them. "The police won't nevah know about it."

With a promise to let the dog back in and return the key, Loren and Frank went to the apartment. "How about that? We got the key courtesy of the manager with no questions asked. Okay," Frank said over his shoulder as he unlooked the door, "let's see what we can find."

Except for Pep's presence, everything inside the apartment seemed the same as before. Just like the photos of it Mona had shown him when she first moved in. Pep came over wagging his tail.

"Good doggie." Frank petted him then glanced up at Loren. "He's as thin as the manager said. We'll have to find him some dog food." He stooped to check two bowls on the floor by the sink. One was empty, but the other had hardened dog food encircling its rim.

"The manager must have given him some water and food, so there's got to be more around." He got up, opened a cabinet door, and rummaged around inside. "Here's some."

After rinsing the bowls, he pulled out a bag and dumped the rest of its contents in one bowl and refilled the other with tap water. Pep lit into it, gobbling it down.

"It's a good thing we came," Loren said. "Evidently, the manager didn't give Pep enough to eat. He needs to make up for lost time."

After he licked the bowl clean, Pep jumped up on Frank then went to Loren, bouncing around, running back and forth to the door. He scampered into the bedroom, came back with a leash, and dropped it at Frank's feet.

Frank laughed. "I guess he's not going to stop till I take him out." Snapping the leash onto Pep's collar, he told Loren. "Look around. I'll just be a couple of minutes."

When they returned, Frank removed Pep's leash and let him tag along as he followed Loren through each room of the apartment. "Find anything interesting?"

"Not yet," Loren said. "It seems to me we have a girl here who's neat, well-organized, and, from this list of things to do, she's dependable." He held up a printout with dates and times of appointments checked off. "You also said she's a good worker. Yet, without warning, she left her job, a decent home, and her pet." He shook his head. "I don't buy it. True, sometimes people do strange things, but even then there's a reason. People just don't change without a motive."

"Some people might say she went off with Rob, even though Mona had another boyfriend and she and Rob showed no signs of having a relationship."

"But from what you've told me about Mona, and Rob, too, neither of them is the type to just disappear. Even if her boyfriend ditched her, it's not likely she'd take up with another guy so quickly. Something very strange is going on here."

"I couldn't agree more." Frank scratched Pep's ear. "Mona wouldn't leave her dog behind to starve to death. I've just been unable to come up with any reasonable answers. Maybe there are none. The answer may be as far out as those spaceships."

"Come on. I don't believe in UFOs. I don't think you do, either. But if it's a hoax, it's a hell of a good job. It brought the media from all over the country to Mobile. Not bad PR, huh?"

Frank bobbed his head.

"Anyway," Loren rubbed the nape of his neck, "so far, none of the reporters have found one shred of evidence to prove the existence of spaceships, much less an explosion in space. Right now, though, what about Mona? I don't see any connection at all. Damn, let's get out of here. This is getting to me." He pointed to the dog. "I've got an idea. What do you say we ask the manager to let us take Pep with us? He'll probably agree. The dog's out of food, and he's got to be fed and watered. Besides, there's no reason for him to stay here."

"All right. Since you're in a hotel, I'll take him to my house."

"Fine with me."

The manager accepted Dees's offer. "I wondered what to do about him anyway." He shrugged. "No telling when Mona'll be back. She's a nice girl. Hope you find her soon."

"Okay." Frank shifted Pep from one arm to the other. "Here's your key. I'd appreciate it if you call me if anything, I mean *anything*, comes up." He handed the man his business card.

Pep didn't resist leaving with them. With his leash snapped on his collar, he let the newspaper editor walk him to the car as willingly as he would have gone along with his owner. Frank smiled. "I guess if his mistress isn't home, Pep doesn't want to stay there, either."

On the drive, Frank asked Loren, "Do you have time for me to stop and get Pep checked at the vet's?"

"Sure. Good idea."

"The only vet I know is one Mona did a feature story on a few months back. About a clinic specializing in small animals, I'll try that one."

When they got there, he didn't have to ask if Pep was a patient.

"Why, hello, Pep," the receptionist said the minute they entered the office with the dog in Frank's arms. She reached across her desk and petted his head. "My, you're thin." She turned to Frank. "Is Mona sick or something?"

Frank's explanation caused the girl to become wide-eyed. "I've been gone a few days. Must have missed that. Mona's missing? I never read a word about it in the paper or saw it on TV. I can't believe it!"

She hopped out of her chair and flung open a door to an examining room. "Dr. Warren—" The door swung closed behind her and shut out the voices, but Frank had a good idea she was telling the doctor about Mona.

A white-haired man in his seventies came out right away. He followed the receptionist who took the pup to a room, removed the dog's collar, and handed it to Dees. With a gentle gesture, he gave the little dog a thorough examination.

"He'll be all right. Just a little undernourished," he told the editor and the newsman. "No malnutrition yet, thank goodness." He put the collar back on the dog. Frank snapped on the leash and took out his wallet.

"How much do I owe you?"

Dr. Warren waved it off. "No charge. Just find Mona."

Next, Frank drove to the police station where he removed Pep's collar as the dog wiggled around on the floor. Then he held it up. "Can you stay here and watch Pep while I take this to have it analyzed?" he asked Loren. "Maybe they'll find some dirt or some other matter to give them a clue as to where the dog's been."

"Sure," Loren scratched the dog's ear.

Although he identified himself and explained the situation, Frank had very little luck with the collar.

"Sir," the officer on duty grumbled. "I don't even know if I should take this." He studied the dog collar as if it were a foreign object.

"But, as I told you, it belongs to the dog of my reporter who's missing, Mona Stewart."

"Mona Stewart?" His eyes widened. "She's the lady from *The Daily Times*." He pulled out an evidence bag. With his handkerchief, he gingerly took the collar, and dropped it into the bag. "I still can't promise you anything, sir. I'll check with my superiors."

Frank handed him a business card. "Call me if you think of something." But he had little hope this visit would be productive. He left, wondering if it would prove anything if the dog had been near the spot where the spaceships had been reported. He hoped that wouldn't happen. Even the thought of it made him shudder.

When he and Loren arrived at the paper, he discovered Hurricane Dennis had taken precedence over his missing reporters. National media members remained on the scene to wind up reports on the sensational news. Also, the storm had subsided, and as soon as they finished giving all the details on the aftereffects, they'd pack up and return to their home bases.

A radio playing in the background gave the latest news. "The evidence of spaceships is inconclusive because no debris was found to authenticate claims, nor were any reliable witnesses located."

"We don't get much respect. They didn't put it in print, but I heard one reporter telling Detective Ramundi, 'This is just a bunch of rednecks wanting to stir something up. Sounds a hell of a lot like a movie filmed here way back—*Close Encounters of the Third Kind.* Maybe somebody watched a rerun and got the idea of this sighting, searching for a little excitement.'"

Frank slammed a book on his desk. "No reliable witnesses, humph! Even if I question the sightings myself, I don't like the national media's superior attitude." He cocked his head. "Worse yet, Ramundi was eating this up and savoring every bite. He told me, 'I think that reporter's right. It's time for me to low-key this investigation.' At any rate—present company excepted—the big-time operator media representatives gave the impression they were positive something had stirred up imaginations and it resulted in false reports."

Frank grinned. "As a comeback, I wrote a piece saying the sophisticated prize-winning journalists acted superior to those they were interviewing. It didn't change things. They were ready to leave town. The storm gave them an out. They even suggest it may have destroyed evidence. I'm glad they're picking up their cameras and tape recorders and moving on."

"Well," Loren said, "you're stuck with me. I'm not going anywhere."

It pleased Frank when Loren stayed to help find Rob and Mona. However, the younger guy had commitments to his job, and he couldn't ignore them too long. Frank was glad to see the rest of them go. As long as they were in his territory, it hampered his paper's efforts. And on this story, he had a lot more at stake than usual. Whether or not spaceships were in the Mobile area, Mona and Rob had not returned. He went hot and cold on possible reasons for their disappearance. One minute, he'd consider some far-fetched but possible explanation—such as their running away together. The next, he'd fear something dreadful had happened to them. *Have they been kidnapped? Are they alive or dead?* He shook his head to clear it. *I don't even want to think about those possibilities.*

But no amount of reasoning gave him the true answer. Whatever the deep, dark mystery was, Frank didn't have enough information to fathom it. He hoped he could pursue the case without the United States government sending their clods down to gum up the works. But because they were dealing with UFOs, he knew they wouldn't miss any opportunity to spend the taxpayers' money. He feared before it was over, a full-scale investigation would take place. He hated the thought of it, but he could do nothing to keep it from happening.

Chapter Thirty

Hearing the news of the investigation concerning the space explosion and her and Rob's disappearance further unnerved Mona. "I sure want to go home and find Pep, but we're not ready to face reporters," she told Rob. "If we show up in Mobile and any national media representatives are still around, they'll descend on us like vultures."

Still a little pale from his ordeal, he narrowed his eyes. "*The Daily Times* should break this story first, if we can make Dees believe it."

Mona nodded. Sooner or later, some hotshot reporter in Pensacola would find them out. They had to make a move. Sitting at the old oak dining table, they discussed the options with Doc while a handyman named Demetrius finished removing the tree that had fallen in the living room and draining water out of the flooded part of the house.

"We can't sponge off of you forever, Doc." Mona sucked in the corner of her bottom lip. "But what are we going to tell people? We couldn't make Dr. McNally believe us. How can we make anybody else? Even Frank Dees...*especially* Frank Dees. He's a total skeptic."

Rob let out his breath. "That's the truth. The circumstances don't give any weight to our story. Making somebody believe us is an almost impossible task. For half a century, others claiming sightings failed in their efforts to be convincing. Why should we be treated any differently?" He ran his hand through his hair. "I remember one of my own assignments and how I reacted. A young Baptist minister in Citronelle claimed he'd seen a UFO. Talk about skeptical. After interviewing him half an hour, I left totally unconvinced. If I didn't believe a man of the cloth, why should anyone believe me?"

"We have to face facts. We probably can't convince anyone to believe us. Makes me doubt the wisdom of even attempting to tell our story."

"You won't be able to live with yourself if you don't try," Doc said. "You're a reporter, and truth is the most important tool of your job. Words may be meaningless to others, but not to you. Your integrity is at stake."

Rob hung his head and shook it. "You're right, but, damn it all, what can I do?" He looked up. "Proof's been on my mind. How can we prove our story? The first thing I ask for when I do an interview is documentation. And here we are without one shred of evidence. If you never had a sighting yourself, would you have believed Mona and me?"

"I suppose not," the doctor admitted. "But there could be some evidence you just haven't found yet. I could go to Mobile with you. Maybe all three of us could return to the scene and find something."

"I doubt it." Mona chimed in. "Even if we wait till we're sure all the commotion has died down and the reporters have left, it's a good bet at least one hotshot will hang around for weeks, hoping to luck out on a big break. He or she will comb the area one more time, and if one fragment of a clue is left, somebody could beat us to it." She bit her lip. Itching to scream out, "I have proof! It's right here in my purse!" she covered he mouth with her hand. *What's wrong with me? For all I know, that damn capsule is still dangerous as hell. Why can't I make up my mind what to do with it?*

"Hang on a minute, young lady." Doc sat up straight in his chair. "You know, there may be proof after all. One of you might have something in your system foreign to known matter. We've been so busy thinking about the implant, we haven't given any thought to residue still being in your body or Rob's. Maybe from those food capsules you took."

The speculation had a double meaning for Mona. If they'd retained something from the capsules, and if it wasn't harmful, it could be good, provided a way could be found to extract it intact. That would be proof. However, they could have harmful elements in their bodies, and it would be bad. It was also possible Rob had something left in his tooth cavity. In any event, this gave her a few more things to worry about. Another disturbing possibility.

She wrinkled her nose and Doc looked at her. "I can guess what you're thinking. But if something is in your body, no symptoms of trouble have shown up. It may be nothing to worry about. If the pills haven't hurt you before, I don't think they will." He placed his hand over hers. "Don't feel bad about dropping the capsule. It might be the best thing that could have happened. It's surely washed away by now."

Doc turned when Jane Croft came in with a pot of hot tea and cheese crackers just as Mona cringed.

"I'm glad to see Demetrius, Dr. Romano," Jane sighed. "I thought I'd never get away from my sister's. That's why he beat me here."

"No problem, Jane. We got along fine. Yes, Demetrius is doing a good job. Oh, I'd better go tell him I want him to haul off that tree."

Relieved the subject had been changed and she didn't have to respond to any talk about the capsule, Mona leaned back in her chair, closed her eyes, and listened to Jane's report.

"He's already removed the tree. He's a hard worker, and I'll bet he's in demand right now after the hurricane. How'd you get him so fast?" Jane asked.

Doc smiled. "You just have to know the right approach."

But Mona knew what had persuaded the handyman to take the job. Doc had handed Demetrius a fifth of Wild Turkey in addition to promising him a fat paycheck and a big bonus.

Mona wasn't hungry after their big breakfast, but eating broke the tension, so she nibbled on a cracker spread with cheese. Rob cast yearning eyes on the food, but she figured he was still concerned it might hurt to chew, so he left it alone.

In the silence, Mona's mind remained awhirl trying to discern what to do next. Doc's medical background may have given him the idea of an angle to find proof, but Mona didn't consider it feasible. Even if foreign matter was detected in their bodies, who could identify it, and what would it prove? Could they find a radiologist willing to lay his credibility—his reputation—on the line to prove something so bizarre? She doubted it. No, Doc's good intentions notwithstanding, it was not the path to take. Their only hope rested in that tiny vial.

The phone rang.

"Doctor," Jane called out, "it's for you."

In a few minutes, the doctor returned. "It was Joe McNally," he told Mona. "He's been listening to all this news, and, well, he had the idea you and Rob had turned yourselves in by now. Maybe I should have kept my mouth shut, but I told him you hadn't."

"I guess it doesn't matter."

Nick rubbed his eyes. "I'm speculating on what he's up to. Maybe he had second thoughts. He might have been influenced by news reports to the point of doubting his own judgment. So, I hedged and felt him out. I asked him why he wanted to know if you were still here."

Please let him have changed his mind and believe us. Mona leaned forward. "What did he say?"

"He said reports were all the media members had left Mobile, and, even though they didn't say you two had been located, he thought maybe you'd owned up to the hoax."

Rob arched an eyebrow. "I guess you told him we're still here."

"I did."

Rob closed his eyes.

"But I didn't give him any other information," Doc rushed on. "By then, Joe was really worked up. He said, 'Well, you can tell them for me I'm tired of bearing this burden of covering for them. If they aren't going to tell the truth, I am. In fact, I almost did last night. I just happened to run into an old friend at Navarre...Frank Dees.'"

Mona gulped. *He knows Frank?*

Doc frowned. "Then he said, 'I'm going to drive to Mobile to talk to him tomorrow. If they want first chance at it, they'd better make it fast. Either way, he's going to hear the truth as I see it.' Without giving me a chance to answer, he slammed the phone down in my ear."

Pushed into a corner, Mona told Rob, "We've got to act. Hell, we don't even know what McNally's truth is! Time has run out. The only edge we have if we want to get to Dees first is we're about twenty miles closer than McNally." She stood.

Rob followed Mona out of the room. "Doc," he said on his way, "she's right. This is it. We've got to go. Want to come along?"

"No, thanks. If you don't want to pursue my theory, I'll pass. I'm tired. I've ridden this problem about as far as I can. It's up to you, now."

The old man slunk in his tattered horsehair armchair. Mona looked over her shoulder and saw him squirming to get comfortable. She felt bad they'd caused the man so much trouble. At the same time, all that happened had vitalized his spirit. It brought him to the point of going back to practicing medicine in a serious way. Laziness no longer fit his image.

Mona gave him a peck on the cheek. "Thanks for all you've done, Doc. We love you."

"No problem." He smiled broadly. "Glad to be of help." Then he removed his shoes, rolled up his pants legs, and waded into his still-flooded office. "Miss Croft," he called in a booming, authoritative voice, "please come take a letter and be prepared to make a lot of copies. I want to let every one of my patients know I'm back in practice."

Mona beamed at hearing those words as she and Rob left the premises.

Chapter Thirty-One

Mona had thought of Pep many times during their stay in Pensacola, but with so many other problems, she hadn't had time to dwell on his welfare. Riding in Doc's car back to Mobile, she voiced her concern.

"Rob," she said close to tears, "I'm so worried about Pep. I wonder what happened to him. I sure hope he got away and he's okay."

"He may have found his way home. He's a smart little dog."

She swallowed hard. "I don't know if he's that smart." She rubbed her temples. The anxiety piled on anxiety had given her a headache.

"You okay?" He glanced at her.

"No, not really. I think your headache's contagious." She smiled. "Or did you just share it with me? My head's throbbing."

She bit her lip. It was time to admit she'd confiscated the capsule. But she couldn't just say she'd taken it; he'd want details of her plans. With her aching head, she couldn't provide them. It would have to wait.

Rob produced two pills Doc had given him and handed them to her. "Try these."

They must have been powerful because in just a few minutes they took effect.

"Feeling better?" He patted her shoulder.

"Much." She shook her head. "But I'm woozy. Those pills must have a relaxant in them."

She leaned back on the seat and let her thoughts drift. She

needed to relax. Even though she wasn't normally a nervous person, the pressures of this experience preyed on her nerves. A few more days like this and she'd be a candidate for an emotional breakdown.

In addition, with her energy depleted, she could barely think straight. They still hadn't decided what to tell Frank, either. It was all too much. The pills took effect and allowed her the blessed relief of falling asleep.

***

Rob's brain buzzed. He'd decided to tell Frank the truth—the whole truth—and let happen what may. If Frank didn't believe him, well, he and Mona might have to get other jobs.

He and Mona. He liked the sound of that. Linking their names seemed natural. He hadn't discussed their relationship with her, but they belonged together. He hoped she felt the same. Did she? Doubt crept in. Was he taking too much for granted? Were they just caught in the passion and excitement of the moment? When all this was over would they still have something in common? Or was it all part of the unrealistic experiences they shared?

No. It was more, at least for him. Thinking back, he'd probably suppressed his attraction to her in the past. At the time, someone else held her interest. Interest? Hell, except for Lee Black, Mona didn't know anyone else existed. But their relationship was over and done with...he hoped.

Soft music coming from the radio ceased. A loud commercial took its place and captured Rob's attention. Then the news came on.

"Reporting from Mobile, Alabama, this is Jim Rush. The recent sightings of spaceships in the area and reports of them exploding in the air have been deemed erroneous. Investigators and members of the media from around the country have left the Port City, saying there is no documentation for these stories. One reporter from New York City called the incident, 'an attention-grabbing ploy to bring the filming of more movies to Mobile.' But others left with doubt, even though they could find no concrete proof. Further investigation is continuing by members of the local media who remain noncommittal."

When the announcer switched to national news, Rob turned off the radio. No need to disturb Mona. But the report bothered him. If he heard it, Frank heard it, too. That kind of influence would make convincing him of the truth much harder.

A loud clap of thunder returned Rob to reality. Surprised at more bad weather so soon after Hurricane Dennis, he turned on his windshield wipers at the first sign of a sprinkle. The clouds emptied, and rain soaked the streets. Mona shifted her position but did not awaken. In seconds, precipitation became so heavy he could scarcely see through the windshield, even with his wipers on high speed. Deciding he should pull off of the road until the rain slacked up a bit, he looked for a hard shoulder. Before he got a chance, an eighteen-wheeler breezed by him and forced him into a soggy spot. He braked the car and got out of it, finding his tires had dug in deep.

Chapter Thirty-Two

The jolt awakened Mona. "What's going on?" She straightened and rubbed her eyes.

"Nothing much. We just can't make it in this driving rain. A truck forced me on the shoulder of the road. I intended to pull off anyway. I couldn't see out at all." He couldn't bear to tell her of yet another problem.

She sat bolt upright. "But if we stop, McNally will beat us to the paper. We can't let him get to Frank first."

"If we can't get through, chances are he can't either."

"He might if he's got an SUV."

"So? Just tough luck." He took a deep breath. "Mona, I hate to tell you, but we're stuck in the mud."

She moaned. "More bad luck. Haven't we already had our share of trouble? Why did this have to happen?"

He had no explanation. They sat in silence as lightning struck all around them. In the woods bordering this stretch of the freeway, he could see the sky light up and the lightning streaking down to the ground. Thunder boomed time and again. Rain poured down in torrents without letting up.

He considered putting boards under the back wheels and trying to spin the car out, but he doubted he'd be able to find any. Also, if he got out of the car in this kind of weather, he might be struck by lightning and Mona would be left alone. So, until the weather cleared, he saw no chance of moving the car.

Mona wriggled in her seat. "Isn't there something we can do? We can't just sit here forever."

Rob shook his head. This inconvenience grated on his nerves more than the foreign object in his tooth had. *Human nature is funny. A person who can deal with facing death without flinching may crumble when trying to cope with life's little irritations.* Leaning back, he closed his eyes.

But closed eyes didn't prevent him from smelling smoke. When he opened them, he saw the woods on fire. They were parked close enough to the edge of the road to put them in a dangerous position—their car could catch on fire. They had to get out of there.

He jumped from the car, yelling to Mona, "Get out, quick!"

She stayed frozen in her seat.

"Oh, God!" he screamed as a flash lit up the sky. "Lightning struck the tree, and it's only a few yards away."

The fire lapped at underbrush and moved in their direction.

Standing by the car's back wheel, Rob told Mona, "I've got to try to get us out of here."

He stooped to see if he could pry the wheel out of the mud. His stomach twisted with dread. An old rusty muffler lying on the side of the road had punctured a small hole in their gas tank. It was raining so hard he could barely see the fluid trickling out.

He squeezed his eyes shut. He had to think fast. What should they do?

"We're in another mess. You won't believe this, but we've run over an old muffler. It tore a hole in the gas tank and most of the gas leaked out. If fire reaches the gas, this car will go up in flames. If we're around, we'll go with it. We're goners. We have two options. We can try to dig out and get away on the gas we have left, or we can make a run for it." Too frustrated to make a decision, he threw up his hands. "I'll leave it up to you."

Without hesitation, Mona grabbed her purse and held it close. "Let's go. Let's get the hell out of here." Without dawdling over the decision, she hopped out of the car.

As they fled the scene, Rob peered over his shoulder. Flames lapped dangerously close to the car. *I hope Doc had it well insured. If the rain doesn't quickly put out the fire, it'll soon be reduced to cinders.*

Panting as he stopped at the crest of a hill, Rob held up his dripping wet hand. "Wait. I think we're okay here. The car hasn't caught on fire yet." He paused, cringing at the repeated flashes of lightning. "Maybe we should have stayed where we were. The lightning sure is close. Leaving might not have been a good idea."

A loud clap of thunder caused Mona to jerk. Her face turned ashen. "What do you mean? The fire could pick up any minute."

Ignoring her last remark, he looked around. "I can't see any kind of shelter or a ditch to crawl into. Damn." He pointed to the left. "There is a bridge ahead. It's safer than walking through those pine trees where we'd be a perfect target for lightning. Let's go." He grabbed her hand. When she balked, he added, "Don't worry, this has got to stop soon."

But he knew that wasn't necessarily true. An electrical storm could last for hours. Rob wasn't afraid of lightning under normal circumstances, but it took on a different perspective out in the open, unprotected. Many a person had lost a life on golf courses around here. He couldn't argue too much; Mona's fear was justified.

When they reached the bridge, cars passed them by and didn't even slow down. One driver glared at them, but he didn't offer a ride.

"I suppose we're lucky he didn't run us over," Rob grumbled, swearing under his breath at the man's lack of feeling for his fellow human beings.

After two more cars drove by without stopping, Rob knew he had little chance of getting help from motorists on this route. If they wanted to get out of this storm, they would have to do so on foot.

"Come on." He nodded toward the west. "Let's try to reach the road up ahead. "We've got to get somewhere dry. At least cars drive slower on a two-lane road. Maybe somebody will give us a lift."

Drenched to the skin, they walked off among the trees where the ground became soggy. Slowing their pace, they continued side by side.

"It's difficult to believe so much unpopulated area exists between Pensacola and Mobile. When you're driving, you don't notice it. But walking is different." He knew since neither he nor Mona was familiar with the territory, finding civilization wouldn't be easy. But he would not let this defeat him. One plus, he had spent so much time in the woods recently, rambling around, these didn't bother him one bit. Mona plodded ahead of him. *Guess it doesn't bother her either.*

"These woods seem like home, don't they? Our noses ought to be able to lead us by now." He grinned. "We've had lots of experience in the woods lately. This ought to be easy."

"Well, I'm not so sure about that," she retorted. "I'm still a bit uncomfortable in a strange place. And we don't seem to be getting any closer to the road you're looking for."

The irritation in her voice grabbed hold of him. "I can't help it," he snapped. "You don't think I want to be here anymore than you, do you?"

Before she could answer, a roaring sound captured his attention.

He turned in its direction. "Listen. I think I hear a train."

The rumbling got louder and louder.

"What the hell?" exclaimed Rob. "It's coming this way. A train track can't run through here." It baffled him. He glanced around, searching for the source of the sound.

Just then, he glanced up toward the treetops. A funnel-shaped cloud loomed toward them, and a terrible, thunderous roar accompanying it rumbled in his ears. *A tornado! No way we can outrun that!* Not knowing what else to do, Rob pulled Mona down and they crouched on the ground.

The powerful twirling cone lifted a pine tree by its roots, dipped down, and picked up a small brush in its path. Without warning, it changed its course as if to say, "I don't want you. You're not big enough."

He pulled Mona flat on the ground beside him as the twister dipped down, swirling a few yards from their bodies. Then, it backed off in an eerie fashion. When it passed, Mona's blank face had turned lily-white.

It took a few minutes before Rob stopped shaking and regained his composure. He panted out the words, "After seeing those spaceships, I thought I'd seen it all. But I've never seen or heard anything like that. I can't believe it." He pulled Mona to her feet and could feel her entire body shaking. "Do you realize we've just been through a tornado? I can't believe it," he repeated. "We both could have died."

Mona opened her mouth to speak, but no words came out. Seeing her fright, he pulled her to him. She laid her head on his shoulder, and his arms tightened around her trembling form. She started laughing, screaming, and crying all at the same time, and then went limp.

"Mona, Mona. Letting your hysteria out broke the tension. That's good. Everything's going to be all right." Rob stroked her soaking wet hair. "I know after all we've been though it's hard to believe anything will ever be all right again. And to be perfectly honest, things won't be the same. But it will get better. I promise you. How could it get worse?" He gave a weak little laugh. "Hey, look." He held up his open palm and no water fell on it. "Good news already. It's stopped raining. Let's go back to the highway."

The tornado seemed to be the climax of the storm. Clouds were still gray, but the lightning moved off into the distance, and along with it, the thunder reduced to a low rumble.

"Well," he said, "at this point, any change in the weather is an improvement. Even in wet clothes and shoes, walking will be easier."

"Something's different." Her words came out calm—which surprised him after she'd just gone through an emotional break. "I can't pinpoint it, but somehow that tornado wasn't like those I've seen in photographs or on television. It was different enough to cause me to have a gnawing feeling of concern."

She stopped dead still and slapped her hands against her cheeks.

Rob stopped beside her and sucked in his cheek. "What's wrong?"

"A face flashed through my mind. Someone I saw in the middle of the tornado. The image was fuzzy, but I...I recognized Torpi. He had a blunt instrument pressed against my head. His eerie laughter echoed in my brain as he told me, 'I've erased Rob's memory, now I'm erasing yours.' He repeated, 'I'm erasing yours,' three times. Then"—she swallowed hard—"he fell dead at my feet." She shrugged. "I feel better, but my head's still swimming. Maybe that's natural. Then again, maybe it's not."

Without warning, Rob slumped to the ground. Fear and confusion twisted through him. *What's happening to me?* He looked up. Mona hovered over him. Her eyes showed terror. He couldn't focus. He barely managed to keep his eyes open and stare back.

"Rob!" She knelt next to him. "Rob, what's wrong?"

He couldn't respond. What had come over him? *I feel dizzier and dizzier. I've lost control.*

When he lifted his arm, reaching up to her, she turned away. She crawled on the ground. "I can't find my purse." She searched for it without any success then scurried to his side. "Look, mister, I've got something very important in my purse." She pressed her hands against her cheeks. "Please help me find it."

He gave her a blank stare. "Did you see that cone-shaped object? What was it?"

As Mona sank down on the ground beside him, the words cone-shaped echoed in his ears. Vaguely, in his trance-like state, he recognized them as a clue to the tornado's true identity.

Chapter Thirty-Three

Mona lay flat on her back in a hospital bed. Frank Dees stood beside it, holding Pep in his arms, waiting for her to awaken. It had taken a great deal of fast-talking to convince the hospital administrator of Mona's psychological need to see her pet, but he'd used his clout as a newspaper editor to pull it off.

Mona turned to the side, and her eyes fluttered.

"I've been taking care of your dog." Frank kept his voice pitched low. "Looks good, doesn't he? And he's fine. I knew you'd want to see him."

Pep squirmed and tried to get out of Frank's arms and onto the bed.

"He's overjoyed at finding his mistress," he said.

Mona smiled and reached out to pet Pep.

Restraining the pup, Frank leaned over and let Pep lick her hand.

"Wha's wrong with me?" she mumbled. "This iz a hospital, izn' it?"

Frank patted her hand. "Yes, it is a hospital." He realized in her condition, she was in no frame of mind to understand explanations. She'd suffered shock and exposure. The sedation she'd been given should be allowed to take full effect. Rest was the best medication she could get.

Against her best efforts to keep them open, Mona's eyes closed. As soon as she fell asleep, Frank slipped out the door.

A nurse entered as he left.

Frank introduced himself and added, "Miss Stewart works for me, and I'm very concerned about her. Is she all right?"

"It'll take a little time, but she's going to be just fine, Mr. Dees."

"Well, she woke up for a minute, but she fell back asleep right away." He scratched Pep's ear. "Seeing her dog gave her a lift." Frank put the dog on the floor and kept a grip on his leash. "She did ask what was wrong and if this was a hospital. I didn't tell her anything except that she's in a hospital. No rush to go into details. I'm glad she regained consciousness. Good sign."

"Yes, but she's exhausted." The nurse pursed her lips and glanced toward the doorway. "More than anything, she needs rest."

Dees gave a sigh of relief. He didn't want to lose his reporter right after finding her again. But he did want to talk to her as soon as possible. He had a million questions he could hardly wait to get answers to. First, he had to check on his other reporter—Rob Parker.

Rob occupied a room in the same hospital but on a different floor, right across the hall from the elevator. When Dees arrived, he eased the door open a crack and peeked into the room.

A man standing next to the bed taking Rob's pulse glanced up. "I'm Dr. Romano. It'll be a while before he awakens."

Dees held out his hand and introduced himself as Rob's boss.

Romano nodded. "I checked the monitor, his heartbeat's steady. No need to try to talk to him now." He spoke in a loud stage whisper. "Let's go to the coffee shop and come back later. I can tell you a few things about your employees."

They left the room and went downstairs. Over a cup of coffee and a piece of pie, Doc told the story. Leaving out the part about the spaceships, he claimed Rob and Mona had a lead on a story in Pensacola, intimating it was about the storm. Then he mentioned Rob coming to him about a toothache and being caught there. He ended with how the police happened to find Rob and Mona after they'd tried to make their way back to Mobile.

"I received this call from the police. They found the car I loaned Rob and Mona stuck in the mud on the side of the road. It had been abandoned. Naturally, I wondered why. I was very worried about them. We formed quite a bond when they stayed with me. So the police told me the location, and I drove my other car there to see what I could find out.

"When I arrived on the scene, the police had found evidence of a fire nearby, which had been caused by lightning. It had hit a tree we saw felled on the road. They also found my gas tank had a leak." He blinked. "I can't believe the car didn't burn up. We all agreed Mona and Rob were scared off by a threat of fire. But where they went nobody knew. Did they wander down the highway or into the woods? Which direction did they take? We had no clues."

He set his jaw. "One of the policemen, a rookie, said bloodhounds were available and they could hunt them down quicker than humans. Because lightning still flashed in the area and they probably had no place to get out of the weather, time was important. The policeman got on the radio and got the dogs out there fast.

"Then, the storm let up a little. The dogs and their handlers began the search. Luckily, finding them didn't take long. Oh, maybe thirty minutes, but, hell, we could have searched for days without those dogs.

"Anyway, when they sniffed out Mona and Rob, both of them were in bad shape—passed out and soaking wet. I saw them when they first brought them out of the woods. I don't mind telling you I didn't think either of them could make it. Exposure can kill, you know. I'm sure we barely got to them in time."

Dees listened to every word, glad Mona and Rob were all right. He waited for Romano to tell the rest of the story, but when a continuation did not follow, he held up open palms. "Great. Wonderful news. Now for God's sake, tell me whatever else you know."

His urgency didn't hurry the old doctor. "Don't rush me." He leaned forward. "I learned long ago to think before speaking and that words are impossible to get back into your mouth. Biding my time became a tool of my trade."

He put an elbow on the table and leaned his chin on his fist. "Let me tell you what an old professor in medical school once told us."

Dees didn't protest; it would do no good. The doctor was determined to tell his tale.

Romano rubbed his chin. "This wise old codger said, 'Second to your degree, poise and planning are essential to a successful medical career. It's popularly called bedside manner. No matter how critical the conditions may be, or how slight the illness, when facing a patent with a diagnosis, always enter the room knowing precisely what you are going to say and how you will say it. Remember, many patients think of their doctor as a father figure to one degree or another. More than anything else, a patient and his family need a firm, strong, convincing doctor to lean on. It makes a difference, gentlemen, it makes a difference.'"

When Romano drummed his fingers on the table. Dees leaned back and folded his arms. He speculated on how much the doctor would reveal. He had a feeling the man would withhold some information. But he couldn't do anything to force the issue. Dees knew circumstances were very different from the norm. He sat silent, waiting for the doctor to make up his mind.

It took several cups of coffee for Romano to complete his story. He told all. At the end, he slumped in his chair, like a balloon with all the air let out of it, and seemed unable to mouth another word. Yet, it wasn't over. "You have any questions?"

He did, but he tried not to show disbelief in his eyes or disrespect in his manner. He'd already heard Dr. McNally's version and about his skepticism. Dr. McNally had been adamant in assuring him "all of it is some kind of a hoax." With the doubt he'd cast, it would take a great deal of convincing documentation to make Dees believe. He had to acknowledge, although Mona and Rob were always truthful reporters, sometimes a lark seemed very appealing. Often the dramatic appeared quite easy. They could seem to be sensible adults, but a great practical joke such as this could have tempted them past their power to resist.

"Hell," Frank cast his eyes upward, "I have plenty of questions, but I don't think you have the answers. There are so many things I don't understand these days. I've heard one side from McNally and another from you. But accepting your bizarre story as true requires too much stretch of the imagination. It can't be. It's more believable they thought this would be great fun."

With his own words, Dees convinced himself and wrote it off. *Nick is an old alcoholic looking for a thrill. According to McNally, he'd "gone down the drain" the past few years. Any form of excitement probably appealed to him. Part of it could have been hallucinations. Romano believes because he wants to believe. It has to be. Old Doc swallowed the reporters' story whole because it made his own life interesting again. Looks like Mona and Rob had their little joke.*

After the session with Nick, Frank couldn't wait to talk to his reporters. He'd find some way to press the issue and uncover their hidden motivation. Too bad it would hurt the old doctor who had befriended them to discover they'd deliberately taken advantage of him. Though being so insensitive did seem against their nature, sometimes young people could be very inconsiderate. Like it or not, Frank had to make his reporters own up to the truth.

But he had to wait to confront them. Rob and Mona were still recuperating. Eventually, he would, though. When they told their side of the story, maybe then he'd find out all he needed to know to make an honest judgment.

***

Two weeks later, Mona and Rob had fully recovered and returned to work. Frank was relieved Dr. Romano returned to Pensacola. *Why disillusion the old man? Maybe he doesn't need to know the truth after all. If he's lucky, maybe he'll never find out.*

His star reporters stood facing him as he sat at his desk. After a polite inquiry as to their health, and being reassured both were fine and back to normal, he asked them point blank, "Please, tell me your story. I want to hear it all."

Mona and Rob looked at each other. In unison, they answered, "We can't."

"Why not?"

"Neither of us can remember what happened." Rob shook his head. "Before the hospital, the last thing I recall is being in a gully, looking for Mona."

"And all I remember is my car crashing through the guardrail and flying into a gully." Mona shrugged.

Frank frowned. "What do you mean?"

Mona glanced at Rob and then back at Dees. "Just what we said. We don't know what happened."

"Come on, you two." Frank scratched the nape of his neck hard. *Why won't they tell me what happened?* "I know better. You made this up. It's all a farce, a stunt to get attention. I'm disappointed you won't admit it."

Rob leaned on the desk, stared him straight in the eye, his expression sincere. "I'm telling you the truth. We do *not* know what happened."

Either Rob has become a professional liar, or he's telling me the truth. As hard as he tried, Frank Dees, who prided himself on being a highly experienced interrogator, could dig no more out of either of them.

When Mona told him, "A new car? I don't remember returning to work after my vacation, much less buying a new car. What did I get?" no amount of questioning caused her to change her story.

Rob didn't budge on his position, either. And both took lie detector tests, which produced no results.

Frank kept the story out of the papers. Other reporters on staff made up their own versions of where Mona and Rob had been. Frank ignored the whispered gossip circulating the office for a while, then it died down only to pick up again when Mona and Rob were seen together constantly after hours. And even more so when they announced their engagement.

For the record, the police called the case unsolved. Frank was told the mysterious deaths of the two deputy sheriffs remained on the books unsolved. Doc Romano called him once saying, "I haven't heard from Rob and Mona. How are they doing?"

"Well," Dees replied, "it's odd, but they both have amnesia."

"Oh, I wondered why they never came back to Pensacola or at least gave me a call. I guess that explains it. Sometimes a harrowing experience brings on amnesia, nature's way to forget a stressful event entirely." He paused. "I've often thought of going to see them and visiting my estranged son in Mobile. However, Tony and I never resolved our differences, and I'm not sure he'd even agree to see me."

***

A year after Mona and Rob were married and expecting their first son, she requested a leave of absence. "I need time off to prepare for the baby."

"You're not due for months. You've got plenty of time." He waved her request away. "Mona, this story could win you a Pulitzer Prize. It's a real scoop. I don't know why, but our paper got the exclusive to break this news. They specified you should do the interview." Excitement danced in his eyes—a rare sight to witness in Frank Dees. "Of course, only time will tell what the outcome is, but a scientist in Pensacola claims he has a cure for cancer." He cocked his head. "From what I've heard, he's an odd-looking duck, and he acts like he's from outer space, but he has very impressive credentials. His name is King. Dr. Eric King."

About the Author

Mary S. Palmer is an established author and member of the adjunct faculties at several colleges, where she teaches English, including Faulkner State Community College, Faulkner University and Huntingdon College.

Throughout her writing career, she has published books in a variety of genres—science-fiction, true crime, novels, fantasy and biographies. She has also authored two play productions, award-winning short stories and poetry. Mary has a BA in English (cum laude) and a minor in French. She also obtained a MA in English with a Concentration in Creative Writing—the first person to receive the degree with the Concentration in Creative Writing at the University of South Alabama.

Mary is an avid traveler who loves adventure. She has visited every state in the U.S. and every continent except Antarctica. Wherever her travels take her, she seeks out people to engage and interact with and loves to hear their stories. Drawing from those experiences, she weaves different elements into her writing.

Mary S. Palmer's short story about Mobile's Mardi Gras, entitled *Raisin' Cain,* won the Southeastern Literary Tourism Initiative Award in 2014. Alabama Congressman Bradley Byrne, made the presentation of a plaque and a $500 prize at the Mobile Carnival Museum October 15, 2014. He also commented on the new genre of writing promoting tourism on the floor of the House of Representatives and his remarks are permanently preserved in the Congressional Record Proceedings and Debates of the 113th Congress, Second Session, September 18, 2014.